Jim Christ

The Day Hal Quit

Although inspired by actual events, this book is a work of fiction.

References to real people, occurrences, establishments, organizations or

locales are included only to create an atmosphere of authenticity, and are

used fictitiously. All other characters, incidents and dialogue are drawn

from the author's imagination and are not to be construed as real.

For Mary

"O my soul's joy…"

One

I need to go home a different way, Hal told himself, so that damn neon saguaro won't be daring me to stop by and have a beer. …trouble is it's the only way home unless I go all the way around the air base…well, I'll just have to drive past it, too expensive anyway, drinking in there--Two beers in there, and then a tip, same as a sixer at home. But nice and cool too, air conditioned and lit low, and Doris might be there tending bar.

Hal drove north on the overpass above the rail lines, wishing he still had the job at the cabinet shop. He had worked there for two years, but he was not surprised when Ernie had laid him off in the slowdown. It wasn't just that he was the last man hired; growing up on a ranch had not really prepared him for making custom cabinets; but then neither had studying history, his favorite subject in school, or marching around Korea. When he had drifted in looking for work, Ernie asked him if he had experience, and he'd said yeah, thinking about the siding he had nailed on at his aunt's house. Of course, most of the time when he was using a hammer in his ranch days, it was after he'd used a come-along to pull a section of barbed wire tight and lashed the broken ends together with more wire, and he'd been driving staples, not finish nails, into split stakes or rough tree branches set upright in the ground. Ernie's second question was whether he had his own tools, and he had said yeah again, then thought to look around the shop to see what sort of tools the other men were using, not really able to tell except for the obvious hammer so he added, "Well, a few." Ernie told him to be there at eight o'clock the next morning, so he drove to a lumber yard and asked one of the counter men what he might need to work in a cabinet shop. He had come away with a thirteen-ounce hammer, a nail set, a tape measure, a few chisels, a Yankee screwdriver, and a ten-point saw, which he lugged to work in a small suitcase the next morning. Ernie gave the makeshift tool box and the new tools a bothered look, shook his head and led him to a low, broad table where a few wooden parts lay. Ernie showed him how the plywood parts went together, how the frame was attached, asked him if he needed to refill his glue bottle...what glue bottle?... and told the assembler next to him, Luis, to help. Ernie walked away mumbling to himself but kept Hal on while he learned to be a decent cabinetmaker--not a wood butcher anyway. ...didn't drink every day when I worked for Ernie...

But that was then. Now he worked for a framing contractor, and he had no need for the more delicate tools he'd used at Ernie's place. He swung a twenty-two-ounce hammer and tried to drive sixteen-penny box nails in two blows like some of the most experienced framers could, the first a tap to start it and the second to drive it all the way into the fir two-by-fours, but he knew he was going to need more time to master that skill. He also needed a few beers every day on his way home, to cool off, to unwind, so he had been pulling into the Saguaro Bowl every day since starting the new job.

He started picturing Doris in the cool, dark Saguaro Bowl barroom then, behind the bar, with her light brown hair that always looked windblown somehow... curly and wild and not quite long enough ...wish she'd let it grow...what am I wishing that for?...she has no idea who I am...about forty, I guess, not much older than me...maybe just a little on the heavy side, and a little paunch to her tummy...not bad though...the kind of gal that gets hired to be a barmaid, with wide hips and strong calves and thighs and enough musty cleavage to make her seem vaguely debauched...must have a boyfriend though, as attractive as she is...won't even recognize me if I stop, so another reason to just drive on past. Even if someone told her I was coming by to see her and just having the beers so I could see her, she'd be bored. "Who?" she'd say…she'd be bored to death, even if I walk in there with flowers…no ring on her…wonder if she ever goes out with customers…well, with a sweaty carpenter.

He wondered if her bosses would notice if she started talking with him too much. I mean, say she is interested…you don't make money in the bar business, he guessed, if your bartender spent too much time on one customer. Then he wondered if he should go home and come back after he showered.…another reason to drive on by. …shower…some after-shave…who knows…

He thought about his aunt then, trying to picture her before she withered from the cancer gnawing her from the inside, when she was about Doris's age. He remembered her on that first leave after basic training. Hal saw himself pulling onto the driveway to the ranch, under the lumber slab sign with her ranch name and brand, and then coasting down to her house, where his aunt came out and greeted him with her smile. Then he pictured Doris behind the bar again, giving him the bored, jaded stare as he came up to a stool and sat down. It was the look he expected…completely bored with another sweaty, straw-hat carpenter who used to be a cowboy…best to drive on by.

It was late afternoon in June and bright-hot, and the parking lot was nearly empty, and the sign's neon lights were not flashing yet, but it beckoned him anyway. Just a couple, he thought. He rolled his pickup truck across the gravel in the parking lot and took a parking spot near the door to the lounge. What he didn't expect was the hand-lettered sign on the door: Help Needed-Bartender.

When Doris approached him at the bar stool, she did not seem bored at all. She looked younger than forty somehow, in a blue print dress that scooped at the neckline to a place just below her bosom, revealing the sides of her round breasts, with green eyes shining a smile right at him, inviting him. Her expression was like a girl's. She looked him over, which she had never done before, he thought, still smiling as he ordered a glass of A-1 lager and walked toward the tap, switching from one flexed buttock to the other as he settled onto his stool and watched her. Looking around for one of the bowls of thin pretzel sticks, he heard her tones aimed at another customer. He found a half-empty bowl and slid it back to his spot at the bar by the time she returned with his beer. She still did not look bored.

"So, Doris, are you leaving or something?" He took two big gulps of the lager.

She gave him a new look with her head cocked, asking what he meant without saying anything, still smiling with her eyes. In the mirror slanting forward behind the bar, her dress plunged low on her back and wrinkled at the waist with her weight on one leg. He could see the overlap of her bra clasp.

He nodded toward the door. "The help wanted sign."

"Oh, that. Well yes and no. I'm moving to the office, takin' the boss's wife's job. Bookkeeper, sort of." She paused a moment. "You know somebody can mix drinks?"

Hal had hoped she'd ask about him, so he said nothing for a moment, thinking hopelessly about the framing job. "The owner's wife? What happened to her?" Keep her here talking, he thought.

"Nothin' only she don't want to work no more. She says it's cuz their daughter is starting high school." She leaned forward with both forearms on the bar, and it pinched her breasts together and deepened her cleavage. She lowered her voice, "Their kid's a little hell-raiser, always gettin' in trouble at school," and then laughed.

"That so?" His eyes bounced from her eyes to her cleavage and back. "What kinda trouble?" …get her talking about herself…

"Tara gets in fights and stuff. Smoking. Really boy-crazy, I hear." She raised her eyebrows. "The stuff kids do that age. Jus' more than most."

"Yeah? You do that kinda stuff when you were a kid?"

"Sure, didn't you?" She smiled crookedly and wide now.

Hal looked at her mouth closely, thinking he'd never studied it before… wide, very wide, thin lips, teeth that were tobacco-stained but very even. It was a nice mouth, he decided. "Yeah, some, I guess," he lied, "didn't get sent to the principal's office much though." What he remembered best about his school days was reading histories and biographies on the long bus rides every day, always wondering whether Macarthur should have acted more like Meade or vice versa. He reminded himself to talk about her. "Sounds like you made a lotta trouble back in the day, huh?" He sipped the beer, thinking he finally had steered the conversation around to her, but then she walked away to where another customer was holding his glass upside-down.

Hell, he thought, pretending not to care if she came back. Then he looked sidelong to see if she was smiling at the other customer, whether she leaned forward to pinch her cleavage. No, she was giving the bored look. He sipped his beer.

When she came his way, she smiled, more flatly this time, he thought, and said, "How 'bout you?" Then her mind seemed to change direction, and she said, "Did you tell me your name? I noticed you called me Doris before." She leaned on the bar again.

"I'm Hal," he said. "I guess I heard somebody use your name."

"I seen you in here the past few days. You on your way home from work?"

"Yeah, well I been laid off for a while but now I'm framing houses out south of here." He sipped his beer and eyed her back again in the mirror, the skin, the exposed bra strap. "I come in here to cool off."

"Yeah, it's hot workin' outdoors this time of year, but I was thinking maybe you was coming in to see me ever day." She winked.

Or did she? Jesus! He felt her watching to see if it embarrassed him, feeling his face change color, and he looked away.

Doris seemed to study him, mulling something over, deciding. "You think you could tend bar?"

"Not really." Suddenly, he wanted the bartending job and he tried to recover, "I mean probly. Done some at barbecues. Didn't seem too tough."

"Raising a head on a glass of beer is easy. Hard part's getting tips." She leaned on the bar again, with her bosom pressed between her arms, and she smiled broadly. "You wanna talk to the boss?"

"Jus like that?" He wondered if she had been playing him for a big tip all along.

"Seems like you got the right temperment—easy-going-like."

He watched her move to the wall phone between the long mirrors and lift the phone and dial, staring back at him, softly smiling now, reminding him of a school girl showing off. Her upper body angled at the hip as she leaned against the liquor shelves, and she rested one foot on top of the other, projecting her round buttock.

He looked straight at her, but he could not tell what she was saying. He wondered why everyone else could read lips and he couldn't.

When she returned to the bar in front of him, she stood with her hands on the bar. "Okay, Judd's on his way."

Judd was a stout, short man with a sharp angular nose, too-serious black eyes, smooth black hair that swept up and back from his ears in a duck tail and a jaw that seemed to be trying too hard not to let go of a double chin. His pects and biceps bulged against the fabric of his gray tee-shirt. He wore a revolver in a belt holster on his right hip. He strode directly toward Hal at the bar.

Hal dropped off the stool and extended his hand.

Judd took his hand for a moment. "Dorey says you can tend bar, yeah?" His voice was too loud for the nearly-empty lounge.

"He's the one, Judd. Was tending bar at Smith's Family Barbecue but got laid off. Jus now walked in here."

Hal struggled not to look at Doris. "Good to meet you, Mr. Judd ."

"Jus Judd is fine. My kid don't even call me Mister. Your name?"

"You can call me Hal, sir."

"You worked at Smith's, eh? Easy enough to give 'em a call. What they gonna say about you?"

Hal hesitated and Doris interjected, "Well, what you think they're gonna say? They had to lay him off. Business is bad everywhere."

"I can't imagine they'd say anything against me." He examined the stout man, trying to read him, wondering if Doris would lie again.

"Well, when can you start, Hal? I need someone right now. Doris is moving to the office."

"I gotta give notice, sir. 'less it's later shifts. I can come in about this time o' day on weekdays, two o'clock or so, if that helps. Carpenter since I got laid off."

Judd stared for a moment, lowering his eyebrows. He didn't seem doubtful really, maybe irritated with Doris for nudging him.

"We need the guy, Judd. We talked about it enough. I can open up at ten like always and this guy--Hal can take over when he gets here. It'll be all right for a couple weeks."

"You'll need to clean up better'n you are now."He sounded speculative, like this was an experiment, but he was accepting the test because Doris wanted him to, like maybe he had something for Doris.

"Yes, sir."

The stout man talked to Doris now, "You wanna give him a try?" trying to make it her decision now, which for some reason Hal thought it was all along.

"Got somebody knows the job right in front of us. Sure I do, instead of standin' here beating it to death."

"All right then," Judd said. "Come back tonight after supper so you can see where everything's at…how we do stuff. You can start tomorrow."

"Thank you, sir."

After Judd left, he sat again, saw Doris's smile and said, "Well now."

She moved away to serve the other beer drinker.

His name was Harold Mull, although he could not remember anyone ever calling him Harold. He assumed it was his mother who had chosen the name for him because he couldn't remember her either. She was the wife of a ranch foreman and had died of pneumonia during a Wyoming winter when Hal was three. He did remember his father, Savor Mull, who had taught him to ride saddle horses and shoot a Henry rifle and rope steers well enough to win two junior team roping titles in rodeos at Casper and Rawlins before he was ten years old. But then Savor died too, gored by a bull, and his Aunt Henrietta had brought him to her own ranch in southern Arizona, where he brought the Henry rifle and a few boxes of old rimfire cartridges, but he drove a pickup truck more often than he rode a horse. Henrietta didn't put no stock in rodeo. He slept in one of the spacious bedrooms that adjoined her living room; they called his room the blue room for the color of its floral wallpaper. He took breakfast and dinner with his aunt, but otherwise spent his days like one of Henrietta's three ranch hands until 1950 when he was a conscript for the United States Army and got to the rank of lance corporal in the Seventh Infantry Division.

After the brass and the suits wound things up at Panmunjom, he came back to southern Arizona, but he wasn't sure he wanted to live there. He drove over to the bar in Arivaca on Saturday nights to drink beers or bourbon-and-gingers, or sometimes Lakeside or Nogales, but always the beers or bourbon. There were always ranchers or cowhands there, sunburnt like old leather and sinewy and smelling like creosote. He knew he looked like them in his hat and his taut skin, but somehow he could never talk to them. They called him hoss and partner, but he didn't feel like either. And sometimes there were hard guys coming in there too, wearing denim and leather and making sure everyone knew they were there and in charge of the bar, always in groups, with beards and shiny sunglasses. The hard guys would talk to him too, calling him man or pal, but he was quiet, and he could tell they would not press him. When he talked to them, he didn't call them anything, just saying yeah, nope, I don't know and maybe and going back to his drink. Assholes, he thought, but no percentage in pointing it out. After drinking a few, he always felt like he knew what his next step would be, but in the morning the next step had been forgotten, and he was in the blue room, staring at the ceiling, wondering why he drank so much and wondering how his aunt felt. The doctors knew it was esophageal cancer by then.

Doris's hotel, Apacheland Court, reminded Hal of places he had stayed when he was on leave, announced on the Miracle Mile by a three-stage flashing neon Indian, red face and brown hands holding a bow and a quiver of arrows, cinder block with flat beige paint, low buildings arranged in a U around the parking lot. The vacancy sign stayed lit continuously. Next to each red door was a covered carport, where Doris pulled her Bel Air hardtop. Hal parked his truck behind.

"You got one of the kitchenettes?" he asked, trying to make it sound like a compliment.

She didn't say anything, carrying a bottle of vodka to the front door, expecting that he would follow. She led him into a room with dark furniture, a Formica table and two chrome-and-Naugahyde chairs. An air conditioner buzzed away from a place below the front window, not really working very well. "Why don't you set and I'll get us a drink. Vodka okay?"

He wanted to ask for beer, but thought it might be rude, and besides thought she might not have any. "Sure, that'd be great. He sat in the chair and looked at the sparseness of the room, no knickknacks, no family photos, no paintings—only a mirror near the door, framed in wood painted a metallic gold. A rattle came from the air conditioner, and then it buzzed again.

While he looked around the room, she somehow released her bra and pulled it off without removing the dress and then tossed it onto a dresser. Now she was pouring Fleischman vodka into glasses she'd filled with ice. "I was thinking about it on the way over here," she said, "You mentioned your aunt's ranch. Made it sound pretty nice. Why'd you leave?"

Hal was watching her substantial breasts straining down, creating a tuck in the fabric underneath. "I wasn't the heir. Her kids inherited it." Her weight shifted back and forth between right and left legs, and he watched the transformation on her buttocks.

"But they never work there? So they're running it from Pennsyltucky or someplace? Why can't you run it for them, like be their foreman?"

"No, they're selling it. They live in Dallas."

"Dayum." Her eyes caught him eyeing her, and he sensed she approved.

"Judd seems like he's a pretty good guy," raising his eyes to her face, pretending he hadn't been caught.

"He's nice to me," Doris said, sounding hesitant, setting one of the glasses down in front of Hal on the Formica table. "But I guess you could tell that."

Hal sipped the vodka and set it down, wondering what it tasted like. "He hired me so's to be nice to you?"

She sat down across from him. "Somethin' like that. He's got a little mean streak though, which his daughter aggravates and his wife tones down. You'll see it before too long."

"What's with the gun on his hip?"

"He'll tell you if you ask," she said, but Hal didn't respond. "He'll tell you it's cuz of the bar and bowling alley. Lotta cash comes in some nights, and he runs it over to the bank in a night deposit pouch every morning after we close—kinda spooky there that late at night. I think he just gets a kick outta wearing it, myself." She swallowed some of the vodka and spit back a piece of ice.

"Gets a kick out of it?"

"He thinks he's a detective. Even has a private investigator license he carries. It's kinda funny in a way, if you don't think about maybe somebody getting hurt. The maintenance guys all make fun of him. Johnny, the lead mechanic, you'll meet him as soon as you start, anyway he calls him Batman."

"Cuz he's a crime fighter?"

"That and his pointy nose, plus he's always wearing a dark shirt, gray or black." Doris grinned. You'll like Johnny. He thinks everything is funny. Makes it seem funny anyways."

"So what's he do? Judd, I mean, to fight crime?"

"Well, for one thing, he's always trying to catch thieves in the parking lot. Goes up on the roof at night and watches." She tilted her head. "He had some guys up on the roof last week installing a boom up there so he can swoop down from there. So he doesn't have to use the stairs."

"What the hell?"

She chuckled. "Sounds crazy, I know, but one thing leads to the next you know?"

Hal figured it was the introduction to a story, so he waited for her to go on.

"One night a couple months ago he gets the drop on this kid down below. Johnny's up there with him, up on the roof behind this parapet, ya know?"

"Johnny's the mechanic, right?"

"Yeah. He told me the whole thing. He'd called him on the walkie-talkie, but it was breaking up, so Johnny went up there to see what he wanted. Judd was up there behind the parapet looking through his binoculars when Johnny comes up, and he waved at him to stay down, so Johnny scrunches down and run over there. 'There's a little shit down there robbin' cars,' says Judd. Johnny said he was so goddamn mad he was glowing in the dark. He sends Johnny to go call the cops, but then he musta heard something down below, so he stands up and hollered at this kid, 'Stop or I'll shoot.' Johnny says he didn't even have the gun in his hand—that big Colt just settin' there on the parapet."

Hal waited, still wondering about the boom.

"So when Johnny pokes his head up and looks, there was this little fat kid down there, just coming out of this Caddy. Had this eight-track in his hand. So Judd grabs his gun, you know?"

"Right."

"Batman draws down on the kid and says it again, "Stop or I'll shoot.' But the kid doesn't even come to a full stop--the kid says,

'Miss and I'll get way,' and runs off. Didn't even drop the eight-track." Doris chucked again. "So he fires, hits the Caddy twice, but the kid gets away."

Hal smiled.

"Johnny tells it way better'n I do. So poor Judd had to pay for the damage to the Caddy and the kid got away anyhow. Everybody in the bar heard the shots and went out there. Talk about mad—that guy with the Caddy had the veins standing out on his neck. And the cops weren't too happy either."

"Probably a good thing" Hal said. "That he didn't hit the kid I mean."

"Yeah, imagine if he hits him." She shook her head, remembering. "Damn, was he mad. Later on, he was yelling at Johnny about making too much noise, but Johnny couldn't keep from laughing about what the kid said. Miss, and I'll get away."

"So what's the boom do?"

"It's got a counterweight. He swings out on this rope, and it lets him down nice and soft onto the gravel. He was practicing with it on Sunday. Sounds like something Batman would do, don't it?"

"You said his wife? She smoothes him out in the rough places?"

"That woman is a saint. Midge is the one got me on a couple years ago. Kept telling him he needed a woman behind the bar to bring in the after-work crowd. She brought me in one afternoon and climbed all over him till he agreed."

"So she knew you from before."

"Meetings." She renewed her smile. "At church. She knew I could use some help getting on my feet after a rough patch."

Hal decided he didn't want to ask about the rough patch, so he sipped from his glass again. "Did she have to fib to get you on?"

Her smile broadened. "No. You didn't mind my little stretcher, did you?" She took a big swallow of the vodka.

"No, ma'am, I didn't. I guess you could tell I wanted the job. You must've been reading my mind."

"Men are easy to read. And yours is easier than most."

"So tell me what else you can see inside my head."

She took his hand with both of hers and turned it palm up, as if she would read it, but then she leaned toward him and looked at his eyes instead. "You're sad about something. You loved your aunt and miss her, miss working for her. And you're wondering what kind of guy Judd is, how it'll be working for him, wondering if it's the right thing. And you're trying to see under my clothes." Her expression did not change as she waited for him to react.

He felt his face redden again, as it had in the bar, but this time he did not look away from her.

"It's okay. I forgive you," she said, "You really want that drink?"

He smiled, "Not really."

Two

One morning, Hal woke up and realized he had been working for Judd longer than he'd worked any one place since the army. Hal became the late shift bartender, and Doris gave up her room at Apacheland court and moved in with him. His furnished apartment was the farthest from the street, impossible to see from the entrance to the small complex because of the long curved driveway that led to it and the overgrown oleander hedge along the street, which had not been trimmed since the landlady's son left for college. Hal offered to do the trimming himself several times, but Mrs. Thadbury always said, "A man like you, Mr. Mull, is too busy to be fussing with the work of a boy." Yet, until Doris moved in, she climbed his stairs each month to vacuum and straighten up for him, always coming while he was at work so that he could not protest.

When Hal had first moved in, he lived on the ground floor behind Mrs. Thadbury's own apartment, and she would hear him squeak open the door just outside her own bedroom when he came home, but when there was a vacancy upstairs at the rear with east-facing windows, she insisted that he move there. More or less oblivious to the bar business, she was convinced that exposure to the morning light would wake him earlier and, she reasoned, get him into bed at a more respectable hour. It did not work however, despite his leaving up the substance-less white curtains that came with the rent. Now, and even though he no longer lived alone, she listened carefully for his truck in the gravel driveway or rose periodically to see if his lights had come on.

The décor of his rooms was sparse and from no particular decade. The Naugahyde couch and chair in the living room had a vaguely Western theme, with braided rope for trim. The bed frame and chest of drawers were blond ash. Three pictures hung on the wall. A late-teen girlfriend had drawn two of them, unsigned charcoal figure drawings, dubious testimony of nearly-forgotten innocence and youth. The third was the hour's work of some nameless Mexican artist—a voluptuous, jet-haired nude painted pinkly on black velvet, with huge staring dark eyes—memoir of a night's trip across the Mexican border with Johnny, who had bought it as Hal watched, swaying slightly, detached and amused with Johnny's bad taste, wondering if he would really have the nerve to face his wife with it. But after their mescal-drinking and their whoring, Johnny gave it to Hal. He thought several days about throwing it away, but finally hung it above his toilet. When Doris first saw it, she raised both eyebrows but said nothing, so there it stayed.

Meanwhile, Tara was driving her father crazy with her hip clothes and freaky friends and her trouble at school, and Midge tried to smooth out rough edges in both her husband and her daughter. Judd wore the Trooper magnum double action revolver on his belt holster continuously, in front of the hip pocket so everyone could see it. The bartenders had access to another pistol, a Beretta 418, which Judd insisted be kept loaded and just out of plain view on a shelf below the cash register. Seven rounds in the magazine and one more in the tube. Judd said every gun he owned held one on the chamber, ready to fire. To run off the jigs and wetbacks, Judd said, I figure they'll get around to us eventually. He even took the bartenders out to the wash behind the bowling alley once a month for target practice, until the neighbors across the wash complained to the police.

Hal never questioned always getting the last shift, especially on Saturday nights, always the biggest cash night. He figured that Judd would send him to make the deposit if he couldn't do it himself for some reason. And in fact, he had, twice—once when Judd and Midge had gone, without Tara, to Puerto Peñasco for their fifteenth anniversary and once when Judd was at a restaurateurs" convention. And he insisted Hal take the Trooper along even though Hal said he'd prefer the .25 Beretta, so both times Hal dutifully made sure the safety was on, stuck the cannon in his belt or his coat pocket so he could carry the pouch, and then set it on the passenger seat of his pickup truck for the runs to the night deposit box. It was dark there, he had to admit.

Tara came to work at the Saguaro when she was sixteen, not because she had finally reached the legal age for work in a restaurant but because she had been suspended from school for distribution of illegal or banned substances and because Midge would neither let Judd beat some sense into their daughter nor send her to a girls' school in Utah.

"She'll be in here every day till eight, so you'll need to make sure you keep her dumb ass busy for the first few hours of your shift."

Hal wasn't sure he could keep Tara's ass busy, and, judging from Doris's stories about her, he was already fairly certain that she wasn't dumb, but he said, "Yes sir."

The first time Hal saw Tara Judd at the bowling alley, a Saturday afternoon, the early shift bartender, Gary, was telling her to make sure to keep refilling the pretzel bowls, especially for the beer drinkers at the bar. From opposite sides of the bar, he and Tara both glanced at Hal, who had just showed up to start his shift.

Tara said, "Honestly, I don't care how many free pretzels these old farts eat or how many beers they buy. I'm just here till my suspension runs out in a couple weeks. Besides, it's so dark and smoky in here, I doubt I'll be able to see when the bowls are empty." Her face was set, firm but not angry, just letting Gary know she didn't like being bossed.

It was pretty smoky but not that hard to see, Hal thought. She was a tall girl, athletic-looking and blond. Her hair was long, parted in the middle and held tight to her head with a green headband and too straight, as if it had just been ironed. She wore jeans covered in patches and a blousy yellow tunic.

Judd had two bartenders besides Hal, one with cleavage, who almost always worked weekdays ten to six, and this guy named Gary who was five-feet-three and that Hal guessed was wearing lifts and strange as a bull's-udder.

"Well, I'm just telling you how to sell a few more drinks to customers. Seems to me this is a marvelous way for you to make a few dollars for the next few weeks, especially with the tips," Gary said. "Your dad expects you to stay busy while you're here." He glanced sideways at Hal again, and Hal could tell the little guy was glad his shift was over.

Marvelous? Hal thought. He actually said marvelous?

"You know, this is bullshit. I get suspended for sharing a little grass and now you want me to come in here and push booze."

"Hi," Hal said, extending his hand over the bar. "You must be Tara. Welcome to our little café. I'm Hal."

She looked at Hal, her expression still set, her blue eyes settling on his face, softly. After a moment, she took his hand.

"We don't really think of it as pushing."

"You see the irony though."

"Sure." No point saying more, Hal thought.

There was a bell, a single ring, from the kitchen area, and Gary said, "You *mind* takin' the burgers to the guys in that booth."

"My therapist says I don't respond very well to sarcasm."

"How's this gonna work if you don't do what I tell you?" Gary asked.

Hal stepped to the little stainless steel counter where the kitchen connected to the lounge and picked up and delivered the greasy cheeseburgers and fries to two men who were dressed in yellow bowling league shirts. When he came back behind the bar, Gary had left to punch his time card and go home. Tara was still standing in the same place.

"I wasn't really pushing, you know."

"Okay."

"I mean I really wasn't. I was just gonna share a joint with a couple friends. I wasn't selling shit to anybody. They wouldn't've even caught me if the lunch duty teacher hadn't poked his head through the window of the car when we left for lunch. He saw the bag of grass on the floorboard. That prick, Mr. McCain knew it too, but he wrote it up as 'distribution of illegal or banned substances' so he could suspend me longer. I told him I wasn't selling and he says it doesn't matter--you were intending to give it to some other kids-- that's distribution."

"Yeah, that sounds like a prick all right." Hal began filling a pitcher with A-1.

"Who gets that?"

"Those three guys at that table. They been waving their empties."

"Give it to me."

He set it on the bar in front of her and watched her carry it away. He watched her butt twitching in the jeans--he thought, hard not to, even if she is only sixteen. He didn't lecture or disagree with her. He didn't even ask her to do anything. What he did was decide she would get around to helping him as much as she wanted to and that would be enough. What he thought was that would keep her from using a sharp tongue on him and Judd off his back. What he said to her often was thanks.

When the bar business was slow, he would ask her if she wanted to help Johnny in the mechanical room. She would say sure and disappear for a few minutes or an hour, and then return and sit on one of the bar stools. Johnny liked her too. Who wouldn't? Hal thought. Well, maybe not Gary.

Tara said, "I'm supposed to do school assignments while I'm suspended, but I work this eight hour shift six days a week, I'm too tired to go home and do homework. I need to unwind after too."

Hal thought about saying, "Well, you could do the homework before you come in," but what he said was, "Yeah, I don't feel like doing geometry when I get home either."

She said, "That your favorite subject way back when?"

He smiled. "Way back when, my favorite was history."

Tara's suspension turned out to be longer than "a couple weeks," but she didn't seem to mind. Neither did Hal. One day Tara said, "I like working here…when it's you here and not the other two." After a pause she said, "I like *you*." She meant it, and she liked that he didn't try to make her comply with anything or tell her that she was learning how the real world worked. She thought of the whole life experience as a rolling river, and Hal didn't try to stop the river, or push it faster like her father; in her mind at least, he let the river carry him downstream, bouncing off its boulders and snags the best he could. He could drink a few whiskeys and it didn't change him into an asshole. In fact, she liked to flirt with him after he'd sneaked a couple of Judd's Wild Turkeys in the middle of the shift, just flirt and no more. She knew he lived with Doris, her mom's friend. He had to be thirty-five anyway, she thought, twice her age after all, but still...she liked him. "You want to do something together sometime?"

"Like go on a picnic with Doris and me? Lake Patagonia?" He struggled to keep an even face. "Or dinner with your mom and dad?"

The edges of her mouth turned up but her eyes didn't smile.

"Didn't mean to be sarcastic."

"Well, you were. I mean like have coffee or something we could do now and then, like friends do. I'm not like most sixteen-year-olds, I don't think."

She wasn't really like anyone Hal could think of. She was not like her mother, who said she rejected her own German mother's definition of a woman's role—Kochen, Kirche und Kindern, simultaneously living it out. Tara did like to cook, but only if a dish interested her, chiles rellenos perhaps, but not the pot roast and gravy her parents liked. Her resistance to the church grew stronger every day, and her parents never did learn why, but Tara had given up faith in God when she was eleven, right after Father John had pushed her down on the floor of the sacristy and took her virginity after the noon mass, panting out a breath of communion wine as he pumped in her and then spraying out his semen on the Minnie Mouse tee shirt she'd brought back from Disneyland, and telling her she was a cheap whore. Whether she would have children or not, well, she had not decided that yet, but she would never give up a job to spend more time on her own kids the way her mother had—giving up what you do, she said, was too much like giving up your soul. She was not like her father either, because he was always right about things, the right way to run a business, the right way to do a job, the right way to shoot a firearm, the right way to be a husband or wife or daughter. Her only brother, four years younger, had died of leukemia when he was six, even though she prayed for his life. So much for prayer. Through sixth grade, she went to the parish school at St. Thomas, where Father John taught religion along with his other duties as curate because her parents did not trust the public schools to educate her and keep her safe, but she was not really like most of the other children there either. She looked like them, she knew, with her white skin and her genuine Capezios, and her father made as much money as any of theirs, and her mother joined the others' moms, volunteering to run the mimeograph machine and answer the phone, but her birthday parties were never quite as special as theirs, and her report cards were never quite as good. She didn't bother to fight with the girls, but most of the boys were terrified to cross her after she punched and stomped the daylights out of Jim Davies, the school's big bully and son of a university English professor, when he called her a slut. Most of the kids in the upper school had been thinking it because, after her time on the sacristy floor, she had done some experiments, wondering if Father John was right about her moral virtue, but no one else but Jim had had the nerve to say it. After she broke Jim's nose and one of his ribs, he didn't either.

"Maybe I could go along with you and Johnny hunting some time. Daddy started giving me shooting lessons when I was seven years old, you know."

He thought about the way Judd always wore the Trooper. "No I didn't know but I believe you."

"You like the idea, don't you baby." It was the first time she had called him baby.

Hal gave a burst of a laugh, letting it sound mocking. He did like the idea, and he liked the way she had called him baby, but he knew he would not admit it to her or anyone else. "What did Johnny tell you about our hunting trips?"

"He said you drink bourbon and smoke cigars and cuss and miss most of your shots cuz you don't want to field dress javelina or mule deer."

"Well, I don't know that he gave you the whole picture then," remembering their last hunt camp near Douglas, where they should have stayed at night instead of going to whorehouses in Agua Prieta. "Doris don't even like me to go hunting with Johnny." Not to mention that me and Johnny would both get fired, he thought.

"Well, something besides working at my daddy's bowling alley. I'm not that good at delivering sandwiches and beers and flirting with old men for tips."

"I can see that."

"And I don't want to get better at it. I can't see myself taking over the family business either. You can probably tell that as well."

"How about dominoes then?"

"C'mon, Hal. I want you for a friend, okay? We could go over to the park some morning before we come in to work and walk around. Feed the ducks maybe."

The motionless pond in Center Park usually smelled rank, with waxed paper trash drifting to the shallow end and kids catching sunfish that Hal hoped they didn't eat, but the way she talked about it made it sound nice. He found himself wondering when Doris would visit her mother in Nebraska next. "Honestly, it might be a little disruptive for everyone if we started being friends like that. Even once."

Tara said, "Maybe your life could use a little disruption. You *evaluate* what's happening all the time, but you never *do* anything about it, like a guy who reads too many editorials in the newspaper. Most of what you do is because of what came before. Like inertia. You know what inertia is?"

Did she think he was ignorant? "Yeah, I've heard of it, even though I didn't much enjoy science homework either. But aren't you always saying it's good to go with the flow."

When Doris did drive back to see her mother in Nebraska in April, Hal asked Tara to go on a day trip. By then, she had served out her school suspension and her seventeenth birthday had come and gone, but Judd still insisted she work Saturdays and two afternoons every week. Hal asked her if she wanted to poke around down south a little and explained again that neither Doris nor her parents would understand this arrangement, and she promised not to tell anyone. He met her at a Mexican restaurant south of downtown, Mija's. They ate menchaca and eggs and drank coffee and had the waitress roll fish burros to take along for lunch. She left her car, an MGB convertible, parked at the restaurant, and they went south in Hal's '58 Chevrolet Apache through Amado and Arivaca, and drove the narrow dirt roads, stopping to prowl at abandoned buildings and old mine sites, where Tara would ignore Hal's warnings and creep close to the half-caved-in shafts and vents to peer in; it had rained the day before, and the air still smelled faintly of wet creosote, which Hal said had to be the best smell in the world. From her oversized bag, Tara produced a joint and asked him if he wanted to share it with her; when he shook his head, she put it away. They ate the burros at Arivaca Lake in the shade of a giant blooming acacia tree, along with a split avocado and Doritos and fresh pears for dessert;

that was when she pulled a bottle of white wine from her bag. "No dope-smoking for you, so how about a taste of pinot grigio?" This time, Hal smiled, so she passed the bottle over to him. "Sorry it's not cold anymore. I like wine when it's super cold, especially this 'cuz it's not so sweet." He got the cork out with a tiny corkscrew that was part of a red pocket knife that he kept in his glove box.

After lunch, Hal fished for bass in the lake with a deep-wee-R and caught a catfish, and a trout too for Christ sake, both of which he released. She teased him about not wanting to clean the fish, but what he was thinking about was Doris noticing the fillets in the freezer and having to lie.

It was early spring, and the sun did not seem hot yet; the creek water supplying the lake flowed in fresh and sweet; the palo verdes were in full bloom, with each branch looking like some crazy giant jonquil, shedding millions of yellow blossoms, piling up wherever the wind took them.

She wondered out loud about her parents, how strange it seemed to her that her mother had married her father and how much stranger that they were still together. Her mother talked incessantly, which always seemed to set Judd's jaw in a hard place, but when she yakked at Tara it was usually advice about how to deal with boys and the kind of boys she should avoid, which always sounded to her like her mother was talking about Judd. Once, when Tara was fourteen and Midge noticed that she had been seeing the same skinny, long-haired boy for three months, she asked, "Do you think it's smart to get serious about a boy like that at your age?" Tara answered, "First of all, it's got nothing to do with smart or not smart. And I sure don't know what you mean by calling him 'a boy like that.' Besides, there's nothing serious about it—Gregory is just a lot of fun." Her mom said, "Well, I see the way he looks at you, and I worry sometimes if his idea of fun is the same as yours. Some men are just salesmen for regrets, boys too. I don't want him to cause you trouble or ruin your reputation." She felt sad for her mom then and put her head on her mom's shoulder and said, "Don't worry Mama, I won't get into trouble, and nothing is going to ruin my reputation." She was sure of both promises. Judd was not a talker but a spanker. And his eyes were always hard. "He might accept your apology, but his eyes never forgave you." She sensed that her father thought of her as sort of a pet that could be trained into proper behavior with the right mix of punishments and rewards. When she was seven, she remembered vividly, he had spanked her for climbing a tree after her mother had told her it was dangerous; now he'd promised her a new car for keeping her nose clean till the end of the school year in June.

They drove to the west until they came to the Diamond Queen Ranch Road, where Hal turned right and took his truck over the wide plateau and a ridge line, the sparse brush and the barbed wire fence looking the same as he remembered. At the ridge they drove under a two-by-sixteen plank where Hal could no longer see much of the painted letters that announced the place, and then he shut off the engine and coasted up to Aunt Henrietta's house with the gear shift in neutral. Cottonwood trees shaded its west side, and a thicket of blooming acacias stood closer, heavy with their fuzzy yellow flowers. Lantana had encroached on the front porch, and a feral rooster strutted around like Henrietta's heir in the yard. The corrugated metal roof had begun to rust but was otherwise intact, and, remembering, he could almost hear the thunderous sound of July rain storms pounding on it as he lay awake in the blue room. The cousins had sold the property to a neighbor, and now Hal was glad for that. No one lived in the house, but Hal could tell that the new owner was making some attempt to keep it habitable, with plywood covering the doors and the lower portions of windows.

"Can we get in?" Tara asked after Hal had sat silent a moment.

"I imagine. You want to look around some?" When she nodded, they climbed out and he found a flashlight and screwdriver in his toolbox and led her to the steps. They heard doves cooing, but for once, Hal didn't find it annoying.

The stairs and the long covered porch were sound, but dozens of the scroll-cut balusters were missing, kicked out and broken up for campfire kindling, Hal guessed, by Mexicans making their way to Tucson and Phoenix. The ones that remained were dusty gray. Aunt Henrietta, like most of her neighbors, had called such travelers wetbacks, and she would hire one or two for occasional work like trenching or picking fruit. Hal had known where their trails crossed Henrietta's property, where they camped or rested on their hike north. Most times they would move on when they saw him, but sometimes they would wait for him to approach, then ask for directions or for food. If it was morning, he would give them his lunch and point them toward the next water tank to the north or east.

As they approached, hummingbirds alternately sucked at the lantana and buzzed Hal's and Tara's faces. They climbed the steps to the long porch, and Hal could not help remembering sitting here with his aunt in the summer Sunday twilight while she sipped her weekly gin ration from a tall glass. Now that they were close, Hal could see that the plywood covering the front door was ragged from being torn away dozens of times; the nails that had once held it were now just anchors for baling wire that held the cover more or less in place. He put the screwdriver in his back pocket and began unlashing it. After the second strand of wire was unwound, he was able to set the plywood aside, and they entered. The top panes of window glass had never been covered, and there was more light in the house than Hal expected, but he turned on the flashlight anyway and handed it to Tara.

The wainscoting was still intact and white in the front room, the parlor Henrietta had called it, but the flowery wall paper was peeling badly. Two bare wires protruded from the ceiling where there had used to be a brass chandelier, and Hal said, "Of course they wouldn't have left the fixtures." There was still the same rag rug on the floor, which Hal remembered had mostly been blue but was now the color of dried mud and urine. He told Tara that they had both sat here most evenings after supper, he in an upholstered chair reading about Hannibal or Washington and she in her spindle rocker browsing the Farm Journal or Reader's Digest with her ancient dog Shep at her feet. He led her through the house and through the memories, Henrietta's room next, where he remembered he had seldom entered because it felt vaguely uncomfortable and orderly, but now with dusty gauze curtains and broken glass near the window and a stained, cigarette-burnt mattress that made Hal wonder aloud if it had been hers…if that was the same bed in which she had died. They crossed the peeling linoleum in the kitchen and dining room and entered the bathroom, the red room, which took its name from the wallpaper, not just red but a sinful scarlet, flocked and somehow suggesting a whorehouse to him since he had turned thirteen and old enough to know that a whorehouse might be of some use to him sometime. The bath tub had been iron and porcelain, with bright brass feet, but it was gone, and Hal found himself saying he hoped the new owner had taken it. The oak pull-chain toilet tank was still in place, and he stepped over to test it. Water whooshed through the bowl, stained with waste and rust. "That's one way of keeping people from peeing on the walls," he smiled. Finally, they came back to the other front bedroom, the blue room, where mice skittered away as they entered. He leaned against the wall and said nothing.

"I bet this was your room," she said and watched him nod. "The blue is like the color of your eyes." She paused. "Yes, I've looked at your eyes a lot--studied them really."

He knew she was watching for his reaction and he knew he blushed then and wondered if the half-lit room was hiding it.

"It looks like a man's room but I can't imagine you here as a little boy."

"I was a little boy before I got here. In Wyoming."

"I can't imagine you as a little boy at all, baby." She hugged him then, suddenly and tightly, with her head turned to the side against his chest and her forearms pressing against his shoulder blades, the flashlight aimed at the ceiling now.

He did not let himself hug her back, although he wanted to, thinking of her age and his age and Doris and Judd and Midge, and wondering if he had been stupid to let her talk him into 'just being friends.'
*****

Until Midge died, Hal enjoyed working Saturdays, partly because that was when Tara put in hours for her dad, but he also liked to have a few Wild Turkeys while he worked and Saturdays were a good day for that, customers tipping him and saying to pour himself one and Gary and Judd and the waitresses too busy to notice that he actually did and Tara noticing but thinking it was clever. After the Diamond Queen tour, Hal took to leaving for work a half hour early and arriving with flowers he put in a vase on the bar near the waitress station. His landlady, Mrs. Thadbury, tried to keep wattle blooming in her garden all the time, and he would clip off two or three yellow heads from her shrubbery and mix it in with flowers picked from her garden, jonquils when they were in season, and otherwise whatever she happened to have in bloom. When Judd asked him why there was suddenly a vase of flowers in his bar, Hal said, "I just thought it would make things a little softer, maybe get some of the ladies coming back." When Doris noticed them, he explained the same way. The first time Tara saw them, her eyes fixed on them and then on Hal's eyes, but she did not ask about them. And sometimes, perhaps once a month, they met earlier on Saturday morning, always at Mija's, for coffee and sometimes huevos rancheros or menchaca and eggs, where they continued telling their stories.

On Saturdays and league nights, the Saguaro's bar served a lot of pitchers of beer, mostly Schlitz, and a fair number of mixed drinks, mainly well bourbon, but one thing they didn't pour a lot of was wine. They always had open jugs of Gallo ready to pour, red and white, but the same gallon bottles would last for weeks, no pinot grigio at all, and Hal had to go to a liquor store to find some. He kept it very cold, and on Saturdays, he would keep a glass of it behind the bar and then set it out on a coaster for Tara when she sat down on a break. She would finish the glass during her shift, never asking for more as if it was a rule she had, and she was almost always gone by seven anyway, Saturday night being her night to go out with friends. There was nothing different that night either.

Hal always obeyed his own rules about the WT's too, no more than four, nothing after eleven and never, ever anything at all if Judd had asked him to make the night drop. His Saturday drinks really didn't have anything to do with Midge dying anyway, he knew. And the police never asked if he'd been drinking that day, though they did ask all about Judd, whose drinking did have something to do with it after all. It didn't matter though; he felt guilty anyway.

Hal noticed the detectives called him Mr. Mull and referred to Judd as Mr. Judd, and both names sounded a little odd, no one else ever addressing them that way. His head hurt where the thieves had hit him, and he was sure that Judd's head hurt from drinking too much and the sting of losing his wife, snatched away like a mouse taken by an owl in the night.

Those first interviews were done in Judd's office, away from the custodians who were cleaning the bowling alley, the restaurant and the lounge. It seemed like he had to tell his story over and over and answer the same questions again and again. He could see Judd was not only broken with grief but also angry, not just with the bastards who had preyed on Midge and him, but with the police too, for not having the bastards yet, and with him too maybe, for not doing enough or not doing the right thing, never taking the night drop seriously enough, not having the Trooper out and ready, not anticipating they would be jumped. Or maybe Judd was mad at himself.

Hal had to admit the detective was asking some questions he didn't like either, almost like he had done the robbery, while the second detective just sat there studying him. Didn't Mr. Judd usually take the money himself? Yes, but I've made the drop before. Why did Mrs. Judd take it this time? She insisted. Why were you accompanying her to the bank instead of Mr. Judd? Judd felt like he had had a couple too many and he told me to go along. Why were you serving him all those drinks? Cuz he ordered them. But the robbers approached when you were getting into Mr. Judd's truck? Yes, but it wasn't really an approach--they rushed from behind. But you turned and saw them and didn't have time to get the .357 out of your pocket? That's right. Mr. Judd has a holster for it, so wouldn't it have been easier to pull from your belt? We always assumed that if there was a problem, it would be at the bank, not here, so I had it in my pocket. I was gonna put it on the seat after I got in the truck. But you saw these guys long enough to recognize them? I told you they were in the bar most of the evening, same guys--at least the two I saw were the same, so I assumed the third guy was the same, the guy over on *her* side of the truck. He looked at Judd when he said *her*, with the sinking feeling. He thought suddenly about Tara then, wondering if she knew yet, if Judd had called her. But of course probably not.

"And I saw them from the ground, looking up at them, with the guy's foot on my neck. You want me to describe 'em? I've been here for an hour and you haven't asked for a description yet. I saw the car too--'65 Impala."

The second detective, the one who had just been watching, leaned forward now and said, "You can let us do our job, Mr. Mull."

That one didn't get past Judd, whose eyes flashed. He said, "We're just waiting for you to start is all. Those assholes are probly in Mexico by now. Hal says he put a slug into the trunk as it was pulling away."

The second detective said, "Mr. Mull better hope he didn't hit one of the guys in the car and send him to the morgue."

Judd said, "Well then at least you'd have a chance of finding him." Hal was relieved to hear his anger directed at the cops instead of him. And these cops *are* kind of assholes, way out of line, no sympathy at all for Judd, like his wife is nothing--*was* nothing. Or maybe they're just trained to be detached…

The second detective stared at Judd, and the first detective went back to the questions as if he hadn't heard a word of this. And they hit you with--what was it again? Lug wrench, one of those single ones with the crook in it. Hal touched the bandage at the side of his head.

Judd couldn't contain his irritation any more. He said, "Well *I* want their fuckin' description, Hal. What did they look like?" and then for the benefit of the two detectives, "These guys may keep my magnum for a while, but I got other firearms."

Hal looked at Judd but hesitated, knowing that this would either annoy the cops or Judd, depending on whether he answered, but he'd been thinking back to what they looked like in the bar now for almost three hours. "They were all in their twenties, but getting close to thirty, I'd say. Tallest guy was about six-one, my height, a white guy, with dark hair and eyes, and the other two were about five-ten, both Mexican I think, long wavy hair. The tall guy was wearing a blue pullover shirt, dark blue and plain, with a collar and buttons just at the top, ya know. He must have been the one…the one that went to the passenger side. One of the Mexicans had a striped shirt--horizontal stripes, and the other had this blue tee shirt that fit him tight, sleeveless, like he was trying to show off his build, big shoulders and biceps. He was the guy who hit me with the wrench. All of 'em wore jeans." He kept his eyes on his boss. "I'm sorry, Judd."

Judd stared back at Hal for a moment, his hard eyes not changing. Then he looked at the cops again and said, "Are you getting this in your notes, or you guys just have a great memory?"

The interviews went on until after seven. By that time, the detectives finally did ask Hal to repeat what the robbers looked like, what they drove away in and whether he could remember the license plate number, which he did. It was probably stolen, they said, and Judd said, "That mean you ain't gonna bother looking for the car?"

When the detectives finally left, Judd asked Hal to follow him home. He said, "I just don't know how she'll react," Tara of course. What he meant was that he didn't know how to tell her. In either case, Hal didn't see how his being there would help, but he said, "Yeah, I can come," wishing that Doris had worked tonight, thinking he could pick her up on the way, but then realizing the news would be hard for her too, and that it would be his chore to tell her. He consented because *he* didn't know how Tara would react, and because he felt responsible. Why hadn't he put the trooper in his belt instead of his coat pocket? Why had he assumed that an attempted robbery would happen at the bank, not in the bowling alley parking lot? Lotta good combat training did him.

When he arrived at Judd's house, it was already past nine. Judd had turned the radio on low but audible, country and western, and started coffee, but he had not waked his daughter. "I called her before I left but I got the answering machine." Hal was thinking, Does he expect me to wake her up? Waiting for the coffee, he told Hal to sit at the kitchen bar on a stool. He got three mugs out of a cupboard and poured about a shot of vodka into each one. "Want some eggs?" he said, still waiting for the coffee. Hal shook his head, wishing at least that they could start. Finally, when both were sitting and silently sipping the spiked coffee, Tara appeared in a yellow terry cloth robe and said, "Where's Momma?"

"Come and sit down, Darlin'. Somethin' happened late last night. She's not here."

"Waddya mean something happened? *What* happened?"

"Come and sit, Darlin'. I'm trying to tell you."

She didn't move. "I never liked her going there to bring you home late at night. *What* happened?"

Judd said, "Oh for God's sake," and stood up. He took her hand and said, "I need you to sit here." There was a silence then except for the DJ saying something about Johnny Cash.

Hal went to the coffee pot and topped off the third mug with coffee and set it on the bar counter. She looked at him, staring at the bandage around his head, but let Judd lead her to the bar stool and sat in it. "What happened, Hal?"

"There were these men. They came at us in the parking lot." He watched her from across the counter, expecting her to break somehow, screaming in denial or sobbing pitifully. He waited on Judd to take over the story of what had happened.

She said, "All right," waiting. She picked up the coffee and slurped it noisily, the way she'd learned from Hal. The radio filled the silence again, "The Ballad of Ira Hayes." Hal remembered once their hearing it together when they had met for coffee. She had asked first who was singing it, and he said Johnny Cash; she said, "Sounds like a protest song. You never hear of country singers singing protest songs;" and he said, "Never thought of it as a protest song;" and she said, "Course it is, but is it protesting the white man's treatment of American Indians or ignorance about alcoholism?" and he wondered why she called them American Indians instead of just Indians, never hearing the term before except when the newsmen were doing stories about those Indian guys out there on Alcatraz.

As they had gotten to know each other, since 'the ranch trip' as she called it, he had told her he didn't think much of protesters. When he said, "I don't remember war protests when I was going in the army," she said, "Maybe our society is getting smarter now." When he said, "I have a hunch that a lot of protesters are more interested in sex and dope than in peace and civil rights," she said, "Well, I know I am," saying it without a smile so that he would know she wasn't joking.

She hadn't wanted him to know right away about her experiences with boys or with dope either--and she was the kind of girl who had done lots more of one than the other, she said, and if she had developed a habit, it was definitely not related to drugs, implying that it was okay for a girl to be promiscuous as long as she didn't get hooked on anything. "Besides, that's how men are, so why not women too, right?" Asking for his approval, and he had said, "Well, my aunt always said if it was good for the goose, it was good for the gander." And it really didn't bother him except it made him reflect on 'the ranch trip.'

Then he was aware of the kitchen again, hearing about drunken Ira Hayes and finally hearing Judd speak. "Your mother was making the night drop for me, took the lock bag, gonna ride along with Hal in my truck and then come back for me. They come at 'em." The words came softer and slower. Judd paused to stuff the tears back. "Two of 'em come at Hal and bashed his head and stood over him…the third one went after the bag, and I guess your mom wouldn't let go…the bastard hit her with somethin'--a pistol probly."

She was looking at her father now, waiting for him to go on, but he wouldn't. After a moment, she said, "Well, she's okay, right? Where is she? Is she in the hospital?" Hal thought, She knows but can't admit it yet, making him say it, hoping it's not so but making him say it.

"Oh my God, Darlin'," Judd said, and that was all he could say, hunching over as he sat in the stool.

She looked at Hal again.

He reached his hand across the Formica counter and touched her hand where it still clutched the coffee mug. "I'm sorry, Tara. Your mother passed."

She sat silent for a very long time so that once again the only sound was the radio, Johnny Cash having given way to Loretta singing gospel, maybe because it was Sunday, Hal thought. The tears came very slowly to her eyes, and she said, "Well, that's it then," surprising him. When Hal squeezed her hand tighter, she pulled the mug away and took another slurping sip. "I want to see her. Judd, you need to take me to see her."

Judd couldn't look up. Instead, he said, "That's not a good idea, Darlin'."

"I need to see my mother. I need to say good bye to her, Judd. If you don't take me, Hal will take me, or I'll go myself." Her voice was calm. She set her eyes on Hal, and he knew he would have to.

"Those guys were in the bar half the night. I should have known something wasn't right with them. I shoulda been ready, Tara. I had the Trooper and it was loaded." It wasn't really enough. "It was my fault, Tara."

"Let me get dressed," she said and left the room.

Hal waited for Judd to say something else, but there was only the radio, Loretta longing to hear that tender voice as then.

As they rode toward the morgue, Hal said, "Your dad is right about things sometimes. Even if they let you in to see your mom, it might be pretty upsetting for you."

There was a pause, but then Tara started telling him about a friend of hers, a nineteen-year-old boy who had joined the army, and Hal thought that she was changing the subject. "It shocked me, shocked all of us. Robert never thought the war was right. He even protested. He was in that protest at the university that got out of hand…when they trashed the police car and everything. When things got crazy, Robert backed away from the trouble, but he didn't leave. He just watched. Up to that point, it was just the campus cops you know, but then they called the sheriffs in and everybody scattered except the crazy guys--this Marxist guy named Conrad and some of the anarchists. And a few of us, me and Robert and some others, we pulled back to watch it all happen. And two weeks later he joins the army."

He felt her inspecting him now, as if she were waiting for a response, so he said, "Okay," aware now that in her mind anyway, the story about the college boyfriend was relevant, but not seeing the connection.

"I tried to talk him out of it. All of us did, his friends. Here he is doing something that he's always thought was wrong…and besides that risking his own ass to do it. For Christ sake, I know a couple guys who went to Canada to avoid the draft, and here he is joining the army and all he can say when I ask him why is he feels like he *has* to."

"So he's gone now?"

"Yeah, so you see, don't you?"

Hal nodded. "They still may not let you in though." The technicians on duty certainly didn't seem inclined to let her in. First they said it was not possible, that the procedures didn't allow for that, no, not even for immediate family, and next that it was not possible on a Sunday, and after haggling and waiting for two hours and making calls to Judd's lawyer Fred and the ACLU and her priest and the Bishop of Arizona, that it was not possible unless she was accompanied by one of the medical examiners. Then it was another hour-and-a-half, her begging the same people to twist the arm of the ME's office to have one of the assistant ME's show up and then waiting for him and finally leaving Hal in the outer room and disappearing through the doors. In a half-hour, she came back, dry-eyed and silent, and that's how he drove her home.

The cops caught two of the robbers a week later, the Mexican ones who, it turned out, were the cousins Ruiz, the older one born in Agua Prieta and the younger one in Douglas. They were living in a south side duplex on a street lined with duplexes, each one a reverse floor plan of the ones on either side, but painted a variety of greens and beiges in different stages of weathering. A patrolman had spotted the Impala with the bullet hole and the matching license plate number parked on the street. Miguel, the older cousin, had done a decent job of disguising the plate with half-inch adhesive tape so that FBE looked like EBE. The patrolman never would have spotted that, but Miguel also tried to make 318 look like 818, with the result that the two 8's looked different enough to catch the cop's eye as he cruised down Thirty-Fourth Street.

Miguel and Josue, his muscular cousin, had been smoking some very good velvet bud the night before and then drinking Cuervo-spiked Budweisers with their chorizo and eggs in the morning as they watched "The Price is Right," so they were asleep in the front room when the cops crashed through their doors and put shotguns on them, and they did not really move very fast after that either. They rolled right away on their partner, before they even left the duplex. They claimed their main man Alex came up with the idea and had been watching how they brought the cash outside to a pickup truck in a big bag at two or three in the morning, always the same guy wearing the big gun, and they'd expected him and not the other guy and the lady, and so there was the big bag and this time no gun, so they went for the score, and yes, Alex had gone to the old lady's side and smashed her head with his Ruger when she wouldn't let go of the canvas bag, too bad.

Alex's arrest didn't go quite as smoothly. Alex Riordan was his name. He was staying in a second floor room on the edge of downtown, upstairs from a blood and plasma donation center and about a block from the Greyhound terminal, exactly where the cousins had said. It was also not too far from where Dillinger had been arrested in 1934. Maybe that was why he tried to shoot his way out of the rented room with his Ruger. When the police hit his door with a battering ram, the lock tore out instantly, but the jamb held, and so did the chain. It was enough of a warning for Alex to field his pistol and roll onto the floor, where he started firing. One of his shots caught an officer in the thigh, but not before the ram had smashed the door a second time, tearing away the chain and a chunk of the oak door. When the policemen outside the door could hear the clicking from his empty Ruger, they poured into the room. One of them, a patrolman named Melton, shot Alex dead where he lay. Tara quit working at the bowling alley after her mother died, and as soon as she graduated from high school, she moved into an apartment near the university. Judd's objections were strong enough that Hal had to wait for him to be out of the house before he would come over and load her things into his pickup.

Three

Caje'eme's uncle had told him many times that he was named after a great man. On Friday, he was riding on the back of a flatbed north-bound for Sasabe with a load of half-seasoned mesquite firewood, wearing a bandana over his nose to block the dust and holding a duffel bag on his lap. It did not make him feel like a great man. But if he were home, what would he be doing after all? Working in a restaurant, or reading in the university library perhaps, or maybe having fun with the girl, so no, this was better--getting money so he could keep going to the classes and keep being with the girl. Maybe be like that first Caje'eme in a few years.

When the flatbed slowed to turn northwest at Saric, where the road separated from the shoulder of the Rio Altar river bed, Caje'eme jumped off, clutching the duffel. He twisted his ankle as he landed, and rolled into the powdery dust. Wincing, he pushed himself up, slapped the dust away and made his way to the clay bank and then into the sandy river bed. As he had on the previous trips, he continued the trek north in the mostly-dry Rio Altar, treading as much as possible in dampened sand, where it was cool and gave only slightly to his weight. He trailed along the western bank where the shade from cottonwoods and mesquites was just beginning to lengthen. About halfway to El Busani, he began to wonder if he'd broken something in his ankle or foot. He set the duffel bag down and knelt to tighten the laces on his Converse high-tops and limped on, but he knew he could not walk all the way to the frontier now. He needed the steps left in him for the hills beyond the border.

When the river bed turned sharply east and told him he was just south of El Busani, he climbed the bank, continuing north through the thick mesquite and onto the alluvium, under the highway bridge, and still north. Broad farmland stretched to his right, but Caje'eme trailed the tree-lined north-bound road until he reached the town.

At the little dark cantina in El Busani, he ate a burro of beans and carnitas and bought a gallon jug of the local mescal. Then he waited fifty yards away in an adobe ruin, with his right leg raised up on what used to be a window sill. He lay back on the duffel as if it were a cushion. His thick black hair lay flat and smooth on his head, his nose was hooked like a bird's nose, and his mustache was fine-haired and wide, rounding the look of his smooth brown face. He wore a long-sleeved white shirt. He would be late now, and he would have to call the girl, he knew, or she would have to wait. He thought about the girl, tall and lithe and blond. She always called him Caje.

After four o'clock, men began entering the cantina, locals, he assumed. He watched the little parking lot, powdery dust rising as each set of tires rolled in, the Sonoran darkness descending. Finally, a little after eight o'clock a vehicle approached from the north. He heard it before he saw it, a noisy clatter coming in from the dirt road. He watched its headlights until they blinked off as the old pickup truck rumbled in. A floodlight beamed out into the darkness from above the cantina's door, and he could see two men get out of their faded red truck. They looked like braceros, with their sinewy arms, hard dark skin and relaxed gait. They would have to be the ones to give him a ride. He limped closer and waited on the outer perimeter of light. He clutched the duffel. A half-moon rose, and the temperature dropped. He opened the duffel and extracted a dark blue sweatshirt and put it on. He waited.

Two hours later when the men came out, their gait was unsteady. Caje lifted his duffel and the gallon jug and approached them. "¿Me puede dar un paseo al norte? ¿La frontera?" The men's eyes were glassy but steady.

"Vamos a El Cumaral," one said.

"¿Es cercano a la frontera?" He held up the jug. "Por favor."

They nodded at the bed and took the mescal and got into the cab. Caje sat in the straw-strewn bed with his back against its side. He rested his right foot on a smooth spare tire. The truck bumped along for several miles, then turned east, crossed a creek and turned north again. He had not crossed the border east of Rio Altar before, and he wondered where he would find himself. He had over an hour to think about it as the little truck made its way slowly among the ruts.

They stopped at a fork, where Caje could smell livestock and water. He saw several low adobe buildings. The engine idled, and one of the men got out from the passenger side of the truck and said, "Es El Cumaral. Jorge le llevará sobre el filo."

Caje said, "¿El filo…La frontera?" He could smell mescal on the man's breath.

The man nodded and walked toward the buildings. He had left the truck door open, and Caje climbed out of the bed and into the cab next to the driver. The truck turned at the fork and began climbing. Caje bounced on the bench seat, clutching the duffel.

In fifteen minutes they were descending again. There was a road of sorts, but it seemed to open up only a few feet ahead of them in the headlights between scrub oaks and piñons. Branches screeched along the sides of the truck and over its roof. Then they came to a small meadow, where Jorge circled around a tall ponderosa. As the truck came around, Caje saw a barbed wire fence with two small signs. One read 'Coronado National Forest,' the other 'United States-Not a Port of Entry.' Immediately to the left of the sign there was wide gap in the wire.

Jorge said, "No entrada," and smiled at Caje.

Caje smiled back and got out of the truck. "Muchas gracias, señor. ¿Donde esta Ruby?"

Jorge pointed. "Norte recta y un poco este. Seguir la huella. Pero tenga cuidado. Hay hombres malos."

"Okay, Jorge. Tengo cuidado." He slung the duffel onto his shoulder and moved toward the signs, limping but moving quickly. The truck's lights shone directly on the gap in the wire, and as he approached it, Caje could see curls of the wire twisted back and wound haphazardly around the T-posts on either side of the gap. He wondered how many times the strands had been cut and repaired and then cut again. He could hear Jorge revving to start the ascent again, and soon the lights of the truck disappeared. A few yards inside the fence, he stepped into a thicket of oak and sat on the thick duff. He checked his watch and waited for a half-hour, moving once to raise his right leg onto the duffel. He remembered his uncle saying that a Yaqui could wait longer and quieter than anyone—better than an Apache. He listened for engine noises, for footfalls, for voices, for dogs, for anything that did not belong to the night. He heard the fluttering of bats, the padding of a coyote and the swishing of puffs of breeze through the leaves. At eleven o'clock, he took a canteen from the duffel and drank and then set out on the trail again, limping.

The moon had risen, just edging over into a waning stage, and he could see the trail about ten yards ahead, twisting between scrub oak and clusters of rock, sloping down to a creek and then following it. He stopped every hour and rested with his ankle raised up on the duffel. At one clearing along the trail, he saw signs of a camp—rocks circled for a fire pit, broken glass, a few rusting pop-top cans, diapers, a torn shoe…

At dawn, he came to a rocky earth dam on the creek with a silvery camp trailer parked in a flat spot on the far side of the pond. The pond looked still and green and cool, inviting him. There was no car or truck at the camp though, and the trailer stood silent. The campers' fire pit looked cold among a pair of camp chairs and a heap of firewood.

He circled wide to the west, upslope and beyond the dam, and found a wide crevice of granite behind a manzanita bush. He pulled his canteen out and stuffed the duffel into the crevice. He studied the place so that he could find it later—the purple-barked Manzanita lush with blooms, the giant twisted trunk of a dwarfish oak, the towering rocks that leaned together in a kiss to form the crevice. Then he walked downslope again to the trail. He could see that the trail was joined by a narrow road on the far side of the dam. It arced over a hill to the east. He knew it must lead to the Ruby Road, but remembered Jorge had told him to stay on the trail. He walked up the creek trail to the dam. There was still no sound from the camp trailer.

Caje stooped to fill his canteen, then sat on a low rock on the dam and started to unlace the sneaker from his throbbing foot, but he saw the swelling there and thought better of it. Instead, he worked from the bottom of the laces and tightened them even more and retied the sneaker. Then he swung his foot out into the pond and leaned back on his elbows. The morning air was cold, and wisps of vapor rose from the tiny pond. His ankle throbbed. He could call the girl when he got to Ruby if they had a phone there, but where could they meet now?

Perhaps he dozed, or perhaps he was thinking of the girl again, but he did not hear the approaching car until it was turning in at the camp to his left. It was a two-tone El Camino with two men in it, no more than a hundred feet away.

Caje could see the passenger stare at him. He turned slowly on the rock, picking up the canteen, and lifted his wet leg out of the water, standing and testing the foot as water bled from his sneaker.

"Mornin!" the man said, but it was really a question, like 'Who the hell are you?' He opened the car door and stood. He was a big man, well over six feet, with long black hair in a ponytail and a beard. He wore a heavy army shirt, sleeves torn away to make it a vest, over a red shirt, jeans and boots. A name patch on the shirt read 'Hicks.'

Caje smiled faintly and nodded. "Buenos dias." Time to act lost, he decided. He fought the urge to run. "¿Donde esta Calabasas?"

The driver from the El Camino went to the camp trailer and tried the door—locked. Then he came around the car and stood next to Hicks. He was shorter, about Caje's size, with a crew cut, in an oversized white tee shirt, and baggy fatigues and sneakers. He wore a revolver in a holster on his belt. His tee shirt covered his belt line except where it was tucked behind the holster. "What's he want?"

"Says he's looking for Calabasas. Just a wetback I guess." Never glancing at the smaller man, he smiled at Caje.

Caje remembered from his lit class: One may smile and smile and be a villain. He said, "¿Donde esta Calabasas?"

"Northeast. Follow the road." The big man motioned behind him with his thumb. "You alone? Solo?"

Caje nodded. "Si, estoy solo." He smiled and moved forward along the dam to where the two men stood, trying not to limp. His heart pounded but he moved ahead. "Gracias." When he got close to them, he moved left toward the road. The big man leaned at him suddenly, and he almost broke into a run. He nodded and said,

"Muchas gracias." He listened as closely as he could, walking up the road as it rose to the east.

*****

The two men turned and silently watched Caje distance himself along the road until he neared the top of the ridge. "So if that asshole's a wetback, where's his stuff?" the short man said. "He's hiding a pack somewhere."

"Yeah," the big man said. "Get up to the perch and see what gives."

The smaller man hurried to unlock the camp trailer and went inside. When he returned, he was carrying a set of binoculars. Over his shoulder, on a sling, was a Ruger Mini-14. He scrambled up the hillside.

"Well, don't shoot him," he called. "Not unless he's already carrying something," he added to himself.

The small man reached an outcropping of rock and stepped to the edge, raising the binoculars with both hands. In a few minutes he came down again. "Still ain't carryin' nothing but he left the road."

"Which way?"

"Back to the west."

"Little shit! He's a mule for sure."

"Circling back for something. Gotta be."

"Okay. Lock up. Let's get on up the trail. He'll probably come back that way till he gets close." He ambled to the spot where the trail touched the road's dead end and waited.

The small man locked their trailer and joined him. "How you want to do this?" They were both looking north, up-trail.

"You get ahead of me with the rifle, and then go off-trail to the right. I'll stay on the trail and meet him coming back. Gimme the handgun."

The small man handed him the revolver. They started together, and then the small man climbed away to the right. He stopped after a few steps and brought the rifle's sling over to his right shoulder, and then resumed. When he was twenty yards away, he waved back to the big man and started making his way parallel to the trail.

The big man had put the revolver into his belt at the middle of his back. He walked slowly, knowing that his partner would have to set the pace. The trail was rough, barely visible in stretches, but still easier to negotiate than the hillside. He began counting his steps, stopping every twenty paces to let the small man get ahead again, looking hard up the trail for any sign of movement and checking to his right to find his partner.

*****

After he had cleared the top of the rise, Caje continued walking along the road for a quarter mile and then turned uphill to his left. He was glad he had not been sitting with the duffel bag at the pond, but he knew he had to retrieve it as fast as he could. The man in Guadalajara and the other man in Tucson did not forgive.

He moved cautiously, staying in the shade when he could. He climbed with difficulty. His ankle hurt, and his shoes kept slipping on the duff. If he had not twisted his ankle, he thought, he would be having an easy walk in the dry wash bed. He would wear boots next time…or he would not be careless and twist his ankle next time…or maybe he would not do a next time. Safer to study literature…easier too, he thought. He passed the crest of a hill and stood in the shadow of a twisted oak. He scanned to his left for movement, but there was none. He listened and looked hard down the hillside for some sign of the trail.

He removed his sweatshirt and tied its arms at his waist. He looked at the sky and the shadows. He knew that he was going in the right direction, so he would hit the trail at some point. Over the next ridge or perhaps the one after that. He planned his route down the hillside. There was cover, but the hillside had a good deal of duff. He started down the slope, sideways to keep from slipping, facing south and scanning. He held the canteen in his left hand. Leading with his right leg was painful, but it was better than falling or losing control of his speed, and better than turning his back to the south, where the two men might be. In a few minutes, he reached the bottom of the slope and began to ascend toward the next crest, now straight ahead, stepping on rocks and other breaks in the duff.

At the crest, there was a promontory of granite. When he crawled onto it, he could see the trail about fifty yards below him. He raised his eyes, just slits, to the south horizon and crawled them slowly back along the route he imagined to be the trail. There was no movement. He checked his watch and lay there listening. He would wait, he told himself.

But he was becoming anxious about the duffel bag. His hiding place between the kissing rocks was a good one, but what if they found it? He sidled down to the trail and began to trace it back toward the duffel.

*****

Hicks stared uphill and waited for the small man to look at him. When he did, Hicks pumped his right fist, telling him to move faster, but the small man responded by stopping and signaling 'fuck you' with his left. He smiled up at him and nodded. It really was as fast as his partner could manage along the slope, but Hicks was starting to wonder if the mule had avoided them somehow. He looked back along the trail, but he could not see past its last hook around a piñon tree. He estimated that they had covered about three-hundred yards. He looked uphill, where the small man had now disappeared. He peered along the trail ahead of him to the next bend and took twenty more steps—still nothing. Then twenty more…

The next time the small man came into sight, he was crouching and holding his left fist up. Yeah, I'm paying attention, he thought. Standing still, he pulled the revolver from his belt and stared ahead to where the trail curved out of sight, ready if their quarry came into view. After a moment, he looked uphill, and the little man was motioning him forward again, out of his crouch and moving out of sight. Nothing.

Hicks put the revolver back in his belt and went to counting steps. In the next four hundred yards, the small man raised his fist twice. Once he even held his left hand up to his eyes. Each time, Hicks pulled the gun from his belt and readied himself, but there was only the momentary pause and then the signal to move ahead again. He jogged forward until he saw his flank man again and waited for eye contact. When the small man stayed in his crouch and did not look at him, Hicks called to him, "Come on down."

The small man stood and glared down. He held his left palm up and moved it side to side.

Hicks waved for him to come down to the trail. "I'm thirsty."

The small man shook his head. He pointed at Hicks and put his hand over his head in the cover sign. Then he pointed at himself and pointed ahead, crouched and moved on.

"All right, ya son of a bitch," Hicks said to himself, "but sure as shit, we missed him." He squatted to wait.

*****

At ten o'clock, Tara said she would not let herself worry until noon, even though Caje was over an hour late. She asked herself again if she might be in the wrong place, waiting at the wrong arroyo while Caje stood scratching his head and wondering where she was. But no, she could see all the markers he had shown her. To her left was the giant boulder sitting atop the three smaller boulders, shiny with mica, where the road crossed the wash. To her right, buried to its window in sand, was the rusty, bullet-riddled car hood. She was sitting on the same blanket in the same shady spot she'd waited on that first time two months ago, when he had arrived fifteen minutes late. She had carved his name into an oak tree while she waited, and he had asked her not to do that again because it had offended the tree's spirit. She found his name there on the tree. He had smiled and said the only way to heal the tree's spirit was to make love in its shade, and so they had.

But it was one o'clock now and way too hot for outdoor lovemaking, and she was worried. Her thin eyebrows straightened as she focused her blue eyes as far up the wide sandy wash as she could manage, hoping for a man's form to appear suddenly from the mesquite and desert broom that stretched along its course. Waiting, she had intermittently heard gunfire, and though she knew the area was a prime hunting area, she also remembered the stories Hal and Johnny told about Ruby and Arivaca and the hard people who lived out here.

She thought about driving the road again, thinking that maybe it was Caje who had taken a wrong turn. She had already driven Tres Bellotas Road for five miles in each direction, stopping at each arroyo crossing, turning off the engine and calling both ways, scanning for him. She wished now that she had brought his Jeep instead of her MG. She had already scraped bottom half a dozen times on the rough road, and she could not take the MG off road. Well, she thought, I have to do something.

She rose abruptly and stepped out of the shade and jogged back to her car. She pulled her wavy blond hair into a tight ponytail and wound a band around it behind her head and climbed into the little car. She turned it around and drove northeast, toward Arivaca. She looked for straight-aways where she could make a little speed, but there were almost none. The engine wound too tight to stay in first gear, and she shifted into second whenever the road permitted, but she kept having to stop the little convertible for low spots and ruts in the road, and she cursed the MG for not being synchromesh into first gear. No synchro, no air conditioning, no headrests— should have listened to her father that time. Of course, he doesn't like Caje either, she thought. "Fuck it," she said and ground the transmission into first again.

It was hot, over ninety degrees, and the sun hit her bare thighs and arms relentlessly. Sweat gathered in her armpits and ran down her neck between her small breasts. In one straight section of road, she got the MG into third gear and rested her arm on the door, but it burnt her, and her arm recoiled. As the altitude dropped, she saw more mesquite trees and whitethorn acacias. She kept hoping Caje would step out from under a clump of the brush and smile at her.

*****

Caje was thinking about food as he walked, guessing it was now about eight o'clock and trying to calculate how long it had been since he had eaten the burro in El Busani, and he heard a voice and froze, listening. He looked ahead first and then right and left. And there it was—a slant of white up the hill far to his left. It did not move, but it did not belong there either. His heart pounded as he took one backward step, slow, then another, feeling exposed on the open trail in his white shirt but afraid to turn quickly. With his eyes never wavering from the slant of white, he shrank slowly into a squat and pulled the shirt over his head and held it in a ball in his right hand. Then, finally daring to snap his eyes away, he started duck-walking to his right. He made for a twisted multi-trunk mesquite, whose hanging branches swept near the ground, resembling a giant parched weed. Twenty feet away, then fourteen, then six and then finally in the mesquite's cover. Caje turned slowly and searched the hill side for the slant of white.

It was several minutes before he saw it again, closer now, perhaps eighty yards down-trail and moving slowly. He knew he was still too close to the trail, so he turned slowly and planned a route. There was another weedy mesquite about thirty yards away, but he would have to move slowly, crouching behind manzanitas and dwarfish junipers, though the man in white drew closer every moment. He wanted to leave his shirt and the canteen there, the sweatshirt too, but he decided he could not. Not this close to the trail.

He waited until the slant of white went invisible again, behind a cluster of trees, and then he scooted, bent at the waist, to the next cover and turned and found the white again and waited for it to disappear once more. And so he made his way to the mesquite. In the time it took Caje to get in a squat behind the tree, the man in the white shirt never changed in his pace, never came closer to the trail. To Caje, that meant that so far the man in the white shirt had not seen him. He was a man now, and not just a slant of white cloth, forty yards away, with a rifle slung over his right shoulder.

The mesquite had two huge trunks separating in a vee about two feet off the ground. A lot of its new spring growth hung near the ground along with its tangled dead branches. Good cover from the trail. Caje pulled off his shirt and folded it and covered it with the dark sweatshirt, laying them out on the grass and the duff beneath the tree, and he lay on them with his arms holding him off the earth so that he could see through the vee. Then he was still.

The man negotiated the hillside slowly, stopping repeatedly to scan and then moving ahead again, maintaining his distance from the trail. Caje began to wonder where the big man was. If they were tracking the trail from opposite sides, then the big man would approach him on the right, and there would be no way he would miss his hiding spot. But he knew he could not move to a new place with the white shirt so close. Maybe I should have run, he thought, remembering his high school cross country team for an instant, state champions—but not with the bad ankle, not while the man held the rifle. He waited until the white shirt disappeared behind a clump of brush before he rotated his head to the right to check for the big man. Not there. He crawled his eyes back between the notch in the mesquite, and saw the man in the white shirt now straight across the trail from him, motionless and scouring with his eyes. The man looked far down the trail and then brought his head around, peering closely. The man's head stopped, aiming at the mesquite below Caje and then rising to scan. His head stopped several times, squinting closely into the shade of every big tree, seeming to stare momentarily into Caje's eyes.

Finally, the man looked back along the trail, waved 'come,' and started forward again, keeping his distance from the trail. Caje watched him thread his way, now farther with each of his steps. Caje moved his head right, past the old tree trunk's mass, and watched the trail.

The trees did not stir. The big man came along after a few minutes, walking upright, scanning right and left, but not intently as the man in the white shirt had, stopping sometimes. The protective shade was deep, but Caje knew that there would be a few moments when his blue jeans and his brown skin would be exposed to the big man's view, his white high-tops too. He breathed slowly and tried to blink only when the big man looked away. He became aware of an itch on his shoulder blade and then another on the bottom of his foot. His forearms were beginning to hurt from the constant pressure of his upper body, and his hands tingled from restricted circulation. The itching was especially irksome. It reminded him of a book he had read, but he could not remember the story that went with it. He was thankful when he heard a dove's love call and tried to concentrate on that. And still the man inched along like a giant worm.

Finally, the man passed, ten yards up trail, and then twenty…

As quietly as he could, Caje rolled over on his back, wriggled his back against the rough ground and extended his arms to his side to let the blood return. He would have to stay off the trail to return to his duffel.

Caje heard a voice again, and this time he could hear the big man's words as he called, "We missed him." He lay still and listened. After a few minutes, he could hear two voices, low. He knew they were coming back along the trail.

"Maybe he went back across the road after you come down from the perch. Went the other way."

"Yeah, or maybe he's just holed up."

"Yeah, watching the road waiting for us to leave, the little shit."

"Reminded me o' chasing gooks."

"'cept a gook woulda shot us."

"Yeah,'specially when you hollered at me," his eyes calling the bigger man stupid.

"Well fuck you and him both. I'm hungry."

There was a short laugh. "Well we oughta at least drive around after breakfast."

Then the words turned into fading tones and soon there was only the sound of the dove again. Caje rolled back up on his forearms and saw the two men ambling down the trail toward their camp. After counting slowly to nine hundred to measure his wait time, he rose and began climbing to the next crest. It would be a slow hike back to the duffel.

Four

It took Tara forty minutes to reach the store in Arivaca, where two cowboys stood talking on the porch as she turned off the engine. One of them whistled at her when she got out of the MG. She smiled a thank you at him, her habit, and he removed his hat as she strode past. A cool breeze greeted her as she opened the store's screen door, forced out by a swamp cooler.

She asked the cashier for change and fed quarters into the wall-mount pay phone. The cashier, a wide, old, gray-haired woman, stared at her.

"Hello," Hal answered from the phone.

"Whatcha doin?" she said, knowing he would know her voice. Her phone greeting to him was always the same but sometimes vaguely suggestive in the inflection. The pay phone was not in the direct draft of the swamp cooler, and she fanned herself with her hand.

Hal smiled into the phone, not expecting her call. "Hey Tara!" His voice resonated a little too eagerly, but he kept it low, glancing at the bathroom door. It was still closed. "Just watching the grass grow here. How 'bout you?"

"I'm down by Nogales. Hey Hal, I need a favor."

"Sure. You moving again or something?" Chuckling, he turned away from the bathroom door.

"No, a big favor. I need you to meet me at Halfway with Caje's Jeep." She kept her voice sweet.

Hal knew he would say yes, but now he was calculating what to tell Doris, and he hesitated.   ...forty-five minutes there and another forty-five minutes back... pick up the Jeep...

"Would you please, baby?"

He knew she was teasing him along, but he loved the sound of it when she said 'baby.' "Is the Jeep at your place?" ...was I as crazy as she is when I was nineteen?...I can tell Doris I'm doing an errand for Judd...or is that too easy for her to check on?...

"Yes it is."   She pulled her blouse front back and forth to cool herself. The wide woman stared her disapproval. She lifted an issue of *Popular Mechanics* off the rack nearby and fanned herself.

"Okay," he said. He heard the bathroom door open and he put a business-like inflection in his voice. "You need me to bring it this afternoon, still?"

"Right now if you can, Hal. I really need this."   She stared back at the wide woman, who apparently did not like her merchandise being used as a fan, so Tara slapped the magazine back into place. She turned to face the wall, unbuttoned her blouse and flapped it, first one side then the other. It felt cool, and her nipples hardened.

"Yeah, I guess I can do that. Where's the key?" He tried to inject some irritation into his voice, as if this was something he didn't really want to do--a huge pain in the ass for him. He turned to look at Doris, reading the look on her face, and rolled his eyes at the phone. ...just standing there... not liking this...

"Don't need one. Just use your pocket knife—the little blade."

"Okay. Be there in an hour." ...better sell this...

"And Hal, one other thing, okay? I need one of Daddy's guns—the one in the middle of the black case in the study—you know the one?"

He hesitated. "Well, waddya need that for?"   ...the Thompson... the fucking Thompson...

"Oh, nothin', Hal. I just wanted to show Caje. Daddy won't mind.   Perfect place down here where no one's around. Can you please? You still have his house key, right, and the key to turn off the alarm?" She heard momentary silence in the phone and, behind her, the store's screen door opening, a man's voice asking about cold beer.

Bullshit her dad won't mind! Can't ask her about it now, Hal thought, but I'll call her on it when I see her. "Yeah, okay. I'll bring the jack too." He felt Doris's eyes staring as she listened.

"Huh? What are you talking about? I really need you to be a friend today, Hal." She turned to see who had come in, forgetting for a moment that her blouse was open. Then she pulled her elbows in close to her abdomen, which only exposed her breasts a bit more and made them seem a little larger. She turned back to the wall.

"Yeah, I'll be there. At Amado?"

"Yeah, Halfway, whatever you call it. I'll meet you by the dry lake." She turned her head. A man stared at her. He was tall, hulking tall, with black hair pulled taut in a ponytail.

"Okay," he said, but Tara had already hung up. He looked at Doris and kept talking while he thought about what he would tell her. "It will take me at least an hour or so. You sure you need the hydraulic jack?" He pretended to listen. Finally, Doris looked away and moved to the kitchen. "Yeah, see you soon." He hung up and turned toward her. "Hey, sweetie, I gotta go bail Tara out of a little jam. Needs Caje's Jeep. She's broke down."

Doris looked at him but said nothing. She ran water for the lunch dishes.

Hal used the bathroom. When he came out, headed for the front door, Doris said, "What kinda mess she make this time?"

He took his hat from the hook by the door. "She's broke down in Amado. Her and Caje. Needs a couple tools from Caje's Jeep." He moved across the tiny room toward the kitchen, intending to kiss her.

"Why's she callin' you? Ain't Tonto got no friends?" She glared at him.

He stopped in front of her. "You wanna go with? Do some shopping in Nogales?" He hoped she would not know he wanted her to say no.

"Don't want to spoil your fun."

"No, really. You been wantin' a coupla chairs to go around the kitchen table."

"No. Don't want to fry in that stupid Jeep either."

He bent to kiss her, but she turned away. "Be back in a couple hours then." He put on his hat and turned and left.
*****

The tall man stared at Tara's unbuttoned blouse and smiled at her. He was leaning with the side of his leg against the counter while a shorter man paid for two six-packs of Schlitz in cans. The wide woman was putting them in a bag and asking him if he wanted ice.

"Nah, we got ice. Just the beer and sandwiches, the short man said.

"Kinda hot, ain't it missy," the tall man said, staring at Tara.

She smiled back, but it was clearly a no-thanks smile, and moved to the door, buttoning her blouse again. She felt the tall man's eyes on her until she was outside. An El Camino was parked next to her MG. She got into the convertible and drove away to the east in first gear, watching her mirror as often as the road ahead. She was relieved when she saw the El Camino pull out and head in the opposite direction, although she would be going back that way herself as soon as she retrieved the Jeep. She shifted into second gear and accelerated. The dirt road was better this side of Arivaca, with twists and narrow stretches that presented no problem for the MG, and only a couple of low rutted crossings, where she had to bring her little car to a complete stop. Still, in the time it took her to negotiate the twenty-three ragged miles to Halfway, Hal might arrive before she did.

She thought about Hal for a few minutes, about asking him to come right away, to bring the Jeep, to bring Daddy's antique Thompson, and knowing he would do it. He was so quiet, so friendly, so willing to help her. He always seemed to know what she was thinking, but never commenting on it, so different from her father. And so different from the boys she had dated in high school too, and the college boys, even Caje. But there was his mournful look, the mournful look that just appeared sometimes. She shook her head as if to get rid of the images there.
*****

Hal was careful not to let his tires throw gravel as he left in his truck. He felt sure Doris was watching and listening for signs of his impatience. He did not speed, and he did not hurry until he was several blocks away.

He would drive by Judd's house first to save time. If Judd's truck was already gone, he could slip in and get the Thompson. ...Jesus!...down by Nogales, but perfect to shoot it with no one around... more bullshit...where was she really? ...I'm going to need a better explanation about that...just won't give it to her...

When he drove past Judd's house, he could see the new truck there, parked in the driveway. ...well, I'll get the Jeep first and come back...he's gotta be leaving soon...

It took him fifteen minutes to make his way through traffic to Tara's apartment on Tenth Street. It was on the end of a red brick building situated perpendicular to the street, facing an identical building across a narrow swept yard shaded by fruitless mulberry trees. When Hal pulled into the parking lot, he could see two young men and a girl lounging in lawn chairs in the yard, purposefully avoiding the shade. The girl held a book, but all three of them stared at Hal when he parked between Caje's Jeep and a bright yellow Volkswagen Beetle. He felt the sunbathers' eyes on him, wondering if they knew Tara and Caje. He stared back at them and straightened his hat, wondering if they would think he was stealing the Jeep. He rolled up his window and locked the truck, still feeling their eyes on him. He tipped the brim of his hat at them and climbed into the Jeep and started it with his pocket knife and left.

This time, Judd's truck was gone. Hal inserted the little key to turn off the burglar alarm and let himself into the house. He stood in the quietness for a moment, knowing what it meant to take the gun. His eyes roamed the orderliness of the high foyer walls, the plush rug, the huge grandfather clock and the doorways leading to other parts of the house, where Judd nowadays roamed alone. The left wall was bright white, with framed family photographs standing out from the wall but somehow blending into each other; the opposite wall was dark and cold in the dim light. He felt tension throughout his body—the feeling that he was close to some terrible thing, though he could not see it or hear it. There was only the silence, the deep ticking of the clock and the almost imperceptible whirr of the air conditioner. Hal knew the feeling. It was part of helping Tara do something her father didn't want her to do, like the time he had helped her move out of the big house, or when he had lied to Judd about her marijuana stash. He had known Judd might fire him for those things, or send around a deputy friend to toss his apartment. But this premonition was different, more powerful, more dire. ...why the hell does she want the Thompson?...maybe I should just show up in Amado without it...

The door to Judd's study was on his right, standing open, and he went in. Judd's gun collection stood prominent in a display case behind his desk, framed in black steel, covered by Plexiglas. There was a Confederate musket and bullet mold, an 1877 Colt revolver, an 1873 Winchester, a Marlin .32 standard pocket revolver, but in the center was the pride of Judd's display—the Savage Arms 1928A1 Thompson submachine gun, which, according to Judd, had been used in the invasion at Inchon, but Hal, remembering the smoke and ice and slaughter at the Chosin Reservoir, had always doubted it. The submachine gun Hal had carried was the M3/M3A1, the grease gun. He believes what he wants to believe, Hal thought, but who knows. What Hal did know was that Judd would instantly miss the Tommy gun when he came into the study.

He felt under the desktop for the key to the display case. He opened the center section and took out the gun and laid it on the desk. From one of the drawers below the display case, he lifted four thirty-round magazines, which he stuffed into his pockets as far as they would go. Then he relocked the case, lifted the gun and left the room. He wondered whether Judd was more likely to discover the missing gun with the study's door open or closed and decided to pull it shut. In the foyer, a photo of Tara with her parents caught him ...when she was about ten years old, her eyes shining willful even then...when her mother's eyes shone with life and her father's with love... He closed his eyes until the image faded, then stepped outside and reset the alarm.

The Jeep ran quiet but tight on the residential streets. Hal made his way to the highway, which was marked for two lanes but wide enough to allow simultaneous passing from both directions, as long as all the drivers let that happen. He cinched the cord of his hat tight against his chin and sped south. He slowed for a long line of southbound cars near the Sahuarita Bar and again for a highway patrolman that he spied hiding in the shade of a billboard. The Thompson lay under the passenger seat, but a few inches of its butt projected into view, and Hal did not want to have to explain it to a law officer.

I can't let her take the Thompson, he thought. ...I'll tell her that we're bound to get caught this time...I'll tell her about that trembly feeling I got standing there in the hall...about the photograph with the shining eyes...

Tara was waiting for him in the shade of one of the cottonwood trees that ringed the depression of the dried-up lake. Her thighs looked wide and lovely, half-sitting, half-leaning against the bright red of the MG's fender. When the Jeep left the pavement, roiling up dust, she stood and smiled at Hal.

Hal let the Jeep roll up next to her and turned off the engine.

"Thank you so much, Hal." She leaned into the Jeep and hugged him around the neck.

"So what's going on, girl?" It was impossible not to smile back at her. "What's the Tommy gun for? I almost didn't bring it."

"Nothing, only I wanted to show Caje how cool it is to shoot it." Her smile faded, but only slightly. "'member how Daddy used to take me out in the hills to shoot?"

"Tara, your dad ain't here. And he ain't gonna be happy when he sees the empty spot in his gun case."

The smile disappeared now. "It'll be fine, Hal. I'll get it back before he even knows it's gone—tonight. Okay? You know he never comes home till after two."

"Hal studied her, trying to look inside her but failing. He saw her eyes and her face, reddened by the sun and the heat. Tractor trailers bolted along the highway behind him, diesel engines reverberating like trumpets. "What's going on, Tara...really?"

"Nothing, Hal. Caje and I are just gonna find a safe spot and shoot the Thompson." She examined his face. "Don't be sad, Hal. It's gonna be fine."

"Well, where is Caje anyway?" He looked around, unsurprised when he saw no one.

"He's waiting for me down south. Wanted to visit some friends across the border. I'm gonna pick him up."

"This side, right? You're not crossing over, are you? The rurales catch you with a trench broom, and you'll never come back." But he knew she had won the argument.

"Yeah, over here." Her eyes shone the same way as they had in the photograph. "Okay?" She held the keys for the MG out to him and he took them. She laid her hand on his arm, keeping it there until he stood in front of her, and then she leaned up to him, stretching onto her toes, and kissed him on the cheek.

He was surprised at how bad it made him feel, wondering why the dread was rising toward him like a pool at the bottom of a waterfall.

In a moment, she was driving away. Still holding the keys for the MG, Hal watched her turn onto the highway, raising a cloud of hot dust as the Jeep's rear tires spun on the last patch of dirt before gripping asphalt. He watched the Jeep until it disappeared up the highway with Tara, and his eyes went to the hard dirt under his feet, then rose again even slower to the hilly country that stretched out before him to the west. He squinted at a pair of red hawks circling in the glare of the descending sun and thought of the photograph again, wondering when he would see Tara. He tightened his hand around the keys and pushed himself toward the MG.

Almost back in town, almost at the traffic light that signaled the end of the highway, Hal winced as he realized Tara had turned *north* onto the highway. She had been going somewhere very fast, but not to Nogales. He pulled far to the right and braked to a stop on the pavement's edge. He shook his head repeatedly as he waited for a break in traffic. When it came, he swung the MG hard to the left and raced south again. …where the hell…

*****

The Jeep had negotiated the road's ruts and crossings much better than her MG, and she was able to keep it in second and third gear for the entire return trip, all the while scanning for Caje. But the Jeep did not corner as well as her MG, and she almost lost control of it on a couple of tight turns, once where the road crowded a steep drop-off, even as its washboard surface savagely bounced the Jeep's rear wheels. Good thing I downshifted, she thought. She knew she was going too fast and told herself to look farther ahead and see the road's snaky bends.

Tara hated the desert wind that blasted heat against hair and skin almost every afternoon in late spring. And by the time she reached the arroyo crossing where she was supposed to meet Caje, it was very windy. She wished it was calm, wished the Jeep had a cover from the sun's relentless hammering, wished she had had the sense to wear a hat, wished she had bought something to drink in Arivaca, wished too that they had not started the monthly cross-border runs, but mostly she wished she would find Caje sitting in the shade of the tree where they had made love. Her heart sank when she did not.

She let the Jeep idle and looked hard both directions at the crossing, then turned left onto the sand and crept along the wash. The Jeep was like a giant desert tortoise, winding among low ragged mesquites, thriving desert brooms and clusters of gray igneous stone. The gorge narrowed. At least there's less wind, she thought. After a hundred yards, she reached an impenetrable wall of rock where centuries of storm water had formed a cataract, perhaps twenty feet high. The sand where she stopped was damp. She found the little pen knife she'd been using for a key by feeling next to her thigh, inserted it into the ignition to kill the Jeep's engine and slid onto the ground, looking back the way she had come. She could not see the road or the stacked boulders. She tossed the pen knife onto the seat. Then she ascended the cataract, following a tiny trickle of water, using rocks and damp roots as rungs. When she neared the top of her climb, she had to pull herself through the narrow vee of rock at the head of the sluice. A pool of water stood among rocks clustered in a catch basin there, about four feet across and a few inches deep, the still and silent source of the trickle she had seen. She scanned upstream again, where her only discovery was more sand and rock, mesquite and cottonwood and desert broom.

She drank. She tried to lie on her stomach with her face down in the pool the way Caje did, but the rock and ground burnt her tummy and chest, so she squatted and lifted handfuls of the wonderful wetness to her mouth. It was surprisingly cool, and Tara wondered if it just seemed cool to her because she was holding so much heat or if the easy flow of the underground stream kept it cool. The slack process of drinking in this way was frustratingly unquenching, but she made herself drink the tiny swallows that arrived drippingly at her mouth. She looked at her watch and repeated the scooping and swallowing for five minutes. No cheating now, she thought, five minutes. Then she rose and stepped forward into the middle of the little pond and sat cross-legged. She scooped water with both hands now, and brought it to her forehead, letting it wash down her reddened face and neck and into her thin shirt until its front clung wetly to her little breasts. Then she scooped little handfuls of water onto the back of her neck until she could feel the water-soaked shirt below her ribcage. After a final scan upstream and a few more of the tiny gulps, she climbed back down the cataract.

She went to the passenger side of the Jeep and pulled the Thompson from beneath the seat by its barrel. It didn't seem as heavy as the last time she'd fired it. How long had it been? Five years? On a someteenth birthday with Daddy west of town where the rifle range had used to be...or no, it was a New Year's Day, early in the morning.

She cradled the weapon in her right hand, holding the pistol grip handle and rotating it to look at the controls, checking for the safe position, selecting automatic firing and sliding the bolt back. She reached under the seat again and found one of the magazines with her hand. She remembered to check to line up the T-slot and slid it into place, feeling and hearing the secure latching. Then she swiveled the control to the fire position, rotated it into position with the stock against her shoulder and fired a tentative burst into the thriving bloom of a big desert broom where it grew against the arroyo bank. There was a rapid series of booms with exploding dirt and shrubbery bits and brass cartridges flying away to her right. "Damn!" she muttered. She knew the Thompson would fire fast, though her father said it was obsolete now because of all the guns that fired faster. It had always reminded her of a rattle, but this was a deafening rattle, intensified here by the enclosing walls of the wash, and she wondered how far the sound traveled. She dropped the piece to what her dad had always called the gangster position, with the stock between her elbow and ribcage, and fired again, for over two seconds, this time moving the barrel tip in an X across her target, some of the brass chinging off rock now. Twelve rounds a second, her father had told her, and calculating that the magazine was almost empty now, she emptied the last few rounds into the bank. Her ears were ringing. Even knowing it would have angered her father, she decided to leave the brass where it lay. She set the gun's switch back to safe and ejected the empty magazine, tossing it into the rear of the Jeep. She felt under the seat again, counting the magazines—three left. She loaded one, made sure the safety was on and laid it on the floor in front of the passenger seat. She searched in the rear of the Jeep and found a torn tee-shirt that she'd seen Caje

use to clean his hands. She mounted the driver's seat then, covered the gun with the tee-shirt and backed the Jeep snail-slow to the road.
*****

Tara had tried to resurrect her faith a couple times since her days as an Episcopal acolyte, most recently in an Intro to Philosophy class, but she could only get as far as telling herself sure, God exists, the universe had to have a creator after all, but not Father John's God, who let ugly things happen, more like a giant scientist in the sky who had started a grand experiment with the universe and then sat observing to see what would happen, loving his creation perhaps, like a sculptor loves the statues she molds, perhaps even relishing the joys and grieving the sorrows in the farce below, religiously ignoring the prayers that ascended. But she prayed now, not exactly knowing why, but pitifully and desperately, praying for Caje's life, what Father John called intercession in confirmation class... and praying for the package too--there was no safety without delivering that. Just let me find him, she begged, and this'll be the last time. They never intended to do it forever anyway, just once they thought, when RJ had asked if she wanted to pick up some cash, RJ the businessman, RJ who always seemed to sit in the same place at the bowling alley, well, not really the bowling alley but the bar where she had worked and where he spent Friday afternoons, RJ who was a friend of Daddy's. Just once was plenty to pay for everything for a while-- school, rent, everything. Besides, people said that was where RJ had got the money to start his business--one sizeable delivery, Guadalajara to Tucson. And it turned out to be so easy, with Caje knowing his way back through the wild country anywhere between Yuma and Douglas, and there was so much money. So there had been the second time, easier than the first, and now a third. She told herself over and over that he was simply delayed--he decided to visit his family in Mascota, or they didn't have the package ready for him in Guadalajara, or he took a side trip to Nogales, or...something she wasn't thinking of. But she prayed and promised this would be the last time.

She continued west for five miles along the road. She decided she would cover as much ground as possible in the Jeep without dismounting again. Her watch read four-twenty. Search until dark, she thought, or until I find him around the next turn. She kept the Jeep in second gear to regulate her speed. Wherever a forest road or a ranch driveway intersected the road, she turned the Jeep and followed the tertiary trail. Sometimes these trails terminated at a ranch home or at a windmill-fed cattle tank; sometimes they rose into the oak forest and simply dissolved into scrubland. Some of them were forest service roads that extended for a dozen miles or more; she followed these until she reached a rise or a turnout where she could survey the country for a few hundred yards, scanned while the Jeep idled and then turned around. She crossed another arroyo that the Jeep could negotiate beyond her field of vision from the road, so she crept the Jeep upstream again as far as the terrain allowed, surveyed the country, and then backed out to the road. At five-thirty, she turned the Jeep around and raced back to the stacked boulders and began searching east. This time I'll go southeast through Ruby, she thought.

*****

Hal turned off the highway and headed west toward Arivaca, knowing he was about an hour behind Tara, provided she had actually come this way.

...she's crazy all right, but I'm crazier, following her like this...maybe it's just what she said, blasting at tin cans out here with her Yaqui boyfriend...like an adolescent showing off... and so, I'm a complete fool for even being here...missing work and pissing Doris off... but then why did she lie?...not heading for Nogales at all...and I'm just assuming she turned back to the west--for all I know, she went east to Elephant Head or Sonoita... but chances are I guessed right...I'll just find her and make sure everything's okay and then head in to work...unless she's got her foot stuck in something, so then I'm her Uncle Hal. Christ! ...maybe I'll find her before I hit Arivaca.

But he did not. And he understood why she had wanted the Jeep now. Damn little car, he thought. ...but more proof that she came this way...roads to the east are way better...so, keep going and miss work altogether or turn back?

He called the Saguaro Bowl from the store in Arivaca and asked for the maintenance office.

"This is Johnny."

"Hey, it's Hal. I'm kinda stuck someplace. Can you get Gary to work the first part of the shift for me?"

"Sure, I guess. I'll hold him over. What's goin' on?" Bowling alley sounds came through the phone along with his voice.

"Nothin', I hope. Down in Arivaca." He knew if he told Johnny he was looking for Tara, that Johnny wouldn't need to know any more, but for some reason he didn't want to tell him that.

"What the hell ya doin' down there? You go by the ranch?"

He knew Johnny meant the ranch where Hal had grown up, his aunt's ranch. "Nah. I'll tell ya tomorrow. Long story. I should be there by seven or so."

"All right, but you know Gary--he ain't gonna like it."

"I know. That's why I'm calling you. Tell him I'll take his shift tomorrow."

After he hung up, Hal called his own number, trying to reach Doris, but there was no answer.

Hal did not know the name of every place between Sasabe and Ruby, but he knew many of the ranches in the area, and old mines and water tanks and ponds. He knew which ranchers kept bass and catfish in their tanks and which ones would let a neighbor fish there. And he knew the spider web of roads, many of which had no name at all or had a name that was only known to the people who lived nearby, and he began driving them. And he knew how the roads connected to one another so that he could search without retracing a road most of the time.

Late in the afternoon and still hot, and he cursed the little MG for being a convertible. … and not even a rag top, where I could put up the top, but a hardtop with the top sitting unused over at Judd's house, no doubt…

He cursed Tara too, for being…what? headstrong? …Aunt Henrietta would have called her balky…like her horse Hazel, who wanted to go downhill straight into a Cholla cactus just because Henrietta was turning her uphill…funny country word…balky!...but that's what she is …gets it in her mind that she's right about a thing and off she goes…like when she picked this damn car…

Hal stopped at a rut so that he could shift into first gear again, noticing that he was close to Henrietta's place--what had used to be her place--the Diamond Queen, Aunt thinking of herself as the queen of diamonds because she thought of herself as good at poker, though she really wasn't, and thinking of him as the jack of hearts because she said he would break a lot of hearts and never marry--well, she got the never marry part right.

He thought about taking the ranch road, driving down among the cottonwoods that shaded the house, to see how different it might be since his visit with Tara, whether the house--long, low mud adobe with a tin roof and its wooden porch--was still standing. Or had the new owners torn it down? Or some asshole set fire to it to watch it burn. Or had someone moved in?...oughta look... only take five minutes...coulda been my place maybe...Henrietta said she'd write me into her will, but I told her no because then the cousins would sue me anyway, and she said I was the only man she had ever known who joined the army to *avoid* a fight...might as well drive down there...

But when he came to the ranch road, he saw the Diamond Queen sign was gone, and he kept driving. ...just no point in it...

He scoured Yellow Jacket Mine Road, then Tres Bellotas Road and then, past Ruby, Warsaw Canyon Road. He was about to turn north on California Gulch Road, back to the Ruby Road, the connection east to the highway and head north, back to work, no sign of Tara or the Jeep, when he heard the Thompson.

There was no mistaking it, the thrumming racket, clattering up a canyon or a wash on his right, a long way from a listening post in frigid Korea, not as loud but a lot like what he remembered. Ahead or behind him? He stopped the car and turned it off. ...so loud for a four-banger... Then he heard the clattering again--ahead! He started the MG and drove as fast as the road would allow, looking for the next place to turn right.

*****

The two men did not know it, but they retraced most of Tara's route when they left the Arivaca store, casually surveying country along the road. With the revolver nestled in his lap, Hicks was working a toothpick down, chewing hard on the tips with his front teeth and tearing away little strands of its wood with his tongue and then spitting them out. The smaller man was driving, occasionally turning a dial on the car radio to reduce static or find another station.

The El Camino bottomed out on the rutty road almost as much as the MG, and it swayed heavily on curves, jiggling the necklace of molars that hung from its rear view mirror.

The rear wheels spun and skidded to the road's edge, spattering dirt and gravel, and Hicks said, "Jesus, take it easy will ya? You gonna wreck your momma's car like that."

"Wish you'd quit callin' it my momma's car. She gave it to *me* when I got home."

They approached a brown wooden sign that said National Forest Road. Hicks lifted the revolver from his lap, aimed out the window, fired at the sign and missed. "Damn it," he said and fired again, punching a hole and tearing away most of the F. "There, you little gook mother-fucker." He put the gun back on the seat.

"I wish you'd quit doing that. We ain't gonna find that guy with you blasting away every couple minutes."

"Yeah, well you know what I wish, JT? I wish we'd find that little blond bitch we seen back at the store. Showing off her little titties like that, she was begging for it. Wonder if she's from around here somewhere." It was the third time he'd mentioned the little blond bitch and her titties.

"Not in that little piece of shit car of hers. Couldn't be. Besides, she went the other way, back to the highway. Probly lives in Tucson."

"I bet she's a college chick, driving that car. If I knew for sure where she lived, I'd kick in her door, go straight up to her, you know? That would be cool, huh, to see the look on her face?...then fuck her, you know?"

JT didn't answer.

"Don't worry, you can have seconds," Hicks said with a chuckle. He bent forward slightly to open the white top of the ice chest that rested on the center hump of the El Dorado. He opened a beer, threw the pull tab out the window and swigged. "What we need is to have a little gal like her around the farm."

JT drove and looked at the road and wondered if he still liked having Hicks for a partner. He believed Hicks would do just as he said if he found the girl, kick in the door and walk straight up to her and do her, staring at her wide eyes the whole time.

He had thought he liked the way Hicks always did what he said he was going to do. Like the time at Dak To when Hicks had said Lieutenant Craig would be coming back from patrol in pieces. Nobody liked that know-it-all ROTC bastard, and then he had called Hicks stupid and a genetic misfire, so it was no surprise Hicks had said it. But then there was Craig's body when they returned, blood-covered and lifeless, not moaning, saying nothing, but not knowing everything anymore. There were wounds in his legs and abdomen and back, mostly his back, and the wounds said nothing either. "Who's the stupid one now?" Hicks had said, not quietly.

Now JT wasn't so sure. They weren't in Dak To now. Hicks had been with him now for three months, living at the camp that Hicks liked to call the farm, taking his turn at checking on their marijuana crop two hundred yards east of the trailer, selling bags of the stuff now and then, pinching mail from the clusters of boxes along the rural roads, taking what they liked from houses and barns when no one was home, mostly cash or jewelry that was often valuable to the people who had made it easy to take but not always important to deputies or anyone else when it disappeared. But lots of people would want to know what happened to a blond bitch with cute titties if she disappeared, and here there would be no fire fights to explain away her corpse. No, if Hicks kicked in her door, somebody would catch up with him, and if they caught up with Hicks, they'd catch up to him too. Hicks either didn't get that or he didn't care. No, something was a little different about Hicks.

JT drove the road back toward their camp according to his nature, deliberately. From the hilltop pines at the limit of his vision, his gaze crept meticulously through the scrub oak and piñon and juniper and then to the mesquite and barren rock a few feet in front of him, then rose again angled slightly to his right now, and slowly down again, and then angled left, and then all over again. He was like a hawk circling and looking for slight movements on the terrain. The ice chest held three more beers as they neared the fork that turned back to their camp. The sun's blast had lowered to late afternoon, past four o'clock, but if anything it was hotter now than mid-afternoon, its heat also bleeding out from rocks and hard-packed dust where it had been collecting for hours. Sometimes he stopped, idling the El Camino and peering hard into one spot for a minute or two, until he was satisfied that the white-shirted Mexican boy was not there, then moving on again.

Five

Hunger was biting hard at Caje now as he alternately limped and listened his way back to his duffel bag. His canteen had been empty for over an hour. Uncle would think I'm a fool, he thought. No, does think. He's shaking his head at me right now, asking why I'm here and why I did not think of anything but the money... and the girl.

If he were a hawk, Caje's route from where the two men had come so close to him back to the duffel bag's hiding place would have been no more than a thousand yards, but since he was a now a careful man half-stepping on a bad sprain and circling back well-separated from the trail, vigilant enough to stop and listen and to climb and observe, the route was close to three thousand yards. Finally, lying flat behind an oak tree on the crest of a ridge, he could see slices of the silvery camp trailer between tree trunks and shrubs. The El Camino was not there. He was about eighty yards away. From here it was easy to find the crevice and the canvas bag.

He scrambled painfully along the crest next to the rock-strewn ravine he had been following, examining the slopes to either side and the ground that seemed to invite him forward, offering the fastest, easiest route to his duffel. He knew he was rushing, but he felt compelled to be rid of this place, rid of the two men and their camp before their car returned. He strained to listen for the sound of tires on dirt or one of the voices, glancing frequently through the brush at the silvery trailer and the dam below him and on his left. He stumbled on a rock and cursed aloud, then reminded himself to be quiet.

He was past the hiding place a few yards when he recognized the low oak he'd memorized. He turned around and saw the gorgeous manzanita bush, momentarily wondering how he had missed the huge kissing rocks. He moved to the crevice, knelt behind the huge shrub. Green canvas lay there between the stones, offering up a sense of relief. He pulled it out and hugged it, feeling to make sure the packages were still there, and sighed. Now he would circle to the south and, like the man in the white shirt, parallel the road toward Ruby and find his way home with the girl.

Except he couldn't now because there was a pistol barrel against his head. The relief left him and in its place was a sickening feeling—a desperate, heartbeat-skipping, weak-in-the-spine sensation.

"Did you find Calabasas, asshole?" Hicks said. The eight beers he had drunk did not make him sleepy, and they did not keep him from talking loud. But now his speech came out slower and slurred. "Drop the bag."

Caje dropped the duffel, slowly, thinking about the gun barrel.

"So what's he got?" asked JT, advancing, the rifle butt under his shoulder now and the barrel angled down, relaxed.

"Sump'n good I bet. Big bag." He kept the steel barrel against Caje, leaning low to lift the duffel and toss it in one motion, like a bear's swat. "What's in it, asshole?" The big man held the revolver in his right hand and patted Caje's waist and torso with his left.

Caje wondered if it was better to answer or not. He waited on his knees.

"Well, have a look."

JT did not care for Hicks's tone, wondering, not the first time, who was in control of this partnership. He laid the rifle down next to the duffel and, kneeling in the duff, unzipped it. He pulled out an oblong package. The wrapping was clear plastic wrapped tight around grainy shapeless lumps. "Mexican mud, looks like," he said to Hicks. "That right, kid?"

Caje nodded.

"Lots of it. I count twelve good-size wads." He looked at Caje. "You need to tell us all about this, kid. You got another bag?"

When Caje shook his head, Hicks rapped him on the head with the steel barrel. "Say sump'n when you're spoke to! We spent all day lookin' for you."

"That's all there is."

"Ya sure?" Hicks said, rapping the top of his head again. "An' what happened to your Mex talk?"

"Take it easy, man. We got a lot more to ask the kid. He's still trying to figure out how we found him....Aren't ya kid?" He wanted to remind Hicks that it had been his idea to hide the car.

"Yes." Caje did not want to be rapped again, but he thought of the way he had seen the empty camp and rushed ahead. And he thought of his uncle's talks about the power of waiting. When did they first spot me? he wondered.

JT stuffed the tight package into his pants, zipped the duffel shut, and stood. "Well, kid, it was pretty easy--just parked the truck outta sight and hoped you'd come close, and that's what you done, all right." He smiled at Caje and then at his partner. "Pick up the bag and follow me on down. You got that?"

"Yes." He noticed the terror had begun to leave him now. He began to wonder if he would see the next hot day, the girl, his Jeep again.

"Well, jus' keep in mind I don't miss much with this."

To Caje, it meant that they had not noticed his limp yet, and he hoped that was some kind of edge. He stepped over to the duffel and lifted it. When he stood, Hicks rapped him again.

"I wish you'd quit doing that," JT said and paused to look at Hicks.

Caje looked at the small man's eyes, knowing that the words meant something.

They walked downhill to the camp single file, through piñon and oak, the small man leading and the big man trailing. No one spoke. Caje wondered about breaking and running, but each step told him he had a sprained ankle, though he continued to pretend he did not, and the weight of the duffel told him that he would be slow. And of course if he left it, he and the girl would die anyway, in

Tucson. And there was the rifle a few steps ahead of him and the handgun a few steps behind.

In the camp, JT went through Caje's pockets and found dollars and Mexican pesos in a wallet, but no cards or papers. "No ID--pretty smart, kid." He stuffed the money into his pocket and took the duffel from Caje and tossed Caje's wallet into it and took it inside the trailer, along with the rifle. When he came back out, he held a length of thin cotton rope, like clothes-line, which he fashioned into a noose for Caje's neck.

"Set here," JT said, motioning toward one of the camp chairs. Caje sat, expecting the rope to be wound from his neck to his hands or feet, but instead, JT held the end of the rope out to the bigger man and asked, "You wanna handle this or me?"

Hicks handed the revolver back to JT, who shoved it back into the holster that had been empty all day, and took the rope and gave it a little jerk to tighten it around Caje's neck. "Feel that, asshole?"

"Yes."

Hicks went behind Caje and leaned against the trailer's side. JT pulled the second camp chair close to Caje and sat and leaned in at him.

"Kid, my friend here wants to learn a trade."

"A trade?"

"He had a trade, but then he couldn't do it no more. You remember the way he kept tappin' you on the head before? Was a habit he picked up over in Nam after they told him he couldn't work. So I said, 'Well, let's find you a new trade. Sump'n that's got lotta responsibility, so it pays you good.'" He paused. "So what about your kinda work, kid? You got a lotta responsibility?"

Caje wondered if they wanted him to answer or if they were just taunting him, until he felt a tug on the rope. "I don't know. I guess so, yeah."

"Yeah, you know so, kid, all that mud you got with you. What's it worth, twelve wads of that?"

Caje shrugged, then remembering the rope, said, "I don't know," hoping that would be enough. It was not so much that the little yanks on the cord were hurting, but he thought of each one as a warning, like shadows of a hawk flashing near a rabbit, and he wondered how many warnings he had left.

Hicks yanked, "Take a guess."

"Maybe twenty thousand."

"No it's more 'n that, kid. It's not even cut. Or you mean each bag?"

He nodded, "Yes, each one."

JT nodded, believing him. "That's what I'm thinking, but more like thirty. Why they trust a kid like you with all that? And where you get all that shit--way down south?"

"Guadalajara." Caje looked at the sky, still washed pale by the sun, with a few thin clouds. "There's more this time."

"So you done this before, huh? They trust you now, huh? Cuz you showed 'em you could get it done, huh?"

"I guess so."

"Well, you got skills, kid. Don't act so bashful--you got a trade you can brag on. Not like my friend here. Me, I'm a farmer, but my friend here ain't no good at it." He looked at the big man and said, "Show the kid what you're good at, eh."

There was slack in the rope as Hicks stepped closer, moving to Caje's side and reaching behind his back. Caje thought he would bring a second gun or a knife, but he did not. Instead, Hicks flipped open his wallet and produced a photograph, folded but still glossy.

"Take it, asshole."

Caje took the photograph and unfolded it. The jagged creases made the images difficult to comprehend at first, but they came into view with a long look. Two black-haired heads, mouths open and rigid in death, but somehow slack-jawed, attached to small bodies slumped against a tree, their unified mass held together with strand after strand of barbed wire. Caje looked hard at it until the big man pulled it from his fingers and put it back in his wallet.

"See, I put the wire there so the gooks couldn't come get their wasted friends so easy. Then, when they did try to get 'em, we'd pot 'em."

"So, whaddya say? Can you share some skills with my friend here?"

"How would I do that?"

"We could go now," JT said, "take a walk back down that little trail--the way you come. My friend ain't ever been to Mexico."

"I been to Mexico. Shit, I been to Guadalajara," Hicks said.

Caje saw the little man's eyes flash at his partner, staring hard.

JT said, "Yeah, but what I meant was he ain't ever walked to Mexico before. So you can show us, right?"

"I just came up the trail this time, from El Cumaral. Pretty easy."

"Cumaral, what's that, a town?" He held out his hands and turned the palms up. "I'll give you the map in a minute and you can show us there. But you said 'this time.' Ain't that how you usually go?"

Caje wondered if he should be telling them everything, if he should be lying. "No, I went another way before, up the Rio Altar."

"'n what's the Rio All Tar? That a town too?"

"No. It's a valley." He wondered if the two men were equally stupid. "River valley, most of it's dry 'cept for the stormy seasons. Lot of farms there though." Then he realized that he was probably stupider than either of the men, since they were holding the length of rope, and he wondered what Tara was doing, if she was still waiting for him at the arroyo crossing.

JT reached forward and touched Caje. "Okay, kid, I'm gonna get the map and you show me." He went back toward the trailer door with Caje's eyes following him. After he'd opened the door, he paused and said, "Hey. Why doncha tell him how you got wounded and shipped out?"

"That's jus' what happened."

Caje turned his eyes and looked at the big man again. He had the idea that at some point the questions would stop because they would know all he knew, and that then he would be dead, and he had another idea that if he listened to the big man, he could be his friend, he could live. "You got wounded over there?"

"Gook booby trap. Punji sticks."

"I've heard of those. I bet that hurt like hell."

"You're an asshole, kid. You got no idea. The trap was deep. I went in all the way to my knee. The first stick went right through the boot and my foot both. When I tried to pull up, there was sticks that caught me pulling up. I had to dig out from the front. They had to get me out with a chopper. Fucked me up good."

"Jesus, that's tough, mister." Caje tried to sound sympathetic, looking for a sign that the big man would soften.

JT was back now, with his map. "He was in the hospital for a couple weeks cuz it was all infected."

"Yeah, the gooks shit on those sticks before they cover the hole," Hicks said.

The map was topographical, with names of towns. Caje found the stream labeled Rio Altar, and he pointed to where he thought Rancho El Cumaral was, vaguely north of El Busani. He noticed the Ruby Road--not far.

"Okay, kid, so how many times you bring this shit in now?"

"This is the third time."

"Which way's easier?"

"Rio Altar, I guess."

"So why'd you change?"

He hesitated, only a second, and he felt the jerking of the rope. "I caught a ride--saved a lot of walking."

"What else? There's sumpthin' else. How come you changed it up?"

The rope jerked again. "Twisted my ankle."

"Look, JT, this is getting old. We got all we're gonna get from this asshole. We don't need all this jabberin'. Let's just take him up the road and waste him."

Again, the smaller man glared hard at his friend. "I think there's a lot this kid can teach us still." Then turning his eyes back to Caje, "Don't you think so kid?"

A strange tremble ran through Caje. He spat out, "Yeah."

"But my friend is right about one thing, kid. This is taking too long, ya know. Now I want you to start at the beginning and tell me everything. Start with the proposal--either you asked somebody how to score or somebody offered to hire you. And don't leave out no names."

After another jerk on the rope, Caje began, "There's this guy in Tucson, Jasper, they call him RJ, owns a business there, distribution business." He was determined not to mention Tara, or anything linked to Tara, if he could help it. "Got to talking one day, and he asked if I wanted to make some real money....I was telling him how I know the border good, how I just go back and forth to see family down there and don't bother with the crossings. He says all I have to do is make a delivery, Guadalajara to Tucson."

"To him?"

"No, he doesn't get involved any more--it's another guy he knows. I don't know his name. I bring it to this motel on Miracle Mile and check in, and he calls for me to come meet him."

"Where?"

"Different place each time. First time there at the motel. The next time I went and met him. I figure it'll be a third place this time."

"Yeah," Hicks said with a jerk on the rope, "or maybe you just never show, eh?"

Then Tara will die too, he thought.

"Yeah," JT said, "but there may be more on the table here. I hate leavin' money on the table for someone else." Then, to Caje, "How does the pickup go in Guadalajara?"

"Sorta the same. I register in this hotel, and they call and bring it to me. Don't know their name either."

"No, I bet not. But what name you use?"

"Portillo. Oscar Portillo. Both places." Caje raised his eyes again, finding the wispy clouds, now turning pink. Evening had come.

"So these meets you have--the guy come alone?"

"I don't think so. I never saw anyone except the guy with the bundle, or the guy I'm giving the package to, but I always figured someone else was watching."

"And that's when you get paid?"

"Yes."

"But you never take cash the other way?"

"No."

"I told you the kid had skills, didn't I?" He looked at Hicks. "Whyn't you hobble him. The kid can build a fire while we talk."

Plan where to dump me, Caje thought, and for the space of two pounding heartbeats, he considered his chances for running, yanking the rope free from the big man's hands, streaking downhill past the dam and outrunning both men with the bullets flying harmlessly by, but then the rope was being wound around and knotted, first one ankle and then the other, so that he could not step farther than eighteen inches. The big man did it in a practiced way and said, "Lay a fire." Then the two men stepped away from him, turning their faces so that all Caje heard was their intonation, not their words.

"What's there to talk about, JT? We got everything we're gonna get from this kid, including the mud. Let's just dump him down in that mineshaft, like the other time. Jus' one less Mexican. An nobody misses a mule. Hell, probly nobody knows he's even out here."

Maybe Lieutenant Craig had been right, JT thought, he is a genetic misfire. "I know, but listen. We got $300,000 worth of smack, but no great way to sell it. We start asking around about dumpin' the whole mess at once, and the word is gonna get back to the guys in Tucson or the guys in Guadalajara. Sounds like the same outfit anyway. Didja think about that?" Hicks's eyes flashed, and JT reminded himself to be careful about how he said things to the big man. "Maybe these guys cut us in if we save their shit or they start payin' us to protect their delivery boys. Or maybe we just blow them up at the exchange and take the cash too."

"I don't like it," Hicks said.

"Okay, well let's just take him up there to that motel. We can off him as soon as he sets up the meet. How 'bout that? If we want, we can bail then and just take the stuff with us."

JT knew he had won when Hicks grunted but said nothing. But now he could hear the sound from a vehicle, throaty, like a truck sound. "All right, I'm gonna get the car." He strode away, rising on the road toward the hilltop.

*****

The wind had eased as the sun's rays slanted more. With so little daylight remaining, Tara gave up the little excursions up arroyos that she found, although she continued to pause at each one and call for Caje. She had driven past Ruby all the way to Peña Blanca lake and followed the road down to the lake itself and then on east all the way to the highway. She peered hard into oncoming pickup trucks, few as they were, even though she knew it was absurd to expect to see Caje riding in one, and the other driver usually waved a greeting. Sometimes she had followed the side roads that branched away to the south, but with night approaching, sometimes she drove past, with the result that now, driving west and north again along the same road, she did not know which branch roads she had checked and which she had not.

There was a desperate recycling going on in her head. This was crazy, she thought, fighting to stay hopeful. Caje was probably drinking cervezas with his cousins in Mascota right now, with the sun sinking in the west the same as it was here. Maybe he had even called and left a message on her answering machine. She should have had Hal listen to the messages when he went to her apartment. Well, maybe it didn't matter anyway, with daylight disappearing and no point in driving around in the dark, so she'd be home soon and she would play her messages. But what if something had happened? she thought, accompanied by a wretched sinking response inside her heart. Maybe they had crossed him on the transfer somehow; but no, they trusted him. They had sent him with more on his last trip, and he expected more still this time, so why would they stop trusting him like that? And he couldn't be lost. Maybe he was just late and he's there now at the crossing waiting for her. She would go back there one more time, dark or not, and then through Arivaca in the darkness and then home.

She came to another fork to the south, sure this time that she had missed it earlier and wondering why, asking herself if she had time to drive it and still get back to the crossing before dark. She turned the Jeep up the branch road, which was broad and flat for a hundred yards, amid yellowed grass in a field that was surrounded by oak and mesquite, and which then rose into a thicket of piñon and juniper and so narrow that she could touch branches from the driver's seat.

The Jeep plodded steadily up the narrow, darkening climb, like a tortoise inside a tunnel. Tara thought momentarily about snapping on the headlights, but then the thicket thinned suddenly, with trees giving way to grass and brush along the road and the sky stretching above with thin clouds beginning to color with the promise of a sunset. On her left was a dry meadow, and on her right the shoulder of a hill. Two hundred yards ahead, parked in the yellow grass just to the left of the road, with trees and brush of the forest behind, shining metallic though covered in dust, just this side of where the road rose again to the next ridge, were the brown and yellow and chrome of the El Camino.

It can't be the same one, she thought, but then it has to be, way out here. She pushed in the clutch pedal and stopped the Jeep's crawl and let the engine idle as she thought about it, scanning for the two men, the big one with the ponytail who had leered at her and the shorter one that she probably would not recognize. She felt exposed again, as she had with pony-tail man staring at her chest, wondering if he was watching her now. She looked uphill to her right, scanning now for three men instead of just one, among the oak and piñon and twisted mesquite. No big deal, she thought, just a creepy guy, and I can drive on past. Then she eased the clutch out and crept forward again, her eyes shifting between the half-truck ahead of her and the trees that nestled around it.

When she had prowled the Jeep alongside the El Camino, she punched the clutch in and idled again, studying the forest behind it, stretching away to her left. Her eyes came back to the car, with the truck bed in shade now, empty and hot-looking with the cab windows open. The odd-looking chain that hung from the rear view mirror caught her eye, and she wondered what it was. She wondered, too, why they would have left the car in such an odd place. They hadn't looked like hikers. No matter, time to find Caje, drive a little farther and then turn around. She eased the clutch back out and climbed the Jeep up the road and over the place where it crested and began to descend.

That's when she saw a man in a white tee shirt ascending the road toward her. When he saw her, he stood still and stared back. She assumed right away it was one of the men from the store, the one who had been buying beer and whose face she had not seen. He was a blond short man, white but tanned, shorter than Caje, sinewy and athletic like Caje, but more rugged with densely packed muscle rippling down his arms, now smiling at her with a smile that could not hide his stony face. A holster and revolver bulged at his right hip. But where was the other one, ponytail, the creepy one? She kept the Jeep moving ahead, straight toward him, braving a glance down to floor of the Jeep on the passenger side where the Thompson lay, checking to see if it was still covered with the rag she had thrown over it. She would roll past, greet him perhaps, no stopping. He seemed to understand her intention because he slanted away from the middle of the road out to its edge to let her pass, still narrowing the distance between them, now down to a few yards. Then he paused in his stride again, giving her a quizzical look. Recognizes me now, she thought, and wondering about the Jeep.

"Well hi again," he said as she rolled past.

"Hi," she said, returning his look and smiling flatly but keeping the wheels rolling, now aware that she was holding her breath.

She breathed as she sensed him moving away from her again, toward the El Camino where it stood over the hill, she guessed. Soon she was aware of the road's dead ending at the bottom of the hill and the small silver trailer up ahead to her left, and she wondered why it had not registered before. Looking at the guy, she told herself.

The pony-tailed man who had leered at her had turned and was standing next to the trailer. She knew him instantly, and she knew that he recognized her, squaring his shoulders at the Jeep full on now, and staring into her face. And as the Jeep rolled on, she saw Caje stooped over a heap of sticks, with a band of white around his neck, seeing her now and suddenly frozen.

Her hand went to the shifter, and she set the Jeep into neutral. She was trying to think of some narrative that would explain it all to herself, the El Camino, the two men, the trailer, Caje half-standing there with a crooked stick in his hands, the creepy guy with the ponytail starting to smile now. She was thinking, oddly, that she might still have time to swing back to the crossing—but of course now she had found Caje and there was no need to look for him there. And of course the little band around his neck was a rope. Next she was thinking that if they had not agreed to make this third delivery, or if Caje had just showed up like he was supposed to—and where was the package?-- but she was here now, just her and Caje and these two…and after all, something like this was why she'd asked Hal to bring the gun—the Thompson.

Ponytail was taking a few steps toward her, smiling broadly now. "Well, hi again Missy," he called.

She didn't want him getting any closer. If he kept coming—she didn't think she could back up fast enough to keep him away, and there was Caje.

With her foot off the brake, the Jeep rolled slowly for a few feet where it hit the low spot in the road and stopped again, rocking her gently. She leaned over and reached the Thompson and came up to watch the man's face go hard, seeing the gun. Pointing the gun down, she stood in the Jeep to make sure he could see it and flipped the safety off.

He began to smile again, crossing his arms. "I was kinda hopin' I'd see you again. You feel the same way, I guess."

Tara stood silent, glancing toward Caje, who was standing straighter now.

"Kind of an old gun ya got there, Missy."

"The bullets are new enough."

Now the ponytail man was silent.

"Maybe I'm just lost."

"I ain't surprised. But hey, I can help you find your way." He shrugged, looking past her and up the road, then at Tara again, his chin raised at her. He said, "Okay, Missy?" and started toward the Jeep again.

She raised the Thompson into the gangster position and held the gunstock tight between her elbow and ribcage.

He stopped, frowning, seeming surprised. "Whatcha wanna point that at me for?"

"Untie him."

"This is our business, Missy. Why don't you let me help you get turned around so you can get outta here?"

"You *better* untie him," she said. "I mean it." She wondered if she sounded like she meant it.

"Or else what? You ain't gonna shoot nobody."

She hated the way he said it. "You better believe I will." The Thompson's magazine was loaded with thirty .45 caliber rounds, and her finger was tight on the trigger. But the weapon would only keep him away another half-second unless ponytail believed she'd use it. Damn you, she thought, full of hatred and anger, but more than anything she was terrified of him, aware of the pounding inside her chest. She was afraid he would not believe she would shoot, afraid that he would not untie Caje, afraid that he would advance again, but she was not afraid she would not shoot. She would have to. He looked at her, smirking and casual, and then looked past her again, up the road.

"Behind you, Tara," Caje yelled.

Yes, the other one, she remembered, her heart skipping and then racing. She spun and saw him closing on her, running down the road now, with the revolver in his hand. She fired then, for over a second, wildly at first and then trying to adjust as the small man ran, and the thunderous rattling surprised him apparently because he veered to his right and slowed, thinking about it. Puffs of dust rose, but nowhere near him, beyond him because the barrel wanted to lift as she fired, and to his right because now she was spinning back to face the big man, also closing on her now.

Caje stepped as far as he could, forgetting he was hobbled, falling, but still managing to throw the stick he'd been holding and hitting the big man square in the back. It unbalanced him for an instant, and now Tara remembered to fire only a burst, boom boom boom boom, in front of the big man and near his feet, turning him and driving him back. She turned to her left again, where the blond man was coming at her again, but stopping now and raising the revolver with both hands to aim. She fired another burst, trying to aim this time, fighting the jumping barrel, and a round caught him right of center below his ribcage, spinning him violently to his left as if he had been swatted. The revolver sprang from his hands in a spasm, sailing into the yellow grass, landing harmlessly.

When she spun back to her right, Tara could see the big man running, but away from her now, to his left, angling for the rear of the trailer. But he was in more of a jog than a sprint, and he looked back at her as he got close to the rear corner of the trailer, as if he were calculating what she would do. She fired at his feet again and then wondered how many rounds remained in the magazine. Her first series of rounds had been too long, she knew, but she didn't think she had spent thirty. Caje had risen to his knees. His hands were at his neck, loosening the rope and pulling the noose over his head. "Hurry Caje," she yelled. Don't sound so desperate, she told herself.

"You know this guy, eh?" ponytail said. "What's with you, Missy?" He stood with his hand against the rear of the trailer, still exposed to her view, leaning in a relaxed way, as if he still did not consider her a threat.

Caje was sitting now, working to release the hobble, but the knots in the cotton rope were not yielding to his fingernails.

She didn't like this--just standing there while Caje fiddled with a rope, ponytail thirty yards away from her but almost ignoring the Thompson, and the blond guy behind her. She spun to her left again and found the blond man with her eyes. He was sitting now, weight on one hip, grimacing and holding his hand against his side, but trying to crawl uphill. Christ, I *did* hit him, she thought, wondering how bad his wound was as she spun back. What if he dies?

Ponytail was still leaning, and Caje was still fumbling with the rope.

"Can you cut it?" she said.

He rocked forward instantly and rose to his feet and hobbled his way toward the trailer, not speaking, the noose that had been around his neck now trailing behind him. It popped into Tara's head that he looked foolish, like a kid. He went into the trailer, leaving the door wide open.

"Hey Missy, you need to take it easy, eh? We were jus' talking to your li'l friend here."

Tara wished he would just shut up. She raised the stock to her shoulder and sighted down the barrel at a spot just below his feet, and, remembering that the gun would try to rise, locked her left elbow hard against her tummy.

"Friend o' yours, looks like." Ponytail was still smiling--a smirk. "Kinda wondered about that, ya know? I mean my partner didn't even ask your little friend how he was gettin' to Tucson. Real smart guy, my partner."

She raised the sight and put it on the center of his chest, fighting the urge to fire just to keep the man from talking. "Why don't you just shut up?" She dropped the sight low again, wondering now about the blond man. Maybe he was dying back there or maybe he had already retrieved the revolver and he was walking up behind her right now. She had an urge to find him with her eyes again, but now she was afraid to look away from ponytail.

"That bother you, Missy? Me talkin'?" his face was straight now, serious. "Let me tell you something, Missy. Your man here done plenty o' talking too. We know a lot about him…a lot about you too."

Tara wanted to be gone now, with this place far behind her, and that was all she wanted, even forgetting about the package Caje should have been carrying. Another wave of fear was taking her now, replacing her anger. She started thinking about what to do next, how to leave the camp, how to keep the man covered and get away from here, away from the camp, away from ponytail and his partner, who lay angrily bleeding behind her somewhere she was afraid to look. She wondered what was taking Caje so long inside the trailer--

had to be something in there to cut that rope with. She would keep the gun pointed at ponytail and make Caje drive, she decided, step down from the Jeep while he turned it around and then back in on the passenger side, or was she tall enough to get her butt up in there and maintain her aim--no, step to the passenger side and train the site on him while Caje maneuvered... She wished she knew how many rounds remained in the magazine, wished too that she had a second magazine in her pocket

That's when she heard her MG, the sound reverberating deep and far away. Caje always said he recognized it from a couple miles away, and it gave him time to hide his other girlfriends before she got there. It has to be, with Hal behind the wheel looking ridiculous in his cowboy hat. She listened close, hoping for the sound to get closer, and it did. She tightened her grip on the Thompson and waited.

*****

Hal was a man whose natural caution had been sharpened some years earlier when dozens of armed men crept past him in the dark while his senses prickled in a listening post in no-man's land, although he thought of it as fear, not caution. He stopped to study the scene when he came across the El Camino. He looked both right and left, scanning for the Jeep and for Tara, scanning for anything that looked like a threat, wondering if the road he'd taken would lead him to the source of the gunfire he'd heard or if the sound had tricked him, wondering too if the abandoned car had some connection. There had been three bursts--a long one and then two shorter ones. Parked, not abandoned, he thought. He checked the MG's mirrors, then drove on.

He saw it through the windshield as he came over the crown of the road, the Jeep resting where the road hit bottom a couple hundred yards ahead and Tara standing up in it holding the Thompson, and to the left of that, the silver camp trailer, its door standing open. From this distance, it looked as if she was aiming the gun at the trailer itself, and perhaps at someone inside it. He studied the ground to his right and left and behind him, coasting downhill in second gear. Then he focused on the scene ahead again, coming closer. A sniff of cordite hit his nostrils.

Tara could have been a Roman statue, he thought, her figure wide at the hips and small-breasted and motionless, except she was wearing shorts and a blouse instead of a draping toga. And the machine gun and the Jeep did not seem to fit a classical picture either. He thought that his approach in the little MG would cause a change in the scene somehow, with Tara turning or words shouted, but it did not. Her eyes remained fixed as the MG rolled closer.

Hal saw a figure spring suddenly from the trailer, brown-faced and short, lugging a green duffel bag, and he knew it was Tara's boyfriend, Caje, trotting to the rear of the Jeep to toss the duffel in, then preparing to mount it from the passenger side. Caje stopped, listening as Tara seemed to speak at him over her shoulder, never changing her rigid stance, never lowering the Thompson, and Caje reached under the seat then and brought up the black magazines, holding them out for her as he climbed into the passenger side.

When the MG rolled up behind the Jeep, Hal braked, now seeing the big man standing near the trailer where Tara pointed the gun. She fired then, three rounds echoing loud on the short burst, and he looked at the man again, expecting to see him struck and spinning back wounded. The big man stumbled, yelling something, without falling but retreating a few steps out of view behind the trailer. So he was not hit. As soon as she fired, Tara rolled the gun to a cradle position in her right arm and dislodged the magazine, and with the spent mag dropping in front of her, reached out and took another one from Caje. The maneuver was fast, as if she had thought of everything she needed to do before starting it, as if she had done it before.

The big man came around the opposite side of the trailer now, lumbering toward the Jeep. Tara pivoted and fired again, the shots pounding dirt close to him so that he dodged behind the trailer again, and now he ran uphill, away from the gunfire. Hal followed him with his eyes as he ran away, perhaps forty yards to where a line of oak and piñon started. And now Hal saw a second man there behind the tree line, a smaller man lying on his side and lifting his upper body with an elbow, staring down but with no inclination to go anywhere. He was handing something to the big man, and Hal could see that it was a handgun. The big man pointed it now and fired at Tara, the bullet striking metal somewhere, either the Jeep or the trailer, and then again, definitely the Jeep this time, and Tara fired again, a longer burst, seven or eight rounds, the big man stepping behind an oak tree that would cover perhaps half his body and the smaller man covering up flat on the ground.

Tara jumped down from the Jeep then, landing in a low crouch. "Turn it around," she said to Caje.

"Hey, Missy. You just shoot people?" the big man remained among the trees, but he stared downhill at them. "You shot him, you know that? You fucking shot my partner."

"Jesus Christ, Tara," Hal managed to shout, but he remained in the MG.

Hal continued to watch as Tara remained in the crouch and Caje made the turn, back and forth twice so that now the front of the Jeep almost kissed the MG's hood. The men above did not move. Hal backed the MG up so that there were about fifty yards between the vehicles, and then he waited again. Tara backed up to the passenger side, still in the crouch. When her buttocks touched the Jeep, she held the gun firmly and fired a three burst, Hal this time sure that she had aimed low, but turning to look anyway. Then she cradled the weapon in one arm again and reached for the Jeep's windshield, turned and climbed in. The big man fired another round, and Hal heard a grunt from the Jeep, but when he looked, Tara and Caje both seemed fine. Tara had settled to aim again, with her right knee on the passenger seat and her left foot on the floorboard, facing up hill.

"You okay?" Hal called, but Tara did not answer him. Instead, she hollered, "Slow Caje." Hal knew he had to get out of their way and climbed the sports car up the road in reverse, guiding himself with its mirrors and glancing back and forth between the crawling Jeep with the crazy blond girl holding the Thompson submachine gun and her Indian boyfriend driving and the men above, until clearing the crest, alongside the El Camino where he could no longer see the trailer and the two tree-shrouded men. Then he squeezed the MG as far onto the road's edge as he dared so he could begin turning. The Jeep sailed past him, but then, with Tara shouting something at Caje, backed up and stopped close. Tara turned and fired at the driver's-side tires on the El Camino, first the front and then the rear, with the sound of bullets pounding through metal and rubber and dirt, until the car listed heavily. She watched as Hal went back and forth across the narrow road three times to get it headed the right direction. When it was, Tara yelled something, and the Jeep sped off.

Hal knew he could not keep pace with the Jeep, so he didn't try, glad that Tara had thought to disable the El Camino.

Night had fallen by the time Hal arrived at the highway, and he could see the Jeep, parked, and the two of them waiting for him. When he got close, they sped north, and he followed.

Later, Tara would tell them both that she never saw what happened to the blond man or his handgun after she'd shot him, not until she chased ponytail up the hill with the bursts from the Thompson and saw him half-lying there, then realizing he must have made his way to the tree line after retrieving the gun. It was as if she was reliving it and telling it to make sure it had really happened the way she remembered. They were at her apartment now.

She wondered aloud why he hadn't fired after picking up the gun, Hal saying, "So he didn't get shot again."

She said she'd seen what she thought was blood on the blond guy's right side as he was handing the gun to ponytail. "I don't know if I even meant to hit him. Just shooting to stop him. You think he'll be okay?" She was looking at Hal.

"Depends where you hit 'im. You know the sheriff will probly come see you."

"I don't think so," she said. "It shocked me to see them again, especially the one with the ponytail."

Both men looked at her quizzically.

"He gave me the eye down at that store in Arivaca, and it made me feel funny--scared even. I kinda wish I woulda hit him instead of the blond guy."

She felt so relieved when he had arrived, meaning Hal, she said, but she didn't remember him yelling at her, just that he'd pulled up close. And she was glad Caje remembered the package because it was the farthest thing from her mind with them all standing there.

"I lost one of the packages," Caje said, realizing it just then, ashamed. "They took it."

Tara looked at Hal, whose eyes narrowed, and decided to talk about something else. "I knew he'd come for me when I fired the last few rounds, so I was gonna have to shoot him unless you came out in a minute. Or unless you," looking at Hal, "got there. He wasn't gonna stand there like that much longer. Had to have the next magazine right there cuz he didn't scare as easy as the blond guy."

"They took what?"

Tara looked at Caje, then back at Hal. "Don't worry about it."

Hal wanted to know more, but he knew that was all she was going to say about it. He would have to wonder about the duffel bag, the strange men, the missing package... He knew it was time to go when she said, "I'll put the gun back, Hal. It'll be fine." And that was all.

"You better get that cordite smell out of it. And cross your fingers he doesn't notice the missing magazines." He left for work then, just past nine o'clock.

*****

They were sitting in the camp chairs now, with fire light flashing off the silvery trailer.

"You're draining out like a hung hog," Hicks said.

"I'll be fine," JT said. "Went on through. Didn't hit nothing." He didn't seem at all afraid, naked to the waist. He was pressing his back hard against the white shirt he had been wearing, now wadded into a dark slimy ball, and holding a terry cloth towel to the entry wound on the left side of his abdomen. He stared at Hicks, sure now that he didn't like him for a partner.

"Musta hit something the way you're bleeding. 'n them VA docs'll wanna check you into the hospital. Report a gunshot wound."

"I just need a couple stitches. In the morning we can go into Nogey and get a Mex doctor. Maybe sell a few hits o' the mud on the American side. Or even a Mex doctor in Tucson. They don't report nothin'."

"You forget we only got one spare? Gonna have to walk outta here, 'n you ain't walking real good right now, case you forgot that too."

Yup--genetic misfire, JT thought. He didn't like the anger that was starting to sound in the big man's voice. "We can take a tire off the trailer--the rims match."

"You got an answer for everything, doncha? Cep't for that little bitch's Tommy gun."

JT decided to say nothing.

Hicks looked him over, then raised his eyes to the wide expanse of sky, dark and starry, not yet near moonrise. He found the north star and brought his eyes down to the treetop line below it, knowing that Tucson lay off that way somewhere, about fifty or sixty miles, though there didn't seem to be a light crown that he could identify, and farther north by a hundred miles or so, Phoenix, not straight north but west and north. He squinted hard, trying to detect a light crown. He thought about what the kid had said--the motel on Miracle Mile to wait for a call and then a meeting. He turned again when he heard a sound from his wounded partner.

JT was drinking water from a canteen, gasping softly with each swallow, showing a grimace. His skin looked orange reflecting the firelight, and his ribs stood out whenever he breathed in because his breaths were deep and long and he held each breath for a long moment before exhaling. Hicks thought his chest looked like a pumpkin, and he grinned.

JT looked up and saw Hicks's grinning face and frowned, wondering what it meant. If the car hadn't been shot up, he could have Hicks drive him to Nogales now, and he could get the bleeding stopped and get on with the business of healing. "Maybe I could take one of the tires off the trailer right now. Save some time in the morning," he said, sounding hopeful. "I can use the car jack and then put firewood under the axle." He wanted Hicks to get the jack, of course, but Hicks had already passed on getting the spare on, just before dark when he had hinted about that.

"It ain't goin nowhere. Only take a few minutes in the morning."

"Fuck it, Hicks." The hopeful note was gone now. He looked into the fire, and worked his jaw, as if he were working something out in his head. "We oughta do some planning, ya know? So we can catch up with the kid and his little bitch, ya know?"

"They'll be easy to find. 'n this time, there ain't no need for talkin'." He looked hard at the bleeding man. "And no getting away with the mud. Give 'em the Corporal Hicks special." He nodded and let his eyes go far away again.

JT forced out a laugh, still trying. "Yeah, the Corporal Hicks special--how we gonna do it this time?"

"Well, maybe get some different wheels first. They may be lookin' out for your mom's car now. And there ain't that many two-toned El Camino's with shot up fenders. So get sump'n looks real different, like a pickup. Then cruise that street till I find 'em. Then jus' take 'em out."

"At's right. We can get 'em in a crossfire. Get a room at the same hotel or sump'n." He sounded tired now. He took more deep breaths, holding each.

Hicks listened to the labored breathing, bringing his eyes back to JT. "Yeah. Or sump'n. Only I don't think you'll be there." He came close to JT, recognizing the hopelessness in his eyes. "Gimme the towel." He held his hand out.

JT did not hand it to him, but his hand fell away. Hicks lifted the towel and shook it with his left hand. Not that bloody, he noticed. He held it like a screen between them, reaching behind at his belt and retrieving the revolver, bringing it past the towel so the muzzle was a few inches from JT's head. When his partner's mouth came open, he fired one shot into it, with the towel catching most of the spatter that came back at him. He threw the towel aside. Returning the gun to his belt, he removed the sopping wad of tee-shirt from behind the little man's back and threw it aside as well and left him just that way, hanging in the camp chair, to drain out.

He slept in the trailer with the windows and door open to bring in the cool night air.

Six

It was mid-afternoon, clear and hot outside, the day after the problem near Ruby had been resolved with the Thompson, with no obvious way to resolve the problem they were going to have at the motel.

There were two posters on the walls in Tara's bedroom. One was a concert poster--Blossom Music Center presents Janis Joplin with special guest the Faces, Friday August 29, reserved seats $2.50. The letters were contoured around the illustration of an attractive nude woman with orange skin, strawberry-color hair and perfect breasts--Tara loved Janis and the Holding Company, but the illustration really didn't remind her of Janis. Tara stared at it often, never wishing for the orange skin or the strawberry hair because she was happy with her own. The other was a movie poster, Nancy Sinatra pretending to be a wild girl on a Harley behind Peter Fonda. When she stared at that one, she would usually remember the movie and think that Sinatra's hair was way too neat for a biker's girlfriend, but this time she was thinking the ponytail guy could have been riding with Fonda.

She was staring at it when Caje spoke about coming clean at the drop. "They gotta believe me. I never ripped them off."

"Tell them somebody stole it? What the hell, are you crazy?"

At first, Caje said nothing, but he felt her anger. "Maybe we could go back and get it. We can borrow the gun again."

"We were lucky last night. Crazy lucky. We wouldn't catch them by surprise again, and those guys are probly both decent shots with that rifle." They stared vacantly for a few minutes. She was rocking and hugging her knees and looking up at the Janis poster and thinking about Dem Old Kosmic Blues. "We either gotta cut it and pass it off as twelve bricks or we gotta pay for it," she said, calm again.

"How we gonna cut it? If it was powder we could cut it, but it's all sticky and gooey. You can't just throw it in a Waring blender. It would just gum things up."

"You got twenty grand?"

After a moment, he said, "Well, we got about half of that left. And we got something coming for this delivery."

"Well, I can't get anything from Judd." She gave him an impatient look. "Can you get something from one of *your* relatives?" She hated her own sarcasm as much as anyone else's and regretted it the moment she said it and leaned forward and kissed him on the mouth.

He had already made a reservation at the Dreamland Inn, but he knew he did not need to be there until five o'clock. They still had two hours.

She let herself stare at the movie poster again, remembering how the Angels came to see the one guy in the hospital, what did they call him?--the Bruce Dern character--Loser, and how they went after the nurse until Fonda's character saved her from being raped-- yeah, like that would really happen--and then later how they went after Dern's wife after he died, and this time no one saved her, and she remembered the hopeless ending when Fonda said there was nowhere to go. "Nowhere to go," came out of her mouth and then she said, "Well, there are *certain* things. We can't not go, and we can't show up short."

He was the one who stared now as she went on.

"You go check in. Take the bag of shit and the money we do have. Wait for the call. I'll talk to RJ to see if he's got any ideas and I'll come later."

"No, I don't want you in it."

"It's too late." She swiveled and rose from the bed. "That's one of the certain things too. Don't forget to call and give me the room number. Leave it on the machine if I don't answer." She disappeared into the bathroom and closed the door.

He listened to the water running in the shower for a moment, and then he swiveled and got up from the bed as well.

*****

Hal was already climbing out of his truck when he changed his mind about going inside. Doris was still pissed off at him anyway, he figured, and she'd probably already had a couple of vodkas, so he might as well let her wait another hour. He had worked his usual six-hour Sunday shift, but all the while he was thinking about the crazy shit that had happened yesterday: Tara's call and the sneaky visit to Judd's and the shootout with the Thompson. Yeah, he definitely wanted to know more about that. He started the truck and eased it back out onto the street, where he turned up the radio, Buck Owens crooning that all he had to do was act naturally. He followed Speedway west, the same way he'd gone the day before, till he turned south on Park toward Tara's place on Tenth.

The day she had moved in, she told Hal that she was lucky to get the place, the location less than a mile from campus, one bedroom and a full bath for two hundred a month. The only thing she didn't like about it was her losing war with the three-inch roaches. She didn't tell him about flirting outrageously with the landlord after she found out that he thought he already had a renter and was just showing her the place as insurance.

Hal smiled when she told him about the giant roaches, figuring that nobody in town ever won that war anyway. He was helping her carry in her mattress at the time. "All you can do is spray and slaughter. Spray a lot and slay a lot." What he didn't like about the place was the location, too close to Broadway with all its traffic and too close to downtown with all its bums. He didn't tell her he thought the place was unsafe, but he inspected the deadbolt carefully, especially after discovering that the passage lock gave way to a little jiggling. He asked her if she had a good flashlight.

Judd was more direct when he finally saw the place. She had told him it was near the Red Shark Tavern, and he had prowled the neighborhood until he found her car. "It's a hell-hole. You'll be lucky to go a month without some rapist breaking in." He wanted her to take one of his pistols, but she refused and told him she didn't want to act paranoid.

Neither the MG nor the Jeep was there. He pulled in next to the yellow bug and shut off the engine. There were sunbathers again. Whether or not they were the same as the ones he'd seen yesterday, he didn't know, but they did stare as he walked to Tara's door. He didn't stare back, but strode straight to the door, acting like he was fishing a key from his pocket, and tried it. Locked, but then he twisted and jiggled, acting like he was using the key, and it opened and he stepped inside.

He didn't know what to look for but he started looking, slowly, picking things up and examining them and then replacing them carefully, waiting for them to tell him something, as if a realization would materialize like summer storm clouds. But they were just things: wall posters, a couple candles and an empty Coke can and two wine glasses on the coffee table, no bottle, a psych book and spiral notebooks on the dining table, and two paperbacks--*The Great Religions* and *Hamlet,* a Smith-Corona portable with two lines typed onto a sheet--something about anti-heroes. In the tiny kitchen: a percolator--half full and cold, a wall-hung phone with an answering machine connected and not flashing, in the fridge a bottle of white wine with milk and cottage cheese and peanut butter. In the bathroom: eye makeup, two toothbrushes, water glasses--stuff you'd expect; some kind of painting or drawing of a small-breasted nude girl done on cardboard but in an expensive looking frame, signed by someone named J Bayles. Hal wondered if Tara had posed for it. In the bedroom: the rumpled bed clothes, the lava lamp with its nebulous galaxies and the odd light, a cheap metal ash tray with a roach clip and the twisted ends of spent joints and smelling of marijuana, a blue princess phone, a pen and pad with phone numbers--the bowling alley's and some he did not recognize, doodles, some guy named Lacho--probably a friend of Caje's, RJ's initials--the same RJ? Probably not... Just things.

He turned on the overhead light and sat in the cheap sofa in the dining room, telling himself he would wait for her, giving her an hour he told himself, continuing to look around the room and wondering if he was missing something, trying to get his questions ready, which he'd been formulating all night and then all day at work, wondering if he could get her to tell him anything anyway, hoping that Caje would not show up the same time she did. If she did.

 …what the hell am I doing here acting like her slave…or maybe her big brother…fuck, that's not it and you know it… Johnny would say I'm a dirty old man…Henrietta would think I was a monster…This is Caje's role, not mine…the boyfriend's place. It's comical: you think of the boyfriend just living out an adventure, going through a phase, going through a girl. What's he to her or Tara to him? And what would he do different if he really cared for her? Make an ass of himself and go looking for her? Leave someone else? Set aside his own future? Hell, that's just what he's doing. But not me. I go on like everything's normal… go to work…have fried steak and potatoes for Sunday dinner…sleep with my woman… pretending is what I'm doing, sitting here in the gathering dusk and moping in her apartment as if that made a difference…me, the guy who let her mother get taken off when all I needed was to be aware and be ready…or just take the damn drop myself…made her stay…first I walk out there like a dunce and get hammered in the back of the head when any PFC would have been more alert and then I just lay there on the gravel like some kid getting bullied in the school yard while those bastards mangled her…and then yesterday letting her go off with the trench broom, going down there without even taking my Henry and then taking her lame ass story about target shooting…rolling down that hill in the sports car while she faced those guys down…well, when did I ever play the man for her?…when did Judd for that matter?…at least Caje tried.

 After fifteen minutes, he decided she wasn't coming home anytime soon. He thought about leaving a note for her, something like 'Came by to see if everything was okay' but decided not to. He locked the door and left, figuring Doris must have had her third or fourth vodka by then.

 *****

 Hicks had dragged JT's body behind the camp trailer before walking up the road to get the jack. He didn't need anyone seeing it, but he also didn't feel like lugging it too far, plenty of lugging still to do. He walked about twenty steps before he remembered he needed to fish the keys out of JT's pocket. He came back and got the keys along with the cash that JT had stuffed in his pockets, keeping the dollars and tossing aside the pesos, thinking the Mex money might mislead the sheriff, and said, "I think you're right about that rim partner. Should fit."

He put the spare on for the rear tire on the El Camino, leaving the holey tire on the dirt, started the engine, and then eased the car back onto the roadway in reverse, the front listing badly to the left. He stayed in reverse all the way to the camp, feeling the rim finally cut through the side wall of the bad front tire about halfway back. Then, as JT had suggested, he jacked up the trailer's right side, the uphill side, and removed the wheel, using a stack of firewood for a jack stand. He removed the wheel and slid it downhill on its side, figuring that was easier than if it got away from him if he attempted to roll it. He put the trailer wheel on the front of the El Camino and left the ruined rim and tire where they lay. The car still listed because, although the rim was a match, the tire was smaller by an inch or two.

In the trailer, he gathered the big bottle of Jim Beam and the package of heroin that the stupid kid had missed and some canned food and his clothes and the heavy steel flashlight and everything else from the trailer that he thought he could use and everything that he thought might identify him and stuffed it into two suitcases and put those in the bed of the El Camino. He put the rifle on the floor of the cab, tilting toward the passenger side door. He knew the sheriff would know a lot just from studying the scene, find his prints and JT's, find the blood all over the chair and the ground, know it was human blood, find the slug from the revolver; but they'd find all the different looking tire tracks too, and the shell casings from the little bitch's Tommy gun, and probably some of the big slugs from it too. Nothing he couldn't explain away in an interrogation room. Last, he opened a sleeping bag all the way and rolled JT's stiff body into it and zipped it closed and carried it to the little truck and threw it in, grunting as he did. Then he thought of something else and returned to the trailer for the coil of cotton rope; he guessed there was still a good ninety feet left.

He thought he might forget the turns they had taken last time to reach the mineshaft because he had been pulling on the jug of Jim Beam quite a bit that afternoon, but then it came back to him--head southeast and then just don't take any ranch roads and look for the reddish tailings on the hillside. "Thanks, partner," he said. When he saw the tailings, he decided to leave the El Camino on the road and lug JT all the way to the vent for the old mine, with the coil of rope lashed to his belt. Better to sweat a little than to get a flat tire driving off road. Shoulda took the second trailer tire for a spare, he thought. It took him forty-five minutes to reach the vent, and he was a little shocked that he couldn't make the climb without resting, twice, the last time within nose range of the vent, foul and putrid, like lifting the lid on a garbage can a couple days after throwing a rat carcass away. He remembered JT saying that a steer must be rotting down there, and he was surprised no one had fenced off the vent yet. He had held JT's hand so JT could lean toward the edge to determine if he could see bottom and he could not.

When Hicks came within ten feet of the jagged vent opening, he threw down his load at last. He tied a double half hitch around the foot end of the sleeping bag and made a wide half-circle around the mouth of the mine vent, uncoiling the rope as he went. When he and the sleeping bag were on opposite sides of the open vent, he halted, triple twisted the rope around his hands and began to heave. It took three heaves to bring the sleeping bag close to the opening. He released tension on the rope and walked uphill another fifty feet until it was nearly all uncoiled. He walked downhill again and picked up the rope and gave it a final tug, this time without twisting it around his hands. When the sleeping bag fell, he kept loose friction on the rope even though it burned his hands going through. He was hoping the sleeping bag would pull all the rope in after it, but it did not. After a couple seconds, the rope stopped in his hands. He pulled it tight again and walked back with it and guessed that what remained was about thirty feet of rope. So it's about sixty feet down, he thought. Finally, he walked as close as he dared to the open mouth of the vent, balled up the rest of the rope and tossed it in.

He drove ahead to the next fork to turn around. "Okay," he said, as if he were talking to JT. "Gonna drive the car across and leave it in on the Mexico side, stash the luggage on this side first. Come back to the American side on foot and find a car, maybe something with some class instead of mama's hand-me-down. Then north and cruise Miracle Mile till we find 'em. That shitty little sports car or the Jeep with the bullet hole. He knew he'd hit it somewhere.

He found lockers at the Greyhound Bus terminal on the Arizona side and used coins to open the largest one available, along with another one, wondering if they were secure enough for a kilo of Mexican mud, but knowing it was better than risking a search when he crossed back on foot. He wrapped the rifle in two of his shirts before carrying it through the waiting room, but he felt like the three guys sitting there knew what it was anyway, staring at him from the sweat-compool easytouch upgrade kitstained wooden benches. He stared back hard until they looked away. He set the rifle in the bigger locker at an angle, where there was barely enough room for it.

At the border, the American agent waved him through but followed the El Camino with a stare as he rolled through the checkpoint. The bullet holes in the fender, he thought and grinned at the agent in the side-view mirror.

The Mexican guards were stopping cars, not every one but every third or fourth, he noticed. One group of guards stood around a stake truck and watched as the poor son-of-a-bitch driver unloaded bags of potatoes for inspection. Stupid fuckers, he muttered, maybe to JT or maybe just to himself, nobody's smuggling shit *into* Mexico. As he drew close, the Mexican guard in his lane began eyeing him, first the El Camino and its bullet holes and then him. He was red-skinned from the heat and mustached and short, and his uniform had wetted at the neck from perspiration, but his face was stony and serious. Hicks grinned, thinking the guy looked like an extra in *The Wild Bunch.*

When he stopped, the guard leaned close, looking past him to the other side of the cab, to the floor. "Buenos dias," he said. He smelled like peppers and cologne.

"Yeah, buenos dee-ass to you too, Santa Ana," Hicks said, but the Mexican didn't think it was funny, pulling away from Hicks and leaning sideways to glance into the empty bed.

"¿Lo que hizo esos agujeros?" the guard said, like calling me stupid, Hicks thought still grinning back at the Mexican. "I got no idea what you jus' said, Santa Ana. No hablo."

"The holes een you fenders?"

"Oh--dumb bunch o' drunk hunters shooting at a buck. Gettin' it repaired down here." The guard stared, not getting it. "Chango's body shop--you heard of it?"

The guard had gotten tired of him and looked away and waved him through.

He looked for a street he thought was wide enough to have some street parking, found one named Álvaro Obregón, and took it three blocks south. He pulled straight into a parallel spot but left the wheels two feet from the curb so that it would get some attention. Five brown children came to the car and started washing its windows, the oldest one doing all the talking and asking for a dollar and then fifty cents and then a quarter, with Hicks not seeing them or hearing them as they used a spray bottle to wet the windows, so that they gave up and went away before using their squeegees. He took the molar necklace off the rear view mirror and dropped it over his head. He left the windows down and put JT's key ring above the visor on the driver's side and walked back north. Shopkeepers, standing in his way on the sidewalk, asked him what he was looking for and told him they had the best prices on tequila and tile and leather and silver jewelry and Santos and mirrors and Elvis or nude woman paintings on velvet and clothes and huaraches and pottery and rugs and serapes and, finally, boots, which he decided he wanted to try on at least. The shopkeeper was holding a pair that he said were alligator skin, which Hicks didn't believe, but he liked the way they looked anyway. He picked a pair with square toes, black and tan, with straps connected by a steel ring on the side, that the shopkeeper said were biker boots.

"Alligator skin?" asked Hicks, and the guy nodded.

"Bullshit," Hicks said, "How much?"

"Fifty," the shopkeeper said.

"I'll give you twenty," but the shopkeeper shook his head and said it cost him more than that, and so Hicks yanked the boots off and walked out. Ten steps out the door, the guy tapped him on the shoulder and held out the boots and took his twenty dollars. Hicks grinned and took the boots and walked on. He saw an A-frame sign that advertised turtle soup up a flight of stairs and climbed up. He had the soup, wondering if the meaty stuff was just chicken, and two shrimp tacos and a draft Tecate, which he thought tasted suspiciously like piss, and then a bottled Tecate, which he thought didn't taste much different, and two shots of Sonoran mescal. He didn't tip. Near the border were the farmacias peddling birth control pills and pain killers and penicillin and sleeping pills and cigars. He bought a box of panatelas that claimed to be Cuban, which he threw into a bag with the alligator boots, and two bottles of Darvon, which he stuffed into his pockets, and stood in line to cross the border. The line moved fast, and neither the Mexican agents nor the Americans wanted to see his driver's license or look inside his bag.

On the American side, he walked up the steep hill to a burger restaurant where a sign announced 'Over a Billion Sold.' Inside, the wall was covered with painted clowns smiling and flying hamburgers. He stood in line, looking over the crowd, a big crowd, more Anglo tourists than Mexicans. Afraid to go any deeper into Mexico than this border town and afraid to eat any of the Mex food, he thought, when Uncle Kermit told them about getting la turista. He ordered a Coke and stood near a window booth where a family of six ate burgers and skinny fries, too close, so that they would know he was ready to sit down when they left. He stared at the man, who was about thirty-five and shaved close and dressed in Bermuda shorts, there with his wife and three brats and an older woman, his mother or his wife's mother, who was talking too much. He set his shopping bag on the floor and waited to catch the man's eyes and grinned at him, twisting his grin to one side and showing his teeth.

When the thirty-five year-old looked up at him, he stared, knowing why Hicks was standing so close, as if he was building up courage to say something to him, deciding whether he should or not. Hicks looked away, studying the parking lot but still grinning, giving the guy some time to decide what to do.

"We'll be done in a few minutes, okay?" the thirty-five said.

The old woman said, "Why is he hovering like that, Josh?" but Josh didn't answer, probably wishing she would shut up for now.

Hicks kept studying the parking lot until Josh said, "We'll be done here in a few minutes if you don't mind standing so close."

Hicks looked down at him again and said, "Oh you was talking to me. I thought you was talking to the old woman."

It shook up the old woman when he called her that, and Josh said, "What!"

"At's all right. I don't mind waiting on y'all. Say, I'm looking for a ride north. Which car's yours?" He widened his grin. The old woman was staring at him now, and the younger woman too, not eating. The kids kept chewing. Josh's face had reddened, but he didn't say anything. "Must be a van, huh? You got room for one more?"

It was the young woman who said, "Let's go Josh." She started gathering up the paper wrappings and the empty French fry envelopes and the half-full cups, stuffing them into the white bags that had held their lunches. Josh stared at Hicks but did not say anything until he stood up. Then he said, "No, no room," like he wanted to say more but was thinking maybe it wasn't such a good idea, with the kids and the women there. They trooped out to a Dodge window van and left, Josh staring till the last second before turning to go, and Hicks laughed. He sat down at the booth and set his bag on the table, which was still messy with salt and ketchup and a half-full sleeve of fries.

What we need now is somethin' with style, he muttered, looking over the inventory in the parking lot. There was a red Mustang, but the driver and another guy were sitting in it. Probly just the 289 with a two-barrel anyway, the way it's marked. Farther away, parked like the owner didn't want any cars close by, was a black Caddy. Don't know why, but never really liked a Caddy. Probly has a big ass engine in there though, and a four-barrel. What he liked best so far, though, was a 67 Chevelle SS, blue and wide with chrome vents on the hood, a 396 he knew. It was parked right near the door with the windows open. That'd be nice but maybe I oughta go through the parking lot and see if anybody left the keys in their car. Take the first one I find and just drive off. Check the Chevy first, maybe get lucky on it, then if not just go car to car. But then he watched a blue Dodge Charger pull into the lot and park. He figured it had the standard 318 engine with a quad, but he liked the rumble sound he heard coming from it when somebody opened the restaurant door and the dark tint on all the side windows and the wide grill with the hidden headlights and the R/T stripes around the back. He liked it well enough to make it his number one now.

There was a passenger in the car, a girl he could see through the windshield, but he watched the driver, trying to see what he did when he turned off the car. When the guy got out of the Charger, he was holding the keys for a moment, then put them in his right pocket after closing the door. He was young and tall and skinny with blond hair that hung down past his ears, which he ran his hand through on his way to the door. Primping with his fairy-looking hippie hair.

Hicks made him for a spoiled-ass kid, probably still in high school, with the Charger a damn birthday present from his old man. And now he used it to impress girls and get in their pants. The girl reminded Hicks of a cheerleader or a fraternity girl, tending to the voluptuous and aware of it and wearing cut-off white shorts, cut off even with her crotch and squeezing her thighs, pushing about an inch of her leg fat down so that it flared nicely below the frayed edges of the cutoffs. The kid waited at the front of the car for the girl and smiled at her as he took her hand and walked her to the door. The kid held open the glass door for her and looked down at her ass when she went past him into the restaurant. This would be easy. Fun too.

He watched the men's bathroom, to see how busy it was, and he watched the kid working on the girl. While they were standing in line waiting to order, he held her close by draping his arm around her shoulders, but then he dropped his hand down and stuck it in her back pocket and then returned it there after getting out his wallet to pay for the meal and kept it there while they waited for their burgers, squeezing the buttock from time to time. And he kept it there as she picked up the bag of food and one of the drinks and led him to a table and sat down with it still there pressed between the bench seat and the girl's cheek. He decided he had to like the kid for getting away with that. He liked him even more when he pulled the hand out and moved it straight to the girl's thigh, eating like a starving hobo but with one hand the whole time so he could keep the right hand free to grope. He would look up and scan the restaurant now and then.

Probly looking to see if there's anyone he knows. Check him out. Probly doesn't even have to work with Daddy paying for the insurance and kicking in gas money too. Daddy's a lawyer or a banker, his job to make money and the kid's to spend it.

He told himself it was for the best what happened to JT, even though that little bitch shouldn't have shot him. Poor bastard wasn't going to make it after that. And no way were they gonna make it growing weed. He asked himself why he wanted to get stuck there on JT's little farm and living in a crappy trailer and driving around in that corny El Camino anyway. And he answered that he didn't want it and there was another reason it was all for the best.

Hicks waited, sipping the Coke through a straw, sure for some reason that the kid would use the bathroom at some point, finishing the fries that Josh's kids had left behind and then folding the empty cardboard sleeve and turning it into a wedge, as thin as the cardboard on one end and thick as his finger on the other, still watching the kid and the men's room.

The girl went to the bathroom with the kid waiting for her to return, and Hicks started to wonder if his plan was going to work, wondering what was next if the kid never went to the men's room. Back to plan A then, he thought, although the nice Chevelle was gone now. But then the girl returned and sat at their table while the kid got up to go. Hicks waited only half a second and then he followed, leaving his shopping bag and his Coke at the table but carrying the little cardboard wedge. Inside the men's room, the kid was at one of the two urinals, just starting. Hicks dropped his wedge as if he had accidentally dropped his wallet or something and went down after it but instead of picking it up, he jammed it under the door, adding a kick when he came up so that it would stay. He strolled toward the second urinal, knowing the kid hadn't paid any attention. When he got behind him, Hicks grabbed his free arm, the left one, and his hair. The kid began to twist, trying to free himself and flailing uselessly behind him with his right hand, but Hicks jerked his left arm behind his back and rocked his head forward into the wall, twice. He yelped the first time, not the second, but he kept trying to twist and reach behind. There was blood on the wall where his head had struck it and running down over his cheek.

"Just shut up and settle down, now, kid, or you get some more." When the kid stopped struggling, Hicks let go of his hair and yanked his shirt up from the waist line and over his head and down over his face. "I did that so you can't see me, kid. Consider it a favor." The shirt was a tank top, so there was no collar, and now he was raising his right hand up and holding his forehead and starting to cry, but he managed to say, "What the fuck! I'm gonna kill you." Hicks grabbed the kid's neck now, since the hair was up under the shirt, and rocked his head into the wall again, hurting his hand and his head both this time. Then he said, "I kinda doubt that, kid." Someone was trying to come in from the restaurant now.

Hicks let go of his neck then, still holding his left arm behind him and now pressing forward with his leg so that the kid was pinned against the urinal, panting and bleeding all over one of the flying burgers on the wall, and went into his right pocket after the keys, the kid squirming a little but knowing now it was useless and giving up. He had completely opened the fly on his jeans to urinate, and the pants came down a few inches as Hicks scrounged inside his pocket. When his fist came out with the keys, he put them in his own pocket and then went into the kid's rear pocket and pulled out his wallet, flipping it open to find the kid's license first, his name Scott something, from Tucson. "Says here you live on a street called Gleneagle. Where the fuck is that, kid?" Still panting, he said, "Tucson." Hicks said, "I know that kid, but what part?" He said, "North. Foothills." Hicks said, "That near Miracle Mile?" and the kid shook his head, grunting out a negative somehow." Hicks pinched the bills with his thumb and forefinger, letting the wallet drop to the floor and stuffing the bills in his pocket with the keys, not bothering to count the cash or even look at it. "Say what kinda eagle is a Gleneagle anyway?" The kid didn't say anything, not getting the joke. Whoever was at the door was trying harder to get in now, and Hicks knew the wedge wouldn't hold more than a few more seconds. Hicks rocked his head into the wall again and then backed up and turned the kid and punched him in the face, twice, the punches making a smacking sound through the fabric of the shirt. The kid went down, unable to catch himself with his arms, but folded up at the knees and waist. Hicks pushed him back so that he leaned against the wall. He kicked the wedge aside and jerked the door open and said, "Oh my God, he hurt himself. Call an ambulance."

He pushed past a short bald man in plaid shorts who had backed up and was now staring at him, his face red, his mouth wide. Hicks walked back to the table where the shopping bag and the Coke still sat. His gait was slow but his steps long. The kid's girl looked over at him and smiled. He paused for a moment to smile back, took the bag and walked out the door and straight to the Charger, which rumbled agreeably to him when it started. "Yeah, way better," he muttered, maybe to JT or maybe just to himself. It took him ten minutes to get back to the Greyhound station and park. There was a small crowd in the waiting room now, but the same three men were there, and he nodded to them.
*****

RJ's house stood along the east side of a desert canyon, nakedly visible to everyone who drove up the two-lane road toward the mountaintop a mile above. His acreage bordered on the national forest to the north. He had owned the property for six years now, and lived in the home for two after spending two years waiting for the contractor to get it built into the hillside. It was probably worth a couple million dollars anyway, Tara thought, money that RJ had generated through his beverage distribution business, his "business of record," the business that sold booze to Judd's bowling alley, the business that Judd so admired him for and the business that put him in the Rotary and the chamber of commerce. The rumor was that he had acquired that business after making one big score in the heroin importing business. If you believed the rumor, then you believed that he had brought in a half ton of heroin with a load of ironwood furniture, right through the Nogales port of entry, risking everything and then cashing in and never involving himself with the importers again. He had proved a guy could do that--score once, cash in, walk away. Judd thought the rumor was a load of BS because there's no way a respectable businessman could have started that way; Tara knew it was BS because RJ still knew people in the import business. Right now, she hoped he knew the right people.

When the door opened, Tara was relieved to see RJ's wife across the threshold. She made this chat harder in some ways but easier in others. She was about twenty-eight, if that even, about half RJ's age, but then so what, wearing a tee-shirt, too busty for it Tara thought, showing nipple the way it did, and a red bikini bottom, with her hair twisted into a bun on top of her head, blond but showing a few days' growth of dark roots. She wore a disinterested expression.

"Roberta? We spoke on the phone," Tara said, smiling faintly and wondering if she ought to extend her hand.

"Figured it was you." Roberta looked her over and walked across the room toward a set of glass French doors that led outside to a balcony. She said, "RJ oughta be down in a minute," and, as Tara entered, slipped out the door, leaving it open a few inches, and sat at a table in front of a few makeup bottles and a mirror. The French door was part of a wall of glass on the west side of the room. Beyond the balcony lay a panorama of the facing hillside, pale rock formations, saguaros, nopal and creosote, which Tara studied adoringly for a moment until she realized that Roberta might think she was studying her as she applied her mascara. She turned and moved to the south wall, another expanse of windows overlooking the desert and the city from several hundred feet; there was Tucson, low and sprawling, and farther south Sahuarita and Green Valley, where the most visible part was the mine tailings. And farther south were Tubac and Nogales and the scene of her recent debacle. She heard someone on the stairs and turned and saw RJ.

His name was Richard Jenkins Jasper, so naturally he preferred RJ, and nobody ever called him anything else. He was born in Massachusetts to an Anglo woman who was dead now and an Iranian man who had Anglicized his name and made jewelry in a small Boston shop until being summoned "home" in 1955, never to be heard from again. After that, RJ came west with his older brother and spent most of his life in Arizona. When he came into the Saguaro Bowl, it was always with a few men who looked like business types, dressed in white shirts and ties, with plenty of belly fat. RJ didn't seem to belong with them, always wearing shorts and sandals and polo; he was thinner and shorter than the guys he came in with, and he always acted as host, paying for the drinks and conveying superiority. He had prematurely white hair too, but for some reason it didn't make him look old. They would all talk, but Tara knew RJ's guests were afraid of him, sensing it even before she had heard the somewhat colorful rumors about RJ. He did tip pretty well, though.

He stepped to the French door and pushed it all the way shut, Roberta glancing up at him. Then he said, "So you say you need to buy some product this time. That was never the arrangement, pretty one." The condescension in his voice, same as with his bar pals.

She hated the tone and she hated 'pretty one,' but this time anyway, she thought it best to try tamping down her irritation. "Yes. Well, what do you think?"

"You said need, so I guess you aren't going into business for yourself. You want to tell me about it?"

"You really want to know?"

He stood looking past her, at the giant sky in his window. Something like a smile played around his lips, but he didn't answer. Instead, he said, "How much?"

"We have ten thousand plus what we were due this time."

"Sounds low. And even if it isn't, they won't like it." His eyes still past her and out the window.

She felt her heart pounding now, suddenly, and she told it to be quiet. "I know. You told me they don't like changes to the plan. We don't either, but it couldn't be helped. How short are we?"

"Five, but that's if you were listening to what I'm saying. They don't want mules who make shit up."

"I'm thinking this guy has something to do with the beverage business."

His head snapped and his eyes narrowed on her, like a bald eagle with his white hair. "Difference does that make?"

"Maybe I shoulda said hoping." I should be asking for help, she thought, not trying to piss him off, but she went on. "I'm thinking he would hate to disappoint you, this guy."

"You and your little Indian friend oughta be more concerned with disappointing me. And your father." It scared her, and she could feel her heart pounding again, but then his eyes went to the horizon in the window again and he added, "You know what? Maybe you should just go fuck yourself." And now she was sure of herself again because he was acting like some teenage punk, RJ getting off on talking that way to impress her, the same reason he brought her into the import business anyway. To him she was one of the lesser people, like the chubby businessmen who hung with him at lunch time, easy to impress, easy to frighten, easy to forget. He was her superior, doing her a favor.

"Maybe I should. At least I'd be getting it from someone who cares about me." She thought about her life in her father's house, the time before Father John and the time since, like a prison run by her father and now another kind of prison living with a man. A child for eleven years and then held down on the floor for five minutes and then the prisoner at her father's house and then in her own apartment, but it was all the same, just a matter of which man tried to own you. Right now, RJ thought he did. She wondered if Hal was any different.

She waited for him to understand her. She watched his eyes come back from the windows and focus on her. His sandals were not Mexican huaraches but Bally, dyed oxblood brown; his long-sleeve polo was Nordstrom's. He moved to his right so that Roberta was behind him, like a three-dimensional painting with her applying rouge now.

"RJ, it's important to make this as easy as we can make it. Caje and I didn't make the trouble--it just came to us. Like a glass of wine that gets dropped on the floor. Caje thought we could explain it to Lacho or whatever his name is while we stand there with a machine gun, but I don't think that would work out very well." She let him have a moment to think about that. "If you don't see a solution, I think that's what he'll do. Make a stand."

RJ frowned. Whenever he frowned, his air of superiority evaporated. "That would be very foolish. Where would he get an idea like that?" Accusing her.

"The movies, I guess. He loved the scene in *Wait Until Dark* when Audrey Hepburn stabbed Alan Arkin. Figures that life can imitate art."

"Pretty one, you need to disabuse him of his fairy tale notions. Lacho is not the Big Bad Wolf, and he's not the one you need to worry about anyway."

"He believes in art. You know if it goes badly, we'll both get shot up over at the Dreamland, and if it goes well, you're saying we'll both get shot up later. I don't know Lacho or any of those people, but I know Caje. He thinks he has to show power--live up to his Yaqui heritage. He decided to carry shit across the border because of me, not because he wanted to live on easy street or to show his spite for white men's laws. That's just something he tells his friends on the rez. But I can tell he's not interested in the American success saga. I suggested this job to him because he has been across the border fifty times on foot and because I knew he'd do it for me. What he wants right now is to feel like he's protecting me from something, especially since I embarrassed him recently. He wants to relive the heroism of his ancestors when they fought the Mexican army. He's got a crazy idea about fighting on behalf of his people. He'll expect that Lacho treat him with respect. He doesn't understand mean people, he thinks of drug traders as a bunch of hippies. I'm not saying I understand everything, but I think smoother is better than rougher. Don't you?"

RJ said nothing. He let his eyes diffuse again through the south window, the frown disappearing, the superior air returning. He stood silent, for at least a minute Tara thought. He turned and moved away without looking at her again, and Tara thought perhaps she was being dismissed, but then RJ sat at a chrome desk and started writing on a note pad. When he finished, he handed her a slip. "Don't tell Lacho you're short until you see him. Then give this to him along with your money."

It was personalized stationery, silver, with black script that said 'A note from RJ'. He had scribbled his initials in blue ink right next to the script. There were three phone numbers, nothing else. She looked at the numbers and then at RJ. "What are these?"

"The first one is if you need someone threatened. The second is if you need somebody's legs broken." Tara put the paper into the front pocket of her shorts and left without saying anything else.

Seven

Hicks told himself that he could have some fun with the Charger for a few days as long as he didn't draw too much attention to himself. Tracking down stolen cars just isn't a police priority, he knew, and the Nogey police would probably assume the car had been driven into Sonora for some quick cash. He loved the way he could touch the pedal and feel the car push him back in the seat, the hood lifting visibly. On the highway north, he had repeatedly let the Charger slow down to just above forty and then punched the accelerator to the floor. The kid had a tach mounted on the dash, and Hicks would watch it as his speed climbed, wondering what his speed would be if he actually red-lined the thing. Once he hit 105, still nowhere near the redline, but he had to slow down for a couple of sedans. Another time, he was above 100 again, but thought he saw a sheriff's car ahead and braked fast. It annoyed some other north-bound drivers, but he knew he'd have to ditch the Charger in a few days and might not get a chance like this again for a while. "Fuck 'em, JT," he said.

He followed Sixth Avenue all the way through downtown and then stopped at an American Oil station to fill the gas tank and ask about the Miracle Mile. He pulled in at the full-serve island, but no one came bounding out to wash his windows, so he leaned on the horn until a short, thin, gray-haired guy strolled out smoking a cigarette, making it a point not to hurry.

The old guy came to the window, only a few inches taller than the roof of the Charger. His name tag said Gillis. He didn't smile, but he took a draw of smoke and spoke as he exhaled. "Well I wish I had this car and you had a wart on your ass." His voice was so low and gravelly that Hicks thought it was a put-on.

"Fill it up, Gillis." He tried to imitate the gravelly voice, but the old guy didn't get the joke. Gillis strolled around the back of the car and started pumping the gas, still smoking. He came forward and used a spray bottle to wet the windshield and began wiping away the streaks of dead bugs. "Hey, Gillis," still imitating the voice, "Which way to Miracle Mile?"

"If ya mean the street with all them whore hotels, it starts here to the west, ya smart alec. 'bout half a mile and turn right." The old guy's voice never changed. When he finished at the driver's side, he took a last puff on his cigarette before dropping it and snuffing it with his shoe. Then he went to the rear of the Charger and topped off the gasoline and put the cap back on. He came back to Hicks and said, "Seven dollars and twenty cents."

"Ain't you gonna do the passenger side?"

"What for? You ain't got no passenger." He pulled a package of Winston's from his shirt pocket and shook one up and put it in his mouth.

Hicks thought about the Ruger Mini-14 in his trunk but decided he liked the old guy while he was lighting his Winston and gave him eight dollars and imitated his gravelly voice one last time, saying, "See ya around, Gillis," and drove west to the next light.

Hicks's plan was to drive the length of Miracle Mile and get an idea of how much ground he had to recon, how many motels he had to watch, then just drive back and forth, cruise into the parking lots if he had to, until he spotted either the Jeep with the bullet hole or the little piece of shit red MG. He turned north where Gillis had told him. The street was not really named Miracle Mile until it made an ell to the west after about a mile and a half, but there were a lot of cheap-looking pre-interstate motels, mostly U-shaped and single-story, every one getting past the run-down stage and all of them posting vacancy signs. He drove slowly past them all, scanning for either one of the cars. When he was almost to the freeway, he pulled into a place called Roadmasters Inn to turn around and start back the other way. He sat in the idling Charger, feeling its soft rumble and thinking. What he didn't like was that there seemed to be so many motels, fifteen that he counted, plus there had to be a few set back from the strip a block or two; and he didn't like the way some of the places seemed to be set up for privacy, a couple places with A-frame signs plugging hourly rates and some with covered, half-hidden parking spots, so that he might have to cruise through the parking area at each place until he found the little bitch or her mule friend. If he had to do that, there was a good chance they'd see him at the same time as he saw their cars. They would obviously be waiting for someone to call or show up for the score and looking outside every time a car rolled past their rabbit hole. "And what we need here is to surprise *them* this time," he said, and now we got the new car and the tinted windows.

He turned off the engine, retrieved the Ruger Mini and two 20-round magazines from the trunk, and returned to the driver's seat, where he injected one of the curved boxes, pulled back and returned the operating slide to chamber one of the rounds and pressed back the safety at the front of the trigger guard with his index finger. There was a middle-aged woman staring at him now through the motel's registration office window, so he smiled. He laid the tip of the rifle barrel on the floorboard and rested the stock on the passenger seat, starting the engine again. But what to do when I find them, he thought, What did JT say--they cut us in or we blow them up? 'They' meaning whoever contacted the mule kid, Portillo--Oscar Portillo, at the motel. JT would want to follow the biggest money. "But that lets the bitch off," he said, "and after what she did, that ain't right." No, I just might have to fix her before I go worrying about the packages. He rolled the tinted windows all the way up and eased up on the clutch and took the Charger back onto the street.

The Charger crawled back and forth along Miracle Mile and the rest of the motel strip in the right lane, occasionally earning Hicks a horn blast or a finger, but he did not respond. He stopped once at a Circle-K for a six-pack of Bud and a bag of pork rinds so he'd have something for his stomach while he looked for the two cars. He scanned parking lots. He was thinking that JT would look the car over and ask him, "What the hell you doing in that splashy car? That car's for hot dogs. It's gonna get you caught." And maybe I'd say, "It's a good plan though, ain't it, looking for one of the cars." And that would shut JT up, since he couldn't have thought of a better one. Or maybe JT would keep on, with a different idea, starting out with 'I wish', like saying 'I wish you'd a thought of this or that'. It was like you had to think of every different way of doing a thing first instead of just taking the handiest way. He remembered seeing two great looking women, with great looking bodies anyway, at that Arivaca bar one time, and hell, you never usually saw any women there, good-looking or not, and he wanted to go over and get acquainted as soon as they walked in, but no, JT insisted, they must wait till they'd had a drink to loosen up and help them relax, lower their inhibitions, he'd said. Okay, so we waited, even though when they went by their perfume smelled good and they were dressed to show off what they had in tight-around-the-ass jeans and tops that stretched just right and they seemed to be giving us the eye. And then, just as they were finishing that first drink, these two cowboys went over there with a pitcher of some slushy stuff and extra glasses and sat down. So they missed the chance to get close to the two nice bodies, and he'd asked JT if he always thought things over so much back in Nam. JT looked at him funny and said yeah, that was how he figured he survived and never fell for any of the booby traps like the ones with grenades inside of empty cans. It made him, Hicks, feel a little dumb for stepping into that conical trap, and he didn't say anything back, but he always thought it was just luck whether or not a guy bought it over there. If Charlie got your name on a bullet, there ain't nothing anybody can do about it, and so yeah, we should have got up and made the move on the women sooner.

Driving south, he came to the Dew Turn Inn Motor Lodge and decided to make a drive-through so he could see into all the parking stalls, which were all recessed between brick veneer rental units arranged in an ell behind the registration office. He pulled past the office and idled along. There was a Jeep parked in one of the stalls, but too new to be the one he was looking for, a couple of station wagons, and just nothing at all in any of the others. He made the circuit, idled back to the front and waited for traffic to clear. Then he saw the MG.

The little bitch was driving it alone, northbound, her blond hair in a ponytail and not really playing in the convertible's air flow. He waited for traffic to clear and turned to follow her in the same lane. He was back over a hundred yards, but he really wasn't worried about losing her at a red light or anything. He knew she had to be turning into one of the flophouses. Like she's kenneling up for the night, he thought, but is the mule ahead of her or still coming?

He did lose her too, where the strip went left, west, where the red light lasted for what seemed like a minute, but it was only momentary. He saw the MG again, parked now at a place called Dreamland Inn, in plain view. He drove past and turned left farther west and found an alley that seemed as if it might back up to the Dreamland on its south side and followed it back to the east. On its alley side the motel was merely a concrete block wall, dull white, with a regular pattern of windows, small ones with steel casements and clouded glass. Probably the bathrooms, he thought. There were no doors, only a passage through a locked gate to connect the parking lot to their dumpster spot. Remembering what he had told JT about just walking in and doing her, he began to wonder about some things. He wondered if she was alone, especially since he had not seen the Jeep; he wondered if she was using the secondary lock, the chain or whatever it was; he wondered if she'd be stupid enough to answer the door so that he wouldn't have to force it open. He pulled around again, spotted the MG in the same place, and then idled past it, lowering his forehead until the windshield passed in front of what he figured was her room toward the front of the east wing, and then staring through the tinted glass. There was about a three inch opening in her drape. He saw the Jeep then too, pulled deep into one of the parking stalls so it would be hidden from the street, and it disappointed him.

The Dreamland was arranged in a U around the office and swimming pool, and Hicks crawled the growling Charger through a complete circuit of the place, figuring he could have his pick of rooms. He parked the Charger close to the office and put on a hat and sunglasses and slipped in to register. A pancake-faced woman at the desk asked him for a credit card but seemed happy enough to take his twenty-two dollars cash for one night when he said he didn't have one. He took a room opposite the bitch's, in the west wing, and far enough back so that the swimming pool fence did not obscure a view of her room. When he parked at the room, he left the Charger in front of the door instead of using the parking bay. Then he lay down across the front seats, his belt buckle against the shifter and his head an inch or two from the rifle. If they're watching the car, they'll think they just missed me getting out, he figured, and it's getting dusk anyway.

He timed himself for ten minutes before getting out to enter the room, carrying the rifle and the last of his meal. The room was stuffy and warm, and he turned on the wall-mount air conditioner, maximum cool. Then he turned on the light in the bathroom and set himself to watch the bitch's room. He opened the drape about a foot and slouched in a mission-style chair in front of it, his boots propped onto the window sill. His gaze took in the open quadrangle formed by the arrangement of buildings, all one story, concrete block painted a light green, an institutional green that reminded him of some sort of army building. There was a slanted porch roof that ran the length of the whole structure, red Mexican tiles, some crumbling at the drain edge now, held up with round support posts every ten feet or so. The sun was gone and the descending dusk gave the whole scene a gloomy look. He sipped beer and ate pork rinds and watched the slit of window across from him. They had turned on lights in the room, and occasionally he would see a flicker or a shadow cross the open slit. Once, someone pulled the curtain back to one side, and he thought he saw a glimpse of the bitch.

He hated the waiting, but he didn't think there was a choice. As he'd driven north, he had all but decided that he was just going to get the brown bricks back and do the girl, the mule too if it was handy, and go into business, but then he realized that JT was probably right about these guys shipping the dope. That damn JT. It was one thing to blow up a delivery and make off with a quarter million worth of heroin, another to advertise it for sale without asking for trouble from the shippers. He was going to have to have a conversation with these somebodies, and to do that he was going to have to react to what the bitch and her mule did. He opened his fifth beer.

*****

It was clear and warm as Tara turned into the Dreamland parking lot. It's not even twenty-four hours since the drama down south, she thought, wondering how the man was, the shorter, blond guy. She wished she had shot the other one. She hadn't bothered to stop by her apartment and check the answering machine, so she looked for the Jeep. She saw it as she rolled past the stall; it was the second unit from the front. She idled for a moment and looked around. She could see into about half of the parking stalls, the Jeep the only car she could see, and she thought maybe they were the only guests. She sensed the movement when the door to fourteen opened, and she saw Caje there holding it wide for her and staring. She killed the engine and took up her oversized macramé purse, which contained two books, fresh underwear and shorts and a top, and as of a few minutes ago, her father's Marlin .32 revolver. It was an antique, but she'd wanted something along for comfort, and the Thompson didn't seem good for that. If Lacho didn't like this deal, the Thompson wouldn't be enough anyway, she figured, because they were dealing with a lot more guys than Lacho, and besides it was crazy loud for in-town if she had to fire it.

Tara kissed Caje in the doorway because she knew he would need that for his own comfort. They were faced with God knew how long a wait and then maybe some sort of crisis when they met this guy, their stupid asses lucky if they came through in one piece, and Caje needed that kind of comfort, like a cuddle. She could not remember a time when she had needed that kind of reassurance. If she waited for a hug or a kiss from Caje or another man or even from her mother when her mother was still alive, it was because she wanted them to feel like they needed *her*. She remembered going to a sorority party once with a girl named Suzy who wanted her to pledge, and telling her, "That's how you know you can get them to do what you want." Suzy, smiling, said, "Sex, right? The one with the pussy gets to decide?" She thought about that for a moment before answering, deciding that it wasn't quite that simple, that instilling need in another person was more about arousing his desire to demonstrate power--superiority even--to compensate for something, more about making other people aware of their weakness but said, "Sure." And a kiss from Hal, well, she was still waiting for that. The gun in her purse was good to have, but she knew the only kind of comfort that meant anything was a resolution, and that would not come until later.

"Did you bring the money?" she asked after the kiss. He nodded, looking like he wanted her to say something more, but she held up her finger as if to tell him to wait a minute and went into the bathroom. She closed the door and sat down to pee and raised her voice. "I guess the guy hasn't called yet." He didn't answer, and she took that to mean yes and went on. "I've been thinking. We're gonna be short on cash for this guy Lacho anyway, right?" He still didn't answer. When she finished on the toilet, she washed her hands and dried them on one of the clean towels and came out and sat on the bed. Caje was in a chair next to the color television.

"So we may as well not give him everything, right? Keep something back for expenses until next time." Two big things for him to think about--'keeping something back' and 'next time'. She watched him react. His face was straight, and he said nothing. "We give him eight thousand and he keeps whatever he was gonna pay you this time." When she saw the big muscle car roll past through the opening in the drape, she stood and moved closer to watch it through the drape opening, but she could see nothing through the windows in the gathering gloom. It grumbled as it idled along the U formed by the buildings and exited behind the front office on the far side of the complex. She apparently had missed something Caje had said because, when she turned, he seemed to be waiting for her. "And the note. We give him this note from RJ." She pulled the slip of stationery from her pocket and handed it to him. "Except we're writing down those numbers first." She retrieved a pen and little note pad from the phone stand by the bed and handed it to Caje. She told him about the meeting at RJ's house--the busty wife, the giant windows, the condescension, the note finally.

As she stood there, he wrote down the numbers and gave her the copy. Then he counted out twenty hundred dollar bills and gave those to her as well. He put RJ's silvery stationery in his shirt pocket. The next time Tara looked out the window, the big muscle car was parked across the quadrangle in front of a room, but she could not see light in any of the windows.

She sat on the bed again and fished one of the novels out of her bag--*Candide*, which had been assigned in her philosophy class, where the prof had been droning on about Leibniz and the problem of evil, and she thumbed past the introductory material and began to read: "In the country of Westphalia, in the castle of the most noble baron..." Caje turned on the television and found *Bonanza*, a rerun episode about a prospector and his daughter and featuring Little Joe and the other young guy, Adam out of the show by then, and they waited for the phone to ring.

By the time the *Bonanza* episode ended, Tara was reading about Candide shooting two monkeys that had been chasing a couple of naked women, and praising God for being able to rescue them, when she saw something move in the room across from her. She hadn't seen any light at all before, but now she detected some, as if a night light was on. She could tell that the drape was wide open over there too, and she scanned along the row of windows to compare. But no, the others all bounced back the ambient light off the light-colored drapes; there was just the one open and dark, with some faint light behind. She was pretty sure someone was over there, away from the window a little so that he was back in the shadows, his form low like he was sitting or bending. Lacho, maybe? Checking them out before he called, maybe? She heard Caje's voice behind her. "You still with me over there?"

She looked at him but didn't say anything about the other guest. Hell, it could be anyone, just a guy driving through who needed to get some sleep, opened the window then crashed in the chair. She thought she'd check over there again whenever the phone rang.

"So if he doesn't come here..." he started. "If Lacho wants us to meet him somewhere, we should have a plan maybe. It's different this time, with the missing brick." His guilt, his embarrassment was showing again, for losing it, on his face and in his voice.

"It's gonna be fine, Caje." She actually thought it would too, with the get-out-of-trouble slip from RJ. "But you're right. If he tells you to meet him someplace, we should know what we're gonna do. I guess I just assumed we'd both go. He might want to ask something about RJ...to prove it was his note."

"What do you think it means? Is it like a threat if Lacho does something?"

"No, it's not a threat. I thought about that on the way over here. I don't think we're important enough to RJ for him to threaten anybody."

"Well, what is it then?"

"He's letting Lacho know…letting Lacho's bosses know that he'll take care of it himself if we fuck up again."

He nodded, becoming vacant-eyed now. "I think I go alone. Lacho's never even seen you, so why would I bring someone new into it now?" He watched her pause to think about that. "And the less things that are different the better, you know?"

She had to admit Caje was right about that. She picked up her book again to see how the naked women showed their appreciation to Candide, and Caje switched over to *Mission Impossible*, where the white-haired guy and the widow-peak guy were both getting mixed up with some British duchess, trying to get her to fall for one of them, men on the make for love of country-- sure. Lacho rang up on the phone at 8:45.

While Caje answered, Tara moved closer to the window and looked hard across the parking lot. Everything was the same, the faint lighting and the low form inside the window, not moving. If it was a man and not just some trick of the lighting, he wasn't anywhere near the phone. So probably not Lacho. She stepped near the door and turned out the room light, letting Caje talk there in the darkness behind her and stepped even closer to the window to peer through the crack in the drapes. The same for a moment and then movement, a shift in the shadows. Caje was repeating some part of an instruction.

"…the picnic table…the last one near the top…yeah, I been there before."
*****

Caje was ten minutes past the last city lights, nearly all the way to the top of the pass and starting to wonder if he'd missed the turn in the blackness. He knew the road and he'd used the very spot to park with girls, a couple times with Tara even, while he was still in high school, as a lot of the west side boys did, but it was utterly dark. The moon had not begun to rise yet. Then he saw amber parking lights to his right. He slowed the MG to a crawl. There was a turnoff leading away from the narrow band of asphalt and through the rocky piece of desert, a rare flat spot on the ascent. He could just make out the chrome and metal of a pickup truck parked there close to the concrete table and benches, a Ford, brown and yellow, pointed toward the road as if its driver had backed in. He pulled next to it and peered up at the front seats, a couple feet above him. Nobody there that he could tell. He killed his lights and the engine and got out of the car to wait, wondering where Lacho was watching from, where he would approach from, whether there was a second guy. He sat on the low front fender facing away from the amber lights, and away from the glow of Tucson back to the east, letting his eyes adjust as much as possible. He was thinking Lacho might come up the dirt driveway behind him, the only way out for the car, but if RJ's little note didn't make an impression on him, he was not going to just stand here and take a couple of slugs. Sprained ankle or not, he would try to sprint away through the creosote and the cholla, the mesquite and the nopal and get back to the road where he knew Tara would be coming along in the Jeep.

Two cars came up the road, just shapes going the same direction he'd been going. The lead car slowed at the turnoff, almost stopped, and he could see some of it illuminated by the headlights trailing it--a big car, a dark color with wide stripes up the side of the rear fender. The second car blared its horn. Both cars drove on to the top of the pass and made the hairpin turn to the left and disappeared, starting the descent into the broad valley to the west.

He let his eyes adjust again. Soon the cacti and scrubby trees began to stand out in contrast to the ground around him, which fell away sharply to the north before rising again to the next hill. A good deal of granite showed ghostly white, even silvery with its mica, but looking downward, it was nearly impossible to plan an escape route. It was very steep here, maybe a cliff. He'd be lucky if he didn't kill himself in a fall, save Lacho the bullet.

He heard the sound of boots on the hard ground, muffled but sure-footed somehow, knowing it was Lacho off to his left, and he turned.   The silhouette was distinct now, against the lighter backgrounds of starlit desert. As Lacho came close, Caje could see his features, recognizing the round face and the long, pulled-back hair, the flattened nose, the large mustache with a toothpick poking through, the powerful arms and torso stretching his jacket.

"Ay hermano, good to see choo again," Lacho said, his lips hardly moving, holding the toothpick in his teeth.

"Hey." He worried about running into a cholla cactus if he started to sprint. He remembered seeing a guy falling into one once, a hod carrier at a construction site, and how he'd lain there till he could be pulled out of the cactus branches, how the masons laughed at him while they pulled the spiny stems out of him with pliers.

"Choo sound a little funny on the phone, hermano. Everything okay?"

"Yeah, things are good." He watched Lacho reach inside his jacket and bring out a package of cigarettes and shake one up and offer it to him.

"Choo still sound a little funny, hermano. Choo packing?" The toothpick moved around in his mustache.

"No. No thanks." He heard an owl now, very close, but he didn't look for it, watching the big man carefully.

Lacho put the cigarettes back and brought out an envelope now. "We wasting time then, hermano. I got something for choo if choo got something for me." He waved the fat envelope in the air and then put it back inside his jacket.

Caje nodded. "In the trunk." He went around the MG, thinking that maybe he could keep the little sports car between them for a few seconds if he started to run, but Lacho followed. He became aware that he was holding his breath and made himself blow out and then inhale again, trying to keep it a shallow breath, controlled, as if he weren't scared. He reached into his front pocket for the key and opened the little trunk and reached down for the duffel bag. There was light from a flashlight now, shining into the trunk from Lacho's hand held high, from his right and behind him, very steady, Lacho still not trusting him entirely he guessed. He pulled the duffel out and closed the trunk lid and set the bag on it and unzipped it and stepped back.

"Choo need to turn around now, hermano, okay. I jus' need to look it over." He aimed the flashlight at Caje now.

"I'm short, man." Now was the time.

Then the light was straight in his eyes. "I can see choo short. You always been short. What choo mean, hermano?"

"I mean we…I mean I lost one of the packages." He tried to see through the beam of the light. "But I can pay for it." Trying to do it the way Tara said, getting the whole thing out while you watch what he does. She had made him practice it for her.

Silent for a moment, Lacho finally said, "Thass no bueno, amigo. Choo need to turn around and lemme look inside. See what choo talking about."

"I will. You just need to let me explain, man." Shit, I'm sounding desperate now. "All the bricks are in there, man." He inhaled deeply. "All except the one we lost." And *don't* tell him somebody took it, she'd said, cuz then he'll want to know who and how and get paranoid about their competition.

"Choo going to turn around?" Not sounding patient now.

"And there's an envelope in there too. That and the new envelope, the one you brought, that's for the one we lost." He wondered if it was the time to run. "There's one other thing too…in my pocket." He brought his hand up from his side. Go slow, she'd said, but don't let him stop you. When he'd frowned, she said that maybe she should come too, but he told her no, that he'd rather have her bringing up the Jeep ten minutes or so behind him and he could do it.

"I need choo to turn around," Lacho said, sounding like he meant 'or else' now, but still not doing anything different, holding the flashlight.

"It's just a note for somebody…for you I guess," he said, pulling the note out of his shirt pocket and holding it out, waiting. There were headlights climbing toward the pass from town again, but not the Jeep's.

"Turn around, amigo." Like there was no more time.

Caje turned, still holding the slip of paper, over his shoulder now, and he saw the owl now, sitting darker than the sky on top of a two-armed saguaro, but the eyes shining ochre. The light changed then, Lacho rummaging in the duffel bag now apparently, with sounds like he'd taken some of the bricks out and laid them on the car to count, and then a sound that Caje imagined was him opening the envelope and looking at the bills in there. The light changed again as if the flashlight had been set down, sounding like all the shit was getting thrown back into the bag and the zipper going shut, and some other kind of shuffling, which Caje guessed was Lacho's gun coming out, and finally the flashlight getting picked up again.

"Choo right, amigo. Choo short."

Caje held his breath, thinking it was time to duck and run, but then the light changed again and he felt the flashlight hand take the note at last, and he waited. He saw the climbing car's headlights slow as it approached the hairpin above.

"Okay. I show this to someone," he said, "and then I don't know, amigo. Choo just can't do this stupid sheet."

"I know, man. Hey listen…"

"Shut up, amigo. I like choo, no? and I hope this work out, but right now just shut choo stupid mouth and hope choo okay. Otherwise, I be back and we don't get to work together no more. Get out choo keys and sit down at the bench. And don't look over this way."

Caje inched toward the bench, fishing the keys from his pocket and then holding them by his ear. The owl sounded again, but Lacho didn't make any noise, waiting. When he reached the concrete bench, he thought about Lacho's gun, not willing to take the seat, thinking that somehow it would make a difference, but then Lacho said, "Sit down," again, without adding hermano or amigo, and Caje sat, still holding Tara's keys by his ear. The coolness from the concrete penetrated his jeans. He listened to Lacho's boots coming up to him from behind and then stopping. The flashlight hand came forward now and took the keys, and then there was a hard tap on top of his head, maybe from the flashlight and maybe from the gun, and it stung.

"Tonto. Okay, Maybe the little piece of paper get choo out of trouble. I see one like it before, one time. I don't know. I leave the keys in the dirt behind choo little car. Maybe choo can find them in the tail lights or when the moon is up. I don't know that either. But choo stay here till I go, amigo, and don't get up."

Caje nodded. He looked up at the owl to keep his eyes busy, thinking that Tara should be bringing his Jeep up the road any minute now, and listened. It sounded like Lacho put the gun back inside his jacket before he turned and moved back to the MG to get the duffel bag. Finally, Caje dared to turn his head enough to watch.

Lacho snapped off the flashlight and tossed it into the duffel bag and rezipped it. He carried it to his truck and tossed it through the window and onto the seat on the passenger side. He retrieved the MG's keys from his own pocket and started walking out to the asphalt to get rid of them, ten yards, then twenty…

Carrying a gun around all the time, scaring the shit out of people--that's what Lacho's life must be, Caje thought. …takes balls

though.   There was a swagger to the way he walked even now.
Delivering envelopes, picking up loads of stuff and taking them back
to somebody with bigger balls still. Look at the arms and legs on the
guy, like he lifts every day, and the thick neck bulging at the jacket.
Caje thought, I don't want this shit…can't do it anymore.

He saw Lacho toss the keys to his right, where there seemed
to be a clump of nopal. When he started back, Caje tuned his head
again and stared at the owl. Great. If I can see them, I still have to
stick my hands into a mess of spines to get them. Even if you don't
get killed in this business, it's like torturing yourself… except there's
the money of course, and the girl, Tara. He tapped his fingers on the
concrete table, first one hand and then the other. He thought of Tara
coming up the road in the Jeep and finding him out at the road,
embarrassed about losing the keys but still standing. He tried to
imagine what it would be like tomorrow, this hallucination over and
starting to fade into the past like some troubled dream, the delivery
made and still having a little of the money, enjoying the girl's lanky
nakedness in her bed, then coming back here with the spare keys to
get the MG. He looked skyward where there was some brightening,
and he knew the moon must be on the rise behind him. Lacho had
his hand on the door latch of his truck now.

Off to his left and above him, there was light in the pass,
illuminating the boulders and brush at the point of the switchback in
the hairpin, a car coming through from the west, impossible to see on
the other side of the ridge but seconds later slithering into view. It
was the dark car with the vertical stripes again, coming back from
wherever. Caje could hear its big engine too, as it began the descent,
still in second gear and engine braking as it approached the narrow
dirt turnoff.

Caje watched Lacho, who had turned on the dome light after
pulling the door closed, settling into the truck's seat and fooling with
the side mirror till he found Caje sitting there, their eyes meeting
again when the mirror was in the right place, his hermano never
changing expression. The truck's brake lights came on, throwing
everything into a bright red, as if Caje were on some stage suddenly
lit with a garish floodlight; its engine started, and Lacho rolled it
forward, no headlights yet, just parking lights, waiting for the dark
car to pass by out on the road, Caje guessed.

Eight

Except it didn't. It lurched to a stop on the pavement in the wrong lane, its front nose even with the turnoff. Caje recognized the car now, the same one that had been parked at the Dreamland when he left, and even in the semi-darkness, he now recognized the guy with the ponytail, Hicks, through the open driver's side window, amber-lit by the truck's parking lights, reminding Caje of that Halloween trick where a guy holds a flashlight under his chin to try to look spooky, and he squinted to see farther inside, looking for the other guy. It was while he strained his eyes that the rifle barrel leapt out, and it did not register until the first bright flash in the dark. He rolled off the bench and kept rolling until he had put the concrete between him and the rifle.

Lacho did not recognize the dark car nor the man in it, but he recognized instantly that he had a problem, so he was already in reverse when the rifle appeared, already throwing gravel and backing up when the first shot came through the windshield and hit him in the neck. He could feel the pain on the left side, and he figured that the wound was through muscle because he still had control of everything, but that it must have hit a vein or an artery because he knew his blood was emptying onto and into his clothes, and he dropped his head to his right before the second bullet came through the glass and struck him in the scalene above his left clavicle, and he spun the wheel right now, still backing up, until he'd slammed the side of his truck's bed into the concrete table.

He kept his head low and listened, getting the pistol out of his jacket, a Walther nine, and punched the safety off. He wondered about the blood, so much of it, as he listened, thinking--hoping it was not from an artery, and he held his left hand against the exit wound on his neck, feeling to find if the blood was coming out in pulses or not, and then he put pressure on it, trying to stanch it, feeling the pain above his shoulder too, still listening for sounds from the other car. Thinking now that he should get out of the truck so the guy wouldn't know where his target was, have the little Indian amigo help him, the chinga puto, desde que jodido. Another round from the rifle sounded, punching through the car metal, making a sound like it had buried itself in something, making Lacho think it was in him before realizing it had hit the duffel bag. He managed to reach over and turn off the dome light, but still he waited. The guy couldn't stay out there shooting from the road like that, with a car coming by every few minutes, and if he knew about the mud, he'd have to come for that; he'd either have to drive in or walk in.

Hicks decided to drive in. He was sure he'd hit the guy, looked like a Mexican guy, once at least, chest or neck, and he thought it might have been enough to do him. He'd hit him ducking down with his first shot and then not so sure about the second one, and then there was no movement, so he fired a third shot now, with the rifle barrel inside the car so that the ejected shells hopped onto the dashboard and ricocheted somewhere inside the car, firing low this time, trying to put one about six inches above where he thought the seat should be, just in front of the door handle but a little lower, and still no movement. He was pretty sure the little dumb ass mule was cowering behind the concrete table too, so really it was better to walk in and finish them both, like walking up on a hooch when you already know where the motherfuckers are and they're just sitting there hoping you don't see them or you leave them alone, like three-year-olds who close their eyes to make you go away, but, shit, can't leave the car out here.

So he set the rifle down on the seat for a moment to maneuver the Dodge onto the tiny dirt road, watching for a change in the pickup truck. It was still idling after it had slammed into the picnic table, and apparently the guy never used the brake because the brake lights hadn't come on, and now the backup lights weren't on either, so he guessed the guy was in neutral and had his foot off the clutch…so still alive then. Hicks lifted the rifle again, got it outside the window, rested it on the mirror bracket, held it in his left hand; he crawled the Dodge forward.

Lacho figured the guy would fire again when he opened the door, and the dome light would turn him into more of a wounded quail than he already was, but he had to move. He heard the car maneuvering, and then its headlights came around and shone through the side window, and then it was rolling toward him, slow. Time to go. He reached back with his left hand, the blood leaking out of his neck again, and lifted the latch and kicked the door open with his foot, and the next shot came high, shattering the passenger side window, and he lifted the Walther and fired blind, wriggling back now, searching for the ground behind him with his feet, pulling the duffel after him. The pain in his upper body peaked with certain movements, and one of the peaks made him think he would go blind or pass out, but he reached out his legs for the ground anyway, found it, and pulled himself down, the duffel landing on his head, and the pain peaked again. He was wondering if the hijo de puta in the car could line up a shot underneath his truck when a round kicked up gravel, but not close, and then another into the metal again, as if the hijo de puta was guessing with the rifle.

"Hermano! Ay hermano, take the bag." He was trying to yell, but the words barely murmured out. He put the Walther down and flung the big duffel up onto the concrete bench, bringing a spike in the pain again. Lacho was aware that the muscle car had stopped, idling now, and he guessed that it was about twenty feet beyond his truck. Then he heard the car's door open, and he knew the hijo de puta would be coming on foot. He reached up and pushed as hard as he could on the duffel bag so that it almost slid to the other end of the bench. "Take it hermano," he said, 'don't let the jodido cabron de puta fucking have it." He lurched his upper body back toward the Walther and got it in his hand and pulled himself under the table, thinking he could still get his hermano to help him. "Hermano!"

But Caje was not there. When the Charger had maneuvered onto the gravel lane, its lights illuminated Lacho's truck, but it also defined the truck's black shadow far into the night, and Caje could see he was inside that shadow and realized it was time to go. He wondered about the other guy, the shorter one, why he wasn't there next to the big guy, whether Tara's bullet had been enough to kill him. But it did not really matter now. All he had to do was stay inside the shadow as he moved down the hillside to the north, and Hicks would probably not see him, even though the moon was now peeping over the Rincons twenty miles east, at least not until Hicks got out of the car. His ankle still hurt, but he used his hands too, reminding himself to keep low and creep, staying slow and quiet to avoid the light from the headlamps and to dodge the nopal and the cholla. He moved past the level area that had been graded for the lone picnic table and down the slope, which was steep and difficult, a broad sweep with breaks created by rock outcroppings, some dropping straight down five to ten feet. Caje looked hard to his right, toward where he knew the paved road was, hoping that Tara would come soon, but not too soon. She was already overdue, so he knew he did not have much time to descend the slope to the wash below and circle back to the road. He tried to move more quickly but almost instantly knew it was a mistake, his calves aching and knotting, and he nearly pitched headlong down the descent.

He was hurrying because of what was behind him, for certain, but he was also hurrying to catch Tara on the road, like a bantam hen scrambling to head off its chicks as they cheeped toward a hole in the fence that kept the dogs out of the chicken yard. He worried that she would drive past before he reached the road, knowing she had to be warned and knowing that he needed her if he was going to get down from these hills alive.

When he reached the sandy bottom, he did not hesitate. He moved faster, though the pain from the wild descent lingered in his calves and shins, maneuvering between the barrel cacti and the palo verde, the dry clumps of grass and the insidious nopal. The wash was a barranca, really, with steep banks. He knew he was loud, moving recklessly down the narrow wash, pushing through the brush, kicking loose rock and loudest of all, his breathing, breathing so loud, he imagined, that Hicks could hear him a hundred yards away.

Then for some reason he remembered running through this pass for cross country, always number one and always leading number two by a couple hundred yards at the top of the pass, at the hairpin. His breath had come easier then, he thought, and his legs had not ached. Of course, that was always in daylight and on the pavement, and more or less straight ahead, when the land surrounding him had seemed sparse with brush, hot and dusty looking, mostly sage green and tan and yellow from the lack of rain. Now, trying to run in the wash, the brush seemed dense and black, cold even, though the moon was up enough now that he could see his way, and he zigged like a bat, changing directions every few steps. The hills towered steep above him, and high above on the ridge lines, round-top saguaros and giant barrels stood out starkly against the sky like black tombstones. That scared him, but not as much as what was behind him and the worry of getting to the road before Tara came along. For a few seconds at a time, he thought he could see the line of the road ahead, but then it would disappear again, because he would have to go around a scrubby tree or some other brush, or he'd drop into a low spot.

After a few minutes, he heard gunfire, and he turned around, for only a few seconds really, to listen and to look back, but he couldn't see anything except some illumination that must be coming from the muscle car's headlights, he thought, from where he'd just come. There were two shots that sounded the same as he'd heard before, and he guessed it was the rifle firing again, and then he heard two shots that were crisper somehow, and he guessed those were from Lacho's gun. He moved on again. There were more shots, but he did not stop any more.

A hundred feet above, Lacho leaned against the inside of the concrete table leg, guessing that the hijo de puta was coming from the west, from his left, from the higher ground, and that the guy would fire first from beyond the patch of illuminated ground there if he had a target. He knew that his hermano was gone now, and it disappointed him that the hijo de puta would get the duffel bag now and he wondered who he was, wondering where he had come from, wondering how his dumb little hermano had managed to be followed. "¿Cómo te cagas, hermano burro? Pero yo lo mataré si puedo, para los dos. It won't help you hermano. Jefe will kill you now, burro." He let his back rest against the concrete, and he extended his legs. He set the Walther on his lap between his legs and pressed his left hand against the neck wound again and tried to peer into the darkness to the west and waited. He was tired.

Right at the edge of the light, in the shadow, was a shape that looked like it could be a man with a rifle, and Lacho waited for the shape to move somehow, for the thing that looked like it could be a rifle to come up, and he wondered how long the guy had been there looking out from the shadow, if it even was the guy and not just a couple of cacti.

The shape came out of the shadow then, in a slow walk, two steps at a time and then pausing as if it were making sure of its footing, edging into the lights' perimeter and raising the rifle but not really sighting with it. Lacho felt for the Walther, still watching the shape as it became a man, and raised the Walther to rest the butt of its magazine on the concrete bench and sighted along it but knowing it would be easy to miss at this range.

The hijo de puta kept moving closer, relaxed but watchfully, looking in hard as if he already smelled Lacho beneath the table and behind the bench and was just waiting for the smell to materialize into a target. If he sees me or the pistol, Lacho thought, he will fire, él con el fusil, while I must wait. You so sure of yourself, keep coming, chinga coño. He pressed his back tight against the concrete and squeezed his eyes shut for a moment, asking himself suddenly why he couldn't be somewhere else or at least have the little hermano there to help him, but then he supposed that the little hermano would fail again when it counted as he had twice now already; his burro hermano would just run, even if he had a gun and had the hijo de puto in his sights, so it was just as well he was not here now; and then he opened his eyes again to check on the hijo de puta, who seemed very big now even though he was crouching as he approached.

He hated the big man, not just for shooting him already, with the blood and the waves of pain, not just for coming to kill him now, but for the way he came. The guy was ready all right, with the rifle seeming part of his hands, but relaxed and confident too, as if he had made an approach like this a dozen times before and already knew the outcome, as if Lacho and the Walther were nothing to even think about. Lacho wanted to fire just to show the man he hated him, but he willed himself to wait. "Unos cuantos pasos más," he whispered. He sighted again.

But the big man did not take any more steps. He did not wait for Lacho and he did not wait until he had come into range of the

Walther. He lunged forward onto the ground, his arms and his rifle that was part of his arms out in front, flat at first to absorb some of the shock of hitting the ground and then up on his elbows with the rifle in his hands, the prone position, and sighting down the barrel and then firing below the bench, where he knew Lacho must be, whether he could see him or not, firing two rounds a few feet apart.

Lacho fired back with the Walther, but now his target was gone, and the first bullet sailed harmlessly into the hill, and he tried to adjust the angle downward, but the second shot was a blind shot with the pistol butt still resting on the bench, and it did no damage either.

And now another round hit him, just above the belt, twisting him as if he'd been pushed, and it was not through and through but there inside of him. He knew the hijo de puta would fire again, but it occurred to him that he did not want to be found dead here with bullets still in the magazine, and he pulled the gun down below the bench and began to empty it at the big man.

But the big man still wasn't making it easy. He was rolling away to his right, which gave Lacho a moving target, though it also put more concrete between the big man and *his* target. One roll to his right, and he came up and fired twice more, then he rolled and came up and fired again, Lacho following with his aim as well as he could and firing the Walther while the rifle bullets zinged off the concrete and into the dirt nearby, harmlessly now, but what he'd had already was enough, he knew. He fired until the magazine was empty, feeling light-headed now but still trying to aim. When the magazine was empty, he laid the Walther down and turned his body back again and leaned his back against the concrete and waited, accepting it. In a couple of minutes, the pain left him.

Hicks lay in the prone position and waited to be sure of the heavy set Mexican. He knew he didn't have to worry about the little one, the stupid pussy mule, pretty sure that he had slipped away again. He would follow him later, whether he'd taken the duffel or not, and he would find the bitch too, but later. He thought he could see part of the Mexican's body there between the table and the bench, but he wasn't sure, all shadow under there and not much light leaking in from the moon or the car's lights. He could wait.

He lay there only a few minutes, though. That was all the time he thought he needed, and he started forward again. He took his time getting up, at first going fast from prone to kneeling and then pausing to aim again, still making sure of the Mexican, then from kneeling to standing and aiming again. Then, sure of the Mexican, he lowered the rifle to his right, one-handed. He came forward in no hurry, careful but not scared, keeping his eyes on the shapes and shadows under and around the picnic bench and ready to dive into the prone position to make himself small again.

"Hey, Mexi-man! You give up? Can you hear me?" he said and kept coming. "No, I don't think so," he said in a lower voice, as if he was talking to a partner. "You ain't talking, Mexi-man, are ya. You ain't talking and you ain't moving either." He took a few more steps. "Looks like I'm a little better shot then, don't it."

Hicks stood at the end of the table, and he could see parts of the motionless Mexican, his leg and his forearm, and the empty pistol on the ground. Blood was seeping from the man and collecting in a little pool in a low spot in the gravel. Then he went to one knee, careful to avoid the blood, and still holding the Ruger Mini with his right hand, leaned in to get a closer look into the shadows and dark shapes behind the concrete. After a moment, his eyes adjusted, and he saw the wound at the front of the dead man's neck, and a dark spot in the jacket shoulder, and peering even harder, he could see the wound in the dead man's side, just below the rib cage. "I did good," he said, "three hits is good." He took the Walther from the dead man with his left hand and set it on the table and crawled between the bench and the table and started feeling the man's pockets. There was no spare magazine, but Hicks found his wallet and stood up. He set the rifle on the picnic table took the cash from the wallet and threw it back on the ground next to the dead man. Then he inspected the pistol, ejected the magazine and dry-fired it to make sure it was really empty and then set the safety and put it into his belt behind his back.

He was only a little surprised to see the duffel bag, the same one as before, and he only glanced inside to make sure the mud was in there. He found a second magazine for the Walther when he looked in the ash tray inside the cab of the pickup and stuffed it into his pocket. He wanted to move fast now, before another car happened along. He carried the rifle and the duffel bag to the Charger. He turned off the headlights, leaving just the amber and red of the Charger's parking lights, and then tossed the duffel bag in, but

he was careful with the rifle, setting the safety and again resting it on the floor and leaning the barrel toward the passenger side window. He took his flashlight with him and walked back to the spot where he had begun shooting from the prone position, looking for his brass.
*****

The barranca turned and wandered east, and Caje figured that it was running parallel to the road now, but he followed it still, with no obvious change in the steep banks, no easy way to climb up to the road. Then he heard the Jeep though, and he knew he had to climb, that the road had to be there just above him to his right and that he had to be standing there when Tara wound her way up the twisting, shoulderless road. He leapt at the exposed roots of a little palo verde tree and pulled as his toes churned at the rock and the dirt in the bank, finding traction on a clump of dry grass; his knee came down hard on a granite outcropping, but he reached again, with his right hand this time and clawed at some rock there and pulled and kept his knee there as he drew his foot up again and found another perch for it and drove himself upward another couple of feet. He could hear the Jeep coming closer, its loud blat fading for seconds at a time and then returning louder. Caje's climb was so steep, it was almost like scrambling up a ladder, but the rungs were thick roots and rock clusters and clumps of grass, and the climb was frustrating in its slowness and painful with skinned knuckles and shins. And all the little while he climbed, the sound of the Jeep grew louder and his hope faded.

Suddenly, the Jeep sounded very close, as if it had rounded the last curve down the grade from where Caje was climbing, and he looked up. He could see the light flooding past the ridge line above him now, still eight feet above, and he knew he was too late to cut off her ascent.
*****

Tara knew she should have left earlier if she was going to visit her mother's place, but it just hadn't occurred to her until she got that dreadful feeling again, which usually came along when she thought about her mother. It was an unnatural, sad rage that was hard to explain, though the only person she had ever tried to explain it to was Hal, and the only reason she had tried that time was he looked so dreadful himself, and she hadn't known if he was still blaming himself or if he thought she was angry with him. So she tried to explain the feeling to him. No, the feeling came from her anger and all her anger was for God because His rules for the universal operating system were so cold and because He never kept promises, not ones that were of any use anyway, and so He probably didn't exist, which was another reason to be pissed off, she had said, and she had no anger left for Hal, even if she did blame him, which she didn't. And it hadn't helped anyway; Hal had looked even more dreadful after her explanation, so she never tried again.

What gave her the feeling this time was the sign she saw after she left the motel. Hope Cemetery, it said, and an arrow underneath, pointing north, white letters on a rectangular green sign, as if green was the symbol for hope in the face of death, which she guessed it was if you believed that life was like an evergreen tree and lasted through the winter. Only a mile or so, she thought, two minutes there and two minutes back, and she could just drive past. She turned north.

Since it was after sunset, a heavy chain hung across the entrance to the cemetery, but her mother's grave was close to the road, and she could see her stone cross, taller than the other markers, from her seat in the Jeep. She had intended to drive up close to it and hesitated a moment, thinking about killing the ignition and walking in, but she knew she did not have time.

Tara's mother's grave had a wide open view in every direction, Aleppo pines a hundred yards away, and most of them nearly a hundred feet high, at both south and north borders. Tara sat there, remembering their last talk. It was just a few weeks after she'd begun seeing Caje, and so of course that's what Mother talked about.

Midge said to her, "You're crazy to take up with an Indian."

Tara answered, "Native American, and you always told me not to judge people by the color of their skin."

Her mom said, "I know, but that doesn't mean you have to take up with someone who's so different. Indians drink you know. Lots of them are alcoholics. I mean it's not their fault, I guess, but they do drink. I never saw an Indian leave the bowling alley sober."

"You should say Native American, Mom. And I hardly see anyone leave the bowling alley sober except you."

"Well, some kinds of mistakes are hard to recover from, Sweetie. You have so much going for you. You're smart, you're pretty, and you could have anyone you want."

"Mom, you say the same thing with every boy I meet. Caje just happens to be Yaqui."

Midge said, "What if he gets you in a family way? Do you want to carry his baby? You want to be like your cousin Viola and *have to* get married?"

"Mama, nobody really *has to* get married. Anyway, I'm not going to get pregnant with Caje's baby or anyone else's. I'm just not. I wish you would quit worrying about that. Okay?"

Midge went on as if Tara hadn't said anything. "Someone like that, sweetie, from the reservation. You don't know what will happen with him."

Finally, the conversation had made her angry, and she said, "Well, at least I'm not going to whore myself to some phony who runs a bowling alley, and if I do get pregnant you can be sure I'll get rid of the little son of a bitch inside," and she turned and left, knowing it would be days until they talked again.

She sat in the idling Jeep and wished for a moment that she could believe her mother was alive somewhere out in eternity, the way they explained in religion class at St. Thomas, and that she could hear her, so she could take it all back. But now it was time to follow Caje. She reached into her bag and withdrew the pistol and laid it on the passenger seat and sped south.

She passed shops and houses with lights on. Straight ahead of her were the taller buildings downtown, not skyscrapers but five, eight, twelve storeys, with lit windows. At the top of the tallest, the time and temperature alternated every few seconds. She turned right on Speedway, the ugliest street in America they had called it, and she could see why, and drove past more buildings and under the freeway and through the barrio. Then the street lights stopped and houses were sparser and traffic lights stopped and the road climbed west, narrower, and then there was only the desert with a house here or there, and then no structures at all. She looked ahead for the MG, which should be coming down now, with Caje in it. The moon was up, but her headlights seemed like the only light.

She knew the place that Lacho had named for the exchange because she and Caje had been there several times while they were still in high school. And she had driven the road dozens of times, and it had never seemed especially tough to navigate in the MG, even at night. But this was the Jeep, and she was pressing a little, trying to make up a few minutes. On one of the curves, she drove her right wheels through a pot hole, and the Jeep chattered and slid sideways about a foot, even with the four wheel drive, and she braked but turned into the slide a little too far and started to slide back the other way, and then the fishtailing stopped as her speed came down, and she downshifted. Almost there, she reminded herself and tried not to speed up again.

She had never noticed how low the steel roadside barriers were because they were at eye level in the MG, but now sitting high in the Jeep, she rounded a wide right-hand bend, the illumination from her headlights shooting far beyond the road's edge, over the formed steel and above the void that must be a dry gulch bed, she figured, with no treetops showing. Then she could see light ahead, too much light for moon reflections and the wrong tint too, and she knew that it was the place, another two hundred yards, and she sped up again.

If there's anything wrong, come out to the road, she had told Caje, thinking that there would be nothing going wrong, and she would see the MG in the next second or the next. Come out to the road on foot if you have to, she'd told him, cuz it would be stupid for me to drive in there if anything isn't right. The road swung back to the right, and her headlights lit up the steep hillside, creosote and saguaro and palo verde standing out green against the brown and gray earth.

When the road brought her back around the next spur, she was within fifty yards of the turn-off, and she slowed down, deliberately now, looking for Caje. She could see more light now, and glints of car metal, chrome and blue and red, and she wondered if the red was her MG. And maybe she saw something move.

She downshifted again, into second, so that she felt like she was crawling up the grade toward the crest of the pass now, hoping that she would see the MG pulling out from the turn-off, or better yet zooming past her downhill, or Caje at least emerging from the darkness on foot. Then she was at the mouth of the turn-off, and she stopped, in neutral now, with her right foot on the brake, and there was plenty of light even though the Jeep's headlights were still aimed up the road. She could see the rear end of a big blue car and past it a pickup sitting sideways, and her MG sitting there too, with its lights completely off. She heard engine noise from there too and knew that one of the cars was idling.

She felt the night closing all around her as she sat there, except where she could see, straight ahead along the road where her headlights shone and over to the right where the spectacle of cars lay. She looked for Caje among the cars, or for anyone, trying to give the scene some meaning, an explanation that would account for everything, but there was a terror seizing her too, like some kind of talons, and she fought the urge to drive on until she could make some sense of it, still hoping Caje would appear. But she thought about someone coming at her from the dark, from behind her or from her left side, and she reached over for the tiny Marlin .32 and pulled the hammer back and held it in her right hand, careful to keep her finger away from the trigger, and called out, "Caje," thinking it was stupid even as she did it, thinking she sounded weak.

Then she saw someone running. A man darted out from behind the truck, scrambling uphill several steps and then disappearing into the dark again. Not wearing white like Caje and too big to be Caje. It may have been a second, perhaps two, before the ponytail registered, but she did not move. For some reason, she thought she needed to first figure out what was going on, as if explaining it would solve it, and as she did, the terror ebbed away from her, and she thought about the way she hated the guy with the ponytail and about what she should do next. She put her index finger on the side of the trigger guard so that all she would have to do was wrap and press, and she pointed the pistol to her left, where she thought he might come if he circled that direction. She stared at the place where she'd seen him disappear but diffused her eyes and told herself that her peripheral vision would pick up movement off to her left. She didn't think he would drop down into the gulch and try to circle to her right, and even if he did, he would find the going pretty rough and it would take him forever. No, he would circle to her left or come out right in front of her, maybe with the gun he'd had the day before and maybe not. But where was the other guy, the short one? And Caje?
*****

At first, what Hicks thought he would do was to come straight at her, go out to the road in the dark and then just run right down on her on the pavement, the hill helping with his speed. He'd be in the light for, what, half a second? See how the little bitch liked that, then just pull her out of the Jeep and slap the shit out of her. But to get to the road, he'd have to cross two hundred feet of hilly desert with just the moonlight, and she was maybe not going to sit there that long just waiting on him to come. And besides, there was that crazy old machine gun she had.

Here was this little pussy of a Mexican kid, and then there's the little blond bitch sending him out on errands and telling him what to do, getting him to haul all that smack, paying him off like a whore would, spreading for him. Hicks didn't know if it was funny or pathetic, but he liked the idea of it, the bitch in control and needing to be taught a lesson. One time, the leave-whore he had stayed with in Saigon had tried to play him like that, wanted him to take her to a better hotel, buy her a dress, treat her like a prom date for Christ sake. He'd said, "Don't start with that shit. I'm treating you good as it is." Damn whores always want more, something JT never understood.

He stood on a broad slab of rock about forty yards above the parking area where the three cars were, the truck still idling, the chrome glinting in the moonlight. He was standing straight and staring down at the Jeep on the road because he was pretty sure she couldn't see him, her there wearing a denim jacket but open in front like she was proud of those little tits of hers. Like, hey guys, check out my tits, like they belonged in *Playboy* or something. Right. He decided he wanted the rifle for this. The pistol had been no match for her gun, but he could shoot the shit out of her at this range with the rifle. See if she was so hot with that trench sweeper when she was staring at the muzzle flash. He began to rehearse in his head what he would do.

He appeared from the dark at a run, heading for the Charger, looking straight ahead.

Like I'm not even here, Tara thought, bringing the little pistol around now and following him as he covered ground. When he got to the front end of the big blue car, with the car between them, he stopped and crouched behind it, and for a moment she hoped he would bolt again, into the dark on the other side because he would fall at the break there and maybe kill himself. But he came forward along the side of the car now, quick but staying low.

She aimed carefully and fired. And heard a thud like the round had hit car metal, and it seemed to freeze him for a moment. She pulled the hammer back and adjusted her aim right a fraction and fired again, and hit him, she knew because he gave a little jerking movement, but not hurting him bad enough because he yelled at her.

"You goddamned little bitch. I am gonna fuck you up." Then he came past the car door and pulled it open and crouched low in front of the open door, reaching for the rifle, but with his head still showing in silhouette.

She cocked the Marlin again and aimed below the outline of the head and fired again and hit something, hoping it was his middle this time, but then she saw him leap out again and charge at her. And now he was firing, not aiming but firing as he came, and she saw the muzzle flash and heard a bullet whine. When a second flash came, she put the pistol down on her lap and pushed in the clutch and jammed the long shifter into first and drove up the incline as fast as the Jeep would go. After a couple of seconds, she shifted, losing a little speed because she couldn't find second right away, but then felt the shifter fit snug and popped the clutch and floored the accelerator. She felt him behind her out on the road, certain that he would aim now, and she began little zigzags, in second gear, still accelerating toward the top of the pass. Then she felt the darkness close around her, and so maybe it was too dark for him to get a decent shot, and she didn't bother with the little tweaks of the steering wheel anymore and shifted into third and accelerated away from the man and his rifle. She heard a sound like a stick breaking and saw a hole appear suddenly in the Jeep's flat windshield, and she knew he'd have to get a lucky shot to hit her now.

She knew how tight the hairpin was, hard left, changing from due west to due east inside of fifty feet, and she knew she could engine brake if she geared down into second about the middle of the turn, and that was always what she had done in the MG, keeping her foot off the brake. The elongated nose of the sports car would veer toward the steel barricade as she pushed in the clutch, giving her passenger the feeling they were about to go flying over the hundred-foot drop, but then the nose would snap back in when the clutch engaged, and the tires would grab, and she would speed downhill on the far side of the pass, smiling and glancing over at the passenger to see how white he was.

But that was the MG. When she plunged the clutch down on the Jeep, she had trouble finding second again, so for a second, perhaps a little less, she was freewheeling, clutch in and foot off the brake and pulling hard left on the steering wheel and moving the long stick on her right hand, the nose of the Jeep aimed at someplace out in the air beyond the barricade, then finding the slot for second and popping the clutch as she realized she needed to put her right foot on the brake but knowing it was probably too late. When the brakes engaged, the nose of the Jeep came suddenly around to face due east the way it should have, but the tail had already begun sliding right, and the little vehicle had already begun to tilt right as it slid into the guard rail, and Tara launched over it, like a dovelet pushed from its nest, the little Marlin .32 still with her. The Jeep's wheels kept churning, and it came to rest on its side about thirty feet down the road from where it had impacted the steel.

Nine

When Hal entered the apartment, Doris was smoking a cigarette and just starting a fresh vodka, neat, the Smirnoff bottle and a shot glass over on the counter. She was sitting in one of the chairs by the Formica kitchen table where they usually ate brunch together, wearing a muumuu with broad purple orchids. There were placemats and napkins and silverware laid out. Empty water glasses too. He hung his hat on a hook near the door, watching Doris watch him.

She inhaled the cigarette deeply and then took up her vodka in the same hand and sipped it and said, "I kept dinner."

Hal thought she sounded okay, and he was relieved she hadn't directly mentioned his being late. He looked toward the stove and saw a box of Rice-a Roni on the counter. He thought of saying it smelled good but instead settled on, "You didn't need to but thanks." He watched her take another drink from her glass, figuring they should start eating before she could finish her drink and pour another one. He took a Coors from the refrigerator, sipped it, and stepped to the stove and lifted the lid on the skillet there. The vermicelli and the ground meat looked very dark. "Looks good, Hon. Want me to get you a plate?"

"Let's have a drink first, 'kay?" The slurring was more obvious now. Don't you wanna have an Ezra first?"

"It's getting too late for bourbon." He looked into the skillet's sizzling mixture. "And I'm hungry."

"Yeah, you're late. You go see your girlfriend again?" She drained off more vodka.

Just being a smart ass about yesterday or really wanting to know? He didn't say anything right away. He got two plates down from the upper cabinet next to the range, the last of his aunt's wild turkey pattern, and set them down and loaded spoonfuls of the dry-looking food on them. She wasn't filling her glass yet.

He set the plates down, one in front of her, and looked into her eyes again. She was waiting for an answer. Well, the half truth hadn't helped yesterday. "No, I hung around with Johnny for a while." At least, Johnny would fib for him—better let him know. He picked up a fork and started eating. The Rice-a-Roni was as dry as it looked, mildly burnt tasting. It occurred to him he should have gotten the cold water from the refrigerator.

"Don't worry, I forgive you."

"I told you I was sorry about yesterday."

"I remember you said that, but you'll still go running off the next time she calls, won't you. Johnny thinks you're making a fool of yourself too. Even Batman is gonna figure out you're too close to her. He's not a total fool, you know."

He got up and got the plastic water pitcher from the refrigerator and poured the water glasses full, though Doris didn't seem inclined to put her vodka aside or start eating. He sat again and ate another forkful. Maybe a little humor... "Hey, you know how to get a nun pregnant?"

She didn't smile.

"Dress her up as an altar boy."

She still wasn't smiling.

"C'mon, Hon. That's a little funny isn't it?"

She stubbed out her cigarette. "You know, I never asked you to come out and say how you felt about me because I thought I could tell." A pause. "You being so easy to read and all, you know?"

She wanted an answer this time. "Yeah, you told me."

"And I never asked you to do anything, did I? I didn't expect a ring or a walk down the aisle. I didn't expect you to quit your crazy trips with Johnny."

What was there to say to that? He wished she would eat. He wished she was sober.

"I never tried to figure out why you're so serious all the time, and why you always wear that I'm-sorry look. And I never looked for anybody else, Hal. I've had offers, you know, even at work." Her eyes glassy, she bored into him to make sure he understood. "You have to think everything over before you do it, if you ever get around to doing anything at all, and then you brood about it afterwards. And I try not to let that bother me either." Another pause. "But you always let on like you're some kinda pleaser, only do what people need you to do." She smiled angrily. "Good old Hal--always trying to help out. 'cept for me of course. I just ain't got that tight little ass, do I?"

He set the fork down. There was no steering her now.

"And that's okay too. But Jesus, Hal, you gotta give me something. You fucked her, didn't you?"

"I already told you I came close one time. I didn't have to tell you, ya know. I told you because I thought you'd see you could trust me to be her friend after that. She can't help it she's too friendly. It's just her nature. The trouble is you think the only way a man can love a woman is to take her to bed."

"No, the trouble is I can tell when a man is cunt-crazy, and if you haven't fucked her already, you're going to."

He said, "You really think that?" but he was wondering if Tara would ever offer herself to him again, remembering how she felt when she had put her arms around him and wondering what it was that had made him resist her.

"Who, me?" she said, mocking him now. She stood up then and lifted the empty little tumbler and stepped to the vodka bottle on the counter. She poured, not bothering with the shot glass now. She sipped and stared at him over the rim.

He rose from the chair then and came to her, trying to sense how she would react, and he put his arms around her, so that her arms were inside his, and pulled her to him. She did not push away, limp in his embrace, but she kept the tumbler at her lips, separating them. He turned his head to the side and down to her shoulder and held her tighter, but she did not respond to him. He said, "I want you in my life," and she stayed passive until he finally eased back from her and let go.

Doris said, "I'm leaving," and lowered the glass and emptied it onto his shirt.

He felt the vodka soak through the thin cotton and smelled the faint alcoholic odor, thinking that it barely smelled at all. "Don't," he said, but knowing there was no stopping her.

"I can't be here right now. That's all." There were tears coming now.

He wondered if she could drive and where she was going and whether she would come back in the morning. "You better let me drive you then." When she coughed out a laugh, he said, "or call a taxi then." When she didn't scoff, he found a number in the telephone book and dialed, wishing that she would stay. They didn't speak again. When the cab arrived, he carried her bag out to the driver, noticing that she was only taking the overnight case, and the cabbie tossed it into the rear seat. He leaned a little closer to her as she approached the open car door, hoping she would kiss him. She looked at him and got into the cab and was gone. The eastern sky was brightening now, the moon hinting that it was about to rise.
                *****

Hal showered and then came back to the kitchen to get a bourbon, but the smell of burning Rice-a-Roni took over. He turned off the stove and scraped the stuff into a newspaper and rolled it up and took it to the dumpster. He left the front door to his apartment stand open and opened his bedroom window and turned on the fan above the range and set all the dishes to soak in a pan of soapy water. He drank a double Ezra sitting at the kitchen table and then poured another and took it with him and set it on the little table by his bed and lay down.

He didn't like the quiet—no rustling sheets from the other side of the bed, no soft snoring. Just him and the bourbon. He didn't expect to sleep. Around midnight, he heard a poorwill outside chirping its name, and he gulped the big shot down, knowing he was letting the self-pity seize him along with the bourbon, and whispered back to it.

Poorwill, poor Will…how bout poor Hal? Poor Hal screwed things up again. What's the use?... Can't keep going like this.

Problems like mountains. So whether to climb the mountains or just give up. My choice. Sweet bourbon and sweet forgetting, like sleeping or dying. Maybe Doris has the right idea about it all, with her vodka. Or Tara with her sweet-smelling, rolled-up joints. Drinking and stoning and sleeping—it's all temporary death, and maybe that's what's wrong with it—just temporary.

He thought about the Henry rifle in his closet, but then he heard the poorwill again, and he thought about getting another bourbon.

Shot of Ezra, shot of Henry. One dulls the pain, the other ends it. Or maybe not, if the Catholics are right. If Tara's right, no hell to worry about, but if Mrs. Thadbury's right…well, that's a problem. So far nobody's come back from over there.

He thought of Henrietta's long illness, her grimaces and her forced smiles, and Judd's terrible loss, the way he seemed to have forgiven him for his failure on the night drop, and Tara's impossible longings, and Doris's empty loneliness, and his self-loathing for the Chinese boys he was sure he'd killed and his failures at the ranch. And he wanted to forget all of them forever. But still, hell would be a hangover that didn't wear off. When he heard the poorwill a third time, he suddenly felt as if Henrietta had to be, somewhere. He looked at a photo of Doris and himself on the bedside table and went into the kitchen and refilled the little glass.

He stepped outside his front door in his boxers and set his drink down on the baluster, listening for the night bird again. The moon was high now, and when he heard the poorwill, he looked for it among the oleanders but couldn't see it. He shivered, not cold but shocked suddenly by the night's ghostly stillness and light, thinking again of the dead. I can do it again I reckon, he whispered, and tossed the last of the bourbon onto the gravel below. In a few minutes, he was driving away in his truck. The old Henry rifle was in a sling on the rack behind him.

At Tara's apartment, there were no sunbathers to fool, but no MG or Jeep either. Hal walked to the door and jiggled it open again, comparing the inside to what he had seen before. All the same except for the flashing light on the answering machine.

"Beep. Hey Tara, it's me. The number at the Dreamland is fourteen. I'm checked in now. See you when you get here. Oh, and I brought the money. Love you. Bye."

Hal listened twice and then erased the message. Then he wondered if that was enough and took the tape. He took the top three sheets from the note pad as well. He went through the place again and saw everything else the same as before. He went to the dresser in her bedroom and took the framed picture there, Tara sitting on Caje's lap, the kind a guy would get at a carnival, wondering if he loved her. He looked up the Dreamland in the yellow pages and left.

Hal passed the driveways at the Dreamland Motor Inn, looking into the lit-up commons area, no cars that he could see. He made a U-turn and drove slowly past again, this time studying the inside of the office, no one visible but a door at the rear. The night manager probably in an apartment behind, he thought. He found a stripper bar a block to the east, still a couple dozen cars there though it was getting to be last call time, and pulled into the parking lot next to a station wagon. Sensible family car, dad blowing off steam. He set his Stetson on the floor of the truck, brim up, and fished a sweaty cap from under the seat and put it on. He opened the tool box bolted to the bed of his truck and took out the Wonder Bar and a pair of pigskin gloves. He worked his hands through the shirred wrists and into the tight gloves. He hung the rifle sling behind him, over his left shoulder, trying to shield it from street view, and walked back to the west. He held the J-shaped end of the Wonder Bar cupped in his hand, with the rest of the bar up inside his sleeve. Near the entrance to a mobile home park, he passed a fleshy hooker leaning against a palm tree who asked him if he wanted a date, and he answered, "No money, lady," eyes straight ahead. End of discussion there. When he reached the Dreamland, he slipped under the eaves of the covered porch and walked to the first door, fifteen, trying to look nonchalant in case someone was looking at him, and continued past. There was a shadow to cover him there, and he looked out over the drive and the commons. It was like an abandoned road through the desert, cracked and buckled and potholed asphalt with tufts of bermuda grass poking through, the red tile roof dull and crumbling but catching the moonlight and darkening the apartments underneath; chain link fence around the pool with sparse Texas ranger shrubs trying to grow. He could see the ends of a couple of cars now, one from New Mexico and one backed in so that its license plate didn't show. This place is about to go belly up, he thought.

There was no movement, no change in any of the lighting, and he moved across a section of asphalt to the next covered porch. No cars parked in the space for fifteen or for the next one, the stall for fourteen, where the MG or the Jeep should be. He stopped for a moment and listened at the door and then tested it. Locked. He knocked quietly, then paused, not expecting an answer, then stuck the short, sharp end of the Wonder Bar between the door and the jamb and drove it home with the heel of his hand and pried. There was a loud crack and the door was open and he stepped inside and closed the door behind him and listened. Maybe a door creaked open somewhere, maybe not. He could hear cars going by out in the street, and pauses between. TV sounds came through the wall, from thirteen, he supposed, or twelve if the owners were superstitious, next door anyway. After a few minutes, he checked to see that the drapes were closed, set down the sling and the tool and turned on the light.

A rug, not a carpet…double bed with tan linens, mussed a little but not slept in, with the pillows at the wrong end …big painting over the bed of a cowboy chasing down a dogie…mugs and Folger's crystals on top of the bureau…couple books and folded girl's panties on the dresser …little jar of Vaseline next to the bed. So they're coming back, looks like. Still, he went through the drawers and looked in the closet. An extra pillow and blanket, a roll-away that smelled faintly of urine, a phone book and Gideon's Bible. He wondered why neither car was there, wishing now he had tried to pin her down the night before about what the hell was going on.

He retrieved the sling and, sitting on the end of the bed, extracted the Henry from it. His dad, Savor, had said it was the oldest rifle in Wyoming, and maybe it was, oldest lever action anyway, the date stamped in it 1863. Savor said it had been used at the Battle of Franklin, and Savor didn't believe in too many fables that came along. He loaded sixteen cartridges from a fresh old box, then closed the box and dropped it back into the sling, thinking that if sixteen wasn't enough, then fifty wouldn't be either. He wondered momentarily if the cartridges were any good, old as they were. Well, he'd shot pigs and mule deer with the last box, so yeah, no doubt they were. He hung the sling on the coat hook on the door, turned out the light again, opened the drapes all the way and cracked the window so that he could hear a bit better. He sat in the dark, in a chair now, taking an angle on the window so he could see them approaching the door. He was holding the rifle atop his legs, trying again to figure it all out.

So Caje and Tara are somehow mixed up with these hard guys, the guy Tara called the ponytail guy and his friend who took one from the Tommy gun. And the bag, that had to be drugs or cash, drugs I'm thinking. And it didn't really belong to them, or to the hard guys either. Unless it was a rip-off. Is that what a rip-off looks like? He'd heard the term lately and wondered why they called it that. The hard guys are supposed to buy the drugs but they plan on just shooting the delivery boy, except they didn't figure on Tara showing up with the heavy artillery? Except the kid said something about losing part of it, so maybe that's the beef. No, maybe that doesn't make sense. Why are they here? Not to meet the same guys. You don't give assholes a second chance to kill you. They wouldn't be here except to hide out from those guys or to make the delivery. And she said she'd seen the assholes earlier in the day but not before that, so it was like they just bumped into each other....That trailer had to be theirs, the two hard cases'. They're holding Caje and the bag of dope there. So Tara was Caje's backup? But then she would have already had a gun and wouldn't have needed me to haul it down there. Those guys must have followed Caje or something. Or overheard something. She was bailing him out--they weren't together, so maybe he sucked her into the whole thing in the first place, or maybe that's just me not wanting to blame her. And maybe they've already finished with the hard guys, and those guys are out of it now. They didn't really have a way to follow her up here, did they? Unless they got their El Camino fixed somehow. Of course they'd try, what the hell else would they do? And then they're driving all over town hoping to see one of the cars. Or maybe they had Caje's ID or something, or maybe he told them something he shouldn't have. Tara is not stupid, but I don't know about her boyfriend. Or maybe that's just me being jealous. But let's say they did know where her apartment is--that explains them hiding out in this little nest. But they didn't come here to stay long--no bags, nothing. And he wouldn't have left the info on her message machine like that then, easy for someone to find. No sense doing that if you're scared they'll find you. Longshot that they're here to hide then. So all this tells me what?

They probably came here, the Dreamland, what a clever name, to meet the man, the right one this time, make the delivery, and that's where they are now. They'll come back here with a wad of money, and they'll be pissed off to see me sitting here. No, not pissed, more like embarrassed for me 'cause I'm thinking I am protecting them when they apparently don't think they need that. So maybe it was stupid to bring the gun, to sit here with it loaded, Tara and Caje doing fine on their own thank you very much. He stared hard out through the gauzy window covering at the spot in front of the door.

But say they're not doing fine. Even if the trailer guys are out of it, they're mixed up with some hard case sons of bitches anyway, or Caje wouldn't be hauling around a bag of heroin or whatever it is. Whoever they're handing it off to ain't no priest--more likely worse than the trailer guys. And that would explain why they were worried about losing part of the shipment. So then they're here so these other hard cases won't find out where they live if they get followed. Or the hard cases come back with them for some reason. Then it's good I got Mr. Henry with me.

But then he got to the idea that he thought he might get to, the idea he liked least of all, that they were not only not doing fine but that maybe they wouldn't come back at all, and having the Henry was just as useless to them as no gun at all, that him even being here was useless. Maybe this is worse than yesterday down south, and she's in over her head. And over mine too.

He didn't like the feeling it gave him, so he set the rifle down next to him and stood up, willing himself to leave his thinking there with his rifle, like it was not part of him, but letting the ideas cook inside his head without concentrating on them, hoping some different conclusions would pop out at him when he took up the gun and the thinking again.

He reminded himself to listen and walked around the room to stretch his legs. Couldn't do *that* in an LP. He took the Gideon Bible from the top dresser drawer, thumbing it in search of the Tenth Psalm, which Henrietta had taken time to memorize when she was near the end, thinking he would read it in the dim light and put it back, but finding that it fell open to Job instead, where there were some hundred dollar bills--twenty of them. He smiled faintly about Tara stashing the bills. Why not the phone book? 'Cause people actually open the phone book, she'd say in her smart ass way. Why Job and not, say, Matthew?... Anyway, they're definitely coming back for this...

He put the Bible back in the drawer and sat down, not taking up the rifle this time and thought, ...if they're able to. But he did feel now like they would probably show up, a mixed feeling for sure, but it was there. Just the feeling more than the idea, like the feeling he used to get in no-man's land just before he actually heard anybody coming but sure that he was about to hear them, crawling over the rocks and the snow about an inch an hour, and he'd get ready to yank on the wire. Just a feeling, but now pretty sure that the feeling was right. So then what? Be ready for the options is what. In an LP you didn't just yank on the wire and duck. No, you ducked all right, but you were ready. Your buddies were going to blast away with everything they had now, but either some Chinaman crawled into your hole or he didn't. You had to be ready to kill him if he did, with your gun if your buddies had begun firing or with your knife if they hadn't. He'd done it both ways and still remembered the look of their Chinese faces as they died. Three options, and you hoped for the first one. Same thing now, sort of. They come back all safe and we all have a good laugh and I go home to my empty apartment, or they come back in trouble and I try to get them out of it with the Henry. Or they don't need my help 'cause Tara's still got the trench broom. So hope for the first one then.
     *****

When Hicks heard the first little pop, he knew she was firing a pistol and he didn't have to worry about the Tommy gun, so when she fired again and the .32 slug hit and he felt the sting just below his nipple, it bewildered him. "The fuck," he muttered, cursing the pain first, and then he cursed at the little bitch out there on the road. He did not bother to feel at the wound, pulling the rifle to his shoulder as he rose and firing at her and then charging. He got off another shot at her before she drove up the road, no better aimed than the first, and then his target was gone until he was at the edge of the pavement, where he stopped to aim from the standing position and hit something this time as she wove the little Jeep up the incline--not her though, he figured, 'cause it kept going. And then a clanking noise from somewhere past the curve, and then silence, and then he thought maybe he did hit her. He stood for a second, straining to hear something more, but there was nothing.

That's when he felt alongside his nipple. Blood, plenty of blood, he thought, looking at his hand and now wondering if the slug had passed all the way through him or if it was still in there or, worse, if maybe it had broken up on a bone or something. More'n one pain spot and blood around the back of the shirt too. And now he could feel the pain all over the left side, like someone had hit him hard in the ribcage with a pipe and broken some ribs. Well, not my heart or lung anyway, or I wouldn't be standing here. "Goddamn little bitch shot me."

Walking back to the Charger, taking it slower than he wanted, he kept his hand over the wound, to assess it more than to stanch it. All right, ain't gonna drain me but I'll need a doctor. Leaning against the Charger, he took off his sleeveless vest and then his shirt. He turned and laid the shirt out flat on the roof of the car and buttoned it. He folded it from the bottom, four inch folds, flattening the shirt out with his hands after each fold, five folds, six thicknesses of cotton. He put the middle of the folded shirt over the wounds, and then, letting out as much air as he could from his lungs, he tied the sleeves together. He put on the vest then.

When his headlights came around, he could see the Jeep lying on the driver side, its headlights shining into the steep ridge, but the girl was not in it. When he passed it, he could see the hole in the windshield and a floor mat on the pavement, but still no girl. He drove past it half a mile, scanning the road for her, to where there was a dirt pullout, made a Y-turn, and came back and put the nose of the Charger within ten feet of the upended Jeep. He turned off his ignition but left his lights on and got out, armed only with the flashlight now. He could hear the Jeep's engine still running, but he didn't smell any gasoline. Still, he looked for a key in the ignition, finding a pen knife instead. He turned it and the engine died. He combed the pavement with his flashlight, looking for something, the pistol, anything, then up the ridge side, not seeing any way for someone to climb. Finally, he stepped over the guard rail and shone the beam down. About a hundred feet down and to his left, he thought he saw a shape that was her, maybe. Maybe a skinny slant of something that could be her leg or her arm and maybe a shape that looked like denim and maybe a little movement too. He stared down and tried to figure out how the shapes could be her body, trying to see if it moved. That's when he heard another car.

He hoped it wasn't a Sheriff's car, and it wasn't. He hoped that they would just keep on going and mind their own business, but of course they didn't. New Mexico plates, they pulled up behind the Jeep to help. A guy got out, fiftyish, bald. He aimed the beam at him.

"Everybody okay?" the guy was looking around, squinting when he looked into the beam. He came up to the guard rail.

Thinks I was involved in the wreck. "Oh man, thank God you're here man! I just pulled up too, man. I think she went over. Maybe you should look too. C'mere and see what you think". He snapped the beam back and aimed it at the form below, waiting.

The guy was short and it took him a minute to get over the rail, get his legs.

Scared to get too close. He heard the window coming down on the New Mexico car and a woman's voice, Be careful, dear. "You think that's her? I think she hit the rail and went over."

The guy leaned out a little and said, "I don't know. What are you looking at?"

"Right there. I think she moved. See the arm?" He wiggled the beam for the fool. "I better go for help. Here you take the flashlight."

"Okay." He reached out for the flashlight but then the wife again, "I'll bring you the flashlight, but you be careful, dear." The car door opening and another beam coming over. The guy held onto the steel rail and leaned a little more. "I guess that could be someone."

"I better go."

The guy took his wife's beam then, still clutching the rail. "I can't see anything. Maybe I should send the wife and stay here with you, try to find a way down."

Leave it to the nosy fool. "No way we're getting down there, man, and I can get to a phone faster. The fool didn't argue.

He left them together, him trying to hold on to the rail, scanning down the incline, her standing on the pavement, clutching her hand to her blouse looking pitiful, neither of them saying much. He drove back through the pass, straight to the Circle K at the edge of town and pulled up to the pay phone.

The yellow pages told him that doctors were listed under 'Physicians.' Column after column, but hardly any Mex names. And the Mexican names all seemed like they had north addresses. North Country Club Road…North Vinson Drive. JT had said south-side, so he kept looking. He finally found a Ruiz on South Sixth Avenue… 2317. He tore out the physicians' pages and left again. He wondered how long those old farts would be there expecting help, trying to see something down the hillside. And he still wondered if that was her down there stuck on a rock or whatever, if she had moved. "Couldn't have survived that," he muttered, at JT he guessed, and started to wonder if he was going to find himself a cash Mexican doctor before he leaked to death.

*****

He could tell that this Doctor Rodriguez, Humberto Rodriguez, M. D. one of the signs on his gate said, lived where he worked. The place looked like a house, a chain link fence around the yard. The other sign on his fence said ¡Cuidado-Pero! But he knew he couldn't wait for Humberto to open up for business. He put the envelope of cash inside the bandage at his chest, got out of the car with the pistol and walked along the sidewalk. He was going to walk past the place to see what kind of dog it was, to see how aggressive it was, but it never appeared, so he stopped at the gate and leaned on it and made kissing sounds, and a bull terrier trotted up to him from the shadow of the front porch. Swinging his dick, wagging his tail, for Christ sake. He stuck the pistol into the rear of his jeans, and put his lips up to the fence and kissed the air, and the dog came close and licked back. Cuidado, hell. The dog trotted alongside him when he approached the front door. He was going to start knocking, go around to a window if no one answered, but he saw another little sign: En caso de emergencia—next to a doorbell. He pushed, waited, pushed again. The dog wagged its tail.

The door came open, stopped by a chain, and a voice came out. "¿Está enfermo?"

"No habla, man. But I need a doctor. I got a cut needs lookin' at." He pointed at his side. "Real bad cut. Emergencia." He said emergency and added uh.

"Hay que ir al hospital."

Hicks understood hospital and said, "I don't want no hospital man, I want a doctor. I want you to clean me up is all. Hurts like hell and I'm bleeding, Doc. C'mon lemme in and take a look. I got money. Dinero"

"No entiendo. ¿Está sangrando? Mmm...You have blood?"

"Yeah I got blood." He opened the vest and pulled out the envelope first and showed the money, not knowing if there was enough light beneath the porch cover for the doc to see it, but then the bug light came on. "See that? I got dinero to pay. I got blood and I got dinero." A moment passed. The doc thinking about it. Hicks put the envelope in his pocket and untied the bandage to show him. He held the bandage in his right hand and pulled the vest back and turned, surprised to feel the weight of the bloody bandage, right now hoping the wound looked bad enough to get the door open.

"Momento." The door closed, the light came on inside and then the door opened again, all the way now. "Come in, sir."

Suddenly the doc was talking English, talking it fine, so like what was all the no entiendo bullshit? Hicks stepped inside. It was a waiting room, reception desk, cheap wood and cloth chairs, Spanish newspapers on a low table. The doc was taller than Hicks thought he would be, younger too, maybe thirty-five, long black hair, hints of a goatee and coarse stubble, a guy who maybe had to shave and trim the goatee twice a day, and eyebrows sharp enough to be asking a question. He was wearing pants and a white shirt but slippers on his feet. There was a woman too, long straight hair, black as his, wearing a light pink robe, eight months along it looked like, holding open a door to another room, obviously for him to go in there. Her eyes were black and direct.

"Doc's been taking good care of you, looks like." He stared into her eyes, checking for the reaction, then grinned at the doc, looking for fear, some nervousness at least, not seeing any. He moved into the exam room and set the bloody shirt on a sink cabinet there.

"On the table, please, sir." The doctor had followed Hicks into the room and now began putting on gloves. "On your side, please. When Hicks had complied, straining and clenching his teeth as he twisted, the doctor opened the vest and worked it down off the shoulder and arm to expose the wound.

Hicks heard a little gasp from the woman and started to wonder how he looked to her. "Sorry about that, señorita. I had a little accident."

"Es señora, sir, not señorita if you please. My wife." A pause, and then, "You have a bullet wound sir, not a cut."

"I know what I got, Doc. I cut myself on a bullet. What I need is you to take care of it." He was holding his left arm out of the way and leaning his head on his right. He didn't like looking up at the man.

"This kind of wound, it would be better if you went to a hospital. I can drive you."

"If I wanted to go to the hospital, I'da drove there myself." He thought about sitting up again, so they would be the same level. "I can pay. You and your señorita don't gotta worry about a thing." He looked at the woman again.

The doctor stared at him for a long moment, and then he said, "This … accident struck your rib and then passed through the body and came out, but you must be examined to determine if there are fragments. From the broken bone… or metal from the accident itself. So that we know there is no ischemia. It must be probed, which can be very painful, and x-rayed, and I do not have that sort of machine."

"Schemia?"

"A blockage. Fragments don't always need to be removed unless they are in a dangerous place. But we must make sure. The bullet might have hit your lung or your heart. I think the rib protected you."

"Just probe it Doc, It'll be fine. Don't want you and the señorita to worry. Her condition and all…" He sat up, straining now and giving out a grunt for the pain, which seemed worse suddenly, and reached behind and pulled the pistol from his waist and handed it to the doctor. "Here. Was that in the way?"

The young doctor stared hard at him and took the gun and laid it on a counter. The woman said, "¿Por qué el hombre disparó a si mismo?... o la policia?"

Hicks said, "We don't need no policia here. What did she say about police?"

The doctor continued to stare at him but spoke Spanish. "Él dice que fue un accidente. Él va a estar bien. Ir a la cama." The woman left then, and the doctor said. "She just wanted to know how you had cut yourself, whether the police might come. Lie down again, please."

"Okay Doc. You not getting any ideas, are you?" He didn't like it that the guy didn't seem afraid. Or the woman either. Rigid maybe, but not scared. Maybe have to kill the guy and his wife, thinking about it, the neighbors, his blood all over the place, the car sitting out there.

"I am not one for ideas, sir. You have cut yourself in an accident, and I will attempt to…make you well again. Do you want an anesthetic? Some of this will be quite painful."

That would be nice, close my eyes, he thought. "I'll manage fine. Just get on with it." He lay down again, left side up, staring at the pistol a few feet away on the counter, but there was a spinning in his head now. Little bitch makes a lucky shot, and here I am.

The woman was back now, framed at the door. "Voy a hacer la comida para él. Y usted. Y el café."

"Seems like the missus wants to hang around," he said and smiled at the doctor again.

"Hay que ir a la cama," the doctor said, not to him and not even glancing at him now, like he was just a doctoring job to do.

The woman was gone again and the doctor was at him. Every light in the room was on, and the doctor had wiped around the wound with a pungent-smelling cloth and now was looking at his side through a big glass mounted on a metal arm, some swabs in his left hand and an instrument of some kind in his right, sometimes pressing or pulling around on him, hurting him, to get a good look inside him, Hicks supposed.

He had put on a white apron and a white mask over his nose and mouth, but his tone never changed. "You are fortunate in many ways about your accident, señor." The bullet that cut you was not a large caliber, and it was fired from some distance." Explaining everything like some kind of an officer would. Some guy who didn't have to be there when the work was getting done, just assessing the value of his work. Only he wasn't. The doc was seeing the little bitch's work, and it was taking longer than he wanted it to, and it hurt more with each passing moment and he wished the woman was there again so at least he could stare at her. He suddenly wished JT was there so that he could just take the anesthetic and wake up when it was over, have JT drive too.

The doctor's voice came again, seeming to drone now. "I have removed some larger fragments of bone and metal and cloth because they were easy to take out, but I think that the worst damage was caused by something I cannot find. And because I cannot find it, it presents a risk, especially if it moves again."

"And what would make it move around?"

"Another injury in the same area…Or a strenuous movement. There is also a vein that needs a suture or two, I think, or it may continue to hemorrhage after the wound is closed." Then he was using other instruments, things that looked like scissors, little hooks and fishing lines. "Perhaps it was nicked by a bone fragment. There are many reasons you should visit a hospital; with the blood loss you probably need a transfusion. And there is risk of infection…I will give you something for that, but always it is better for such wounds to be monitored."

The woman appeared again, this time with a tray with coffee on it, which she set on the counter next to the pistol. She said, "Está sucio. Huele muy mal. ¿Como se explica el daño?" She touched her hand to her right side.

"No es importante para nosotros."

"What's she saying, doc? She getting a long nose?"

He was suturing the exit wound now, and he did not hesitate. "Debemos olvidernos de él." And then, "No, she says you are dirty and you smell bad and wants to know if you will have an infection."

He could feel the little needle pricks and the tugs on his skin. He eyed the doctor and tried to look in his eye, wondering if he was lying. The woman was leaning on the counter now, resting her hands on the counter behind her, as if she was trying to lift the weight of her belly from her legs, watching her husband work. "That's good, Doc. You don't want a woman who's too interested in other people's business, even if she is a fine one." This time the doctor did stop working, just for a moment, glancing at him. Maybe a little bit scared now.

"My wife is quite right; your skin is dirty. I only hope that the dirt has not stayed inside you. Infected you." The doctor went back to stitching, and no one spoke until he said he was finished dressing the wound, wrapping a broad bandage around his chest. "The wrap is not much protection, I'm afraid. You must try to restrict your movements. If you do not rest, you could die." Finally he gave Hicks an injection in the armpit below his left arm and another in the vein at his elbow. Then he removed his gloves and his gown and the mask and picked up the coffee and sipped it. "It is no longer hot, señor, but you may want some of this if you are able to sit now."

"You trying to shake me, Doc?" He sat up and felt suddenly nauseated and dizzy. "No harm is coming to me, Doc. Ever." The skin around the wounds felt taut and pinched.

"My wife has made some food for you too, I think." His dark eyes didn't waver. He handed the coffee to Hicks. "You should rest, señor. Perhaps not here, as I think you wish no one to remember your visit here, but somewhere you must rest, very soon, limit your movement."

"What did you give me, Doc?"

"One injection was to inhibit infection, the other for pain. I will give you some pills as well. For now, you will be able to stay awake, but soon you will not want to."

Hicks stared, at the Doc and then at the woman and then at the Doc again, thinking about doing it when he got the Walther back, but he did not look at the pistol.

"Perhaps you would like to sleep here, and that is all right, but you should know that this neighborhood rises early. There are many men who work early in order to beat the sun."

"I just don't want to forget anything, Doc."

The doctor didn't say anything. He seemed to be waiting. Hicks slipped forward off the exam table and stood up, waiting for a moment to see how dizzy he was. The woman picked up the Walther then and held it out to him, making her hand seem small. Hicks wondered what would happen if there were gunshots in the house. Crummy neighborhood sure, gunshots all the time, but this was the doc's house… Probably were roofers and masons going to work by now …and the Charger out front that everybody would notice. Hicks took the Walther, thinking that this was the time if he was going to do it, but he put it into the rear of his waist band again and told himself he would think about it some more. He took up the coffee and sipped and said, "You got anything to go in it? Whiskey or something?"

They led him into the rear of the house then, to the kitchen, where he could smell garlic and lard and peppery smells. He sat at a wooden table there, and set the coffee down. The pregnant woman brought him a plate that had been in the oven, brown mashed beans and yellow squash and some kind of meat that he thought was chicken but turned out to be pork. The doctor poured Kahlua into his coffee and set the bottle down and sat and watched him eat. The woman watched too until he said, "Ir a la cama y cerrar la puerta. Voy a ver hasta que se vaya." She said, "Espero que paga bien," and disappeared down a hallway. Hicks looked up at an electric wall clock. After four. He swigged from the bottle and took swallows from the mug and ate spoonfuls from the plate. "What'd she say now?"

"She says that you should not forget to pay."

Hicks smiled. "Yeah?" He swigged and ate more. ""So what do you think I should pay, Doc? What's it worth?"

"My patients pay what they can afford, señor."

"Well, this is different, Doc. I ain't one of your other patients. I wanna know what *you* think I oughta pay."

"I believe that one can only know the price of a thing if one knows its value."

The doc was starting to piss him off. "What the hell's that mean? What *thing* are you talking about?"

"That is what I am not sure of, señor. You have come here worried about your life, I think, not the price of an emergency office visit. So if you want me to put a price on such a thing as a midnight office visit, it is quite easy to say a hundred dollars or some other number. But if the thing we are talking about is a human life, your life or another's, then its value cannot so easily be set." The doctor sipped his coffee. 'The price of such a thing as that may be more than you or I, or anyone else, is willing to pay."

Yes, really pissing him off now. "Doc, you're gonna have to excuse me if I don't swallow the horse shit. You know you're caught up in something here. You knew it when you opened the door, but you seen the money and you said why not. But let me tell *you* something now. See, we all of us caught up in things we didn't plan on. It maybe started out as our own scheme but then it got away from us like a crow that flies into the house to steal your biscuits but can't find its way out again. And I mean everyone. From the grunts in the rice paddies right on up to the hottest shit general. So don't preach to me about anything." He thought about using the Walther again, first the doc and then the defiant little wife.

The doc was scared then, finally. Hicks could see it. He reached behind him and brought out the envelope, peeled out two hundred dollars, and set it on the table. "It's good you think your life is worth so damn much, but if I was you, I'd be hoping other people thought the same."

Ten

Somebody was skulking up to the door, a short guy, Caje, tentative but getting ready to put the key in the brass lock, and Hal moved, fast. He jerked the door open with his right hand and pulled Caje in with his left, almost lifting him off the floor by the belt. He pushed Caje back, maybe too hard, against the wall and covered his mouth and said. "It's me, Hal, Tara's friend." He waited for Caje's eyes to get narrow and for his hands to quit struggling against him, and then he eased up on Caje's mouth and belt. When he took the hand away and turned on the light, he didn't say anything but studied him, as if he'd never really paid attention to him before. The kid reminded him of a burrowing owl, with eyes a little too high on his head somehow, a round, almost puffy face, and the little black mustache. "I just grabbed you 'cause I thought you might run off. Where's Tara?"

His eyes looked away from Hal. He said, "I'm not sure. I think she's coming back here."

"So she's okay, right?"

Caje was silent, still looking away.

"All right, Caje. I wanna know what's going on. I didn't walk away from a perfectly good glass of whiskey so you could play dumb." He brought his hand back up and raised the owlish face. "You said Tara's coming back here?"

"She must be. It's what she'd do, I think." Caje twisted away and turned out the light. "We're gonna want to keep that off in case one of those guys come back. One of 'em might even be over there now."

"What guys? The assholes from Ruby? The trailer guys I saw yesterday or someone else?" Caje's body shook several times, and it took Hal a moment to understand the kid was sobbing.

"Yeah, it was them, the big guy anyway. And he might be coming back here too. I seen a car over there before," Caje looking out the window then, "and then the same car shows up at the exchange, and the big guy's in it--must have followed me." Caje was shaking his head, slowly, like he didn't understand how it could happen, how he could be a college boy banging his girlfriend one day and a spider caught up in its own web the next. Hal wanted to make a remark about owls being wise and knowing better, but he didn't want to have to explain it.

"What car? That El Camino?"

"No, it was a big ass muscle car, a blue one, Charger I think." He had stopped the sobbing and the headshaking, but his voice was low and hopeless. "I noticed it when I left for the meeting, and then it just showed up there. And then that bastard was shooting at us."

"Us? But Tara wasn't hit. You said she would probly show up here, so she wasn't hit, right?" He seized the kid's chin again and pulled the owl's face around to look at him. "What about Tara?" Why couldn't the damn kid just tell him everything at once.

"No, man. She wasn't there, not at first. I met this guy there, another guy, the guy I always meet." He thought of Lacho, the way his big barrel body must look now with the life gone from it, draining blood into the hard-packed earth under the picnic table, and he squeezed his eyes shut trying to make the vision disappear.

"And then what?" He tapped Caje's cheek with his fingers. Louder, he said, "Then what?"

"She came up fifteen minutes later in the Jeep. It's what we planned." Then he was sobbing again. "I tried to warn her off but I was too late. She was shooting at him then, the big guy, trying to find me, I think, and then he was shooting back, and she drove up through the pass. I was a couple hundred yards below on the road, and I could see."

"You saw all this? She have the Tommy gun?"

"No. Pistol she had in her purse."

"So how you know she's coming back here?"

"She's gotta be. The guy followed her up the road and through the pass, but it was like she had too much of a head start I guess, 'cuz he came back down, and I hid 'til he went by. She never came back down, so I figure she went south, you know to US 86 and back to town that way."

"But if that guy's coming back, why would she come here? Why are you here?"

"Cuz I think that guy was checked in here too, and maybe she didn't know it. I don't know if she seen that car or not, 'cuz she didn't leave right away. He'll kill her." He looked straight up into Hal's face now. No need to be held steady. "I guess it don't matter though, since Lacho didn't get outta there with the shit. His guys'll come for us now."

"The hell you talking about?" Hal said, but then he shook his head. "Never mind. I don't need to know all that. It's heroin, right? Who's got it now?"

"That big guy, man."

"He's already got what he was after. What makes you think he's still after her?"

"I don't know, man, but he went after her…up through the pass. Don't you see? Why's he do that?"

Hal sighed, shaking his head side to side. "Let's sit down a minute." Hal got the Bible from the drawer chest again and tossed it to Caje. He set the chain for the door in place and said, "That maybe gives us a second or two warning if they show." Then he sat in the chair again and took up the rifle and set it across his knees again and looked out the window. "Blue Dodge, you say. Which room?"

"I dunno. It was parked straight across. I could see the rally stripes through the pool fence when I left." Caje took the bills from Job and put them into a front pocket.

"Well, which room do you think it was?"

Caje stood closer to the window and pointed. "That one, probably, where the inner curtains are open, but the light's off."

"So how long ago was all this?"

"I think maybe about midnight when all the shooting happened…and then it took me a while to find the keys to the MG. I thought maybe she'd be here already…course it's so far going south of the mountains. All the way around."

"But what if she did figure it out? What if she saw the same thing you did? Would she come back here to check on you? Or just for the money? Thinking she could just get in and get out again?"

"I don't know. Maybe."

"Unless they were waiting for her here, and they're already gone." They didn't speak for a time, thinking about that. "You said you never saw the second guy? Tonight I mean?"

"No." Again there were a few minutes of silence.

"Well, I don't know where he is, but odds are he ain't over there. So where'd you park? Didn't hear the car." Hal wasn't looking at him, just staring out the window.

"About a block north. Across Miracle Mile."

"So she'd come here or go back to her place. Anywhere else? Not Judd's house, right?" He figured Caje would not answer. "Say you get outta this. Then what? Can you get her out?" He glanced at him then, and Caje put his eyes on the floor. He thought about asking him if would go to his classes today and cross his fingers for luck, but he didn't say it.

"Maybe go to Mexico. A village I know."

"I can't picture it. Tara, I mean, in a Yaqui village."

"Got a grandfather lives there. He's a Shaman." He caught Hal's puzzled look and said "Mystic healer."

They were sitting a few feet apart, Hal still in the chair and Caje on the end of the bed, both of them stiff-backed and rigid, and seldom looking at each other, with feet flat on the floor: Hal in Justin ropers, black and polished, Caje in canvas high-tops. "Tara told me you thought you belonged in that world more'n the one you're in. That so?"

That caught him off guard, Hal supposed, because Caje didn't answer right away. Then he said, "She knows I want to help my people. And maybe sociology ain't the way."

"Maybe drug-running ain't either," Hal said. My turn to be a smart ass. "Anyway, seems to me that Tara wouldn't belong. Just saying."

"I just mean till it cooled off."

He had to resist the urge to call him boy. "Caje, I don't know a lot about it but I don't think a thing like this ever cools off. Maybe if you pay. You got some way of paying up on a debt like this?"

"Do you?"

Hal looked at him through the semi-darkness, thinking everyone is a smart ass. "I already owe plenty of debts. More'n I can pay too, I guess." He shifted, trying to find a more comfortable way to sit. "Tell you what. One thing we're doing right now is stupid, and that's both of us sitting here waiting. We need to check on her place, one of us wait there for her. You, I'm thinking, since I got the rifle in case your pals from Ruby show up." Caje stood, but not in any hurry, staring at Hal like he didn't want to leave but couldn't think of a reason to disagree. "You see the sense of it, don't you?"

"I'm not sure," frowning then.

"Don't worry. I'll call you there if she shows here first."

"I'll do the same."

"You might need his room number over there. Depends where I wind up. Be good to know where she is. But I got something I gotta do either way." Then he snapped his head at Caje and said, "One thing I need you to do before you leave though."

*****

Caje went in to report the broken door. The idea was for him to get the manager out, away from the office while Hal, Tara's old-guy friend, waited in one of the empty parking stalls on the opposite side. "Get the night manager to come with you," Hal had said, "and I'll come in and get the key for the big bastard's room." But there was nobody even in the office, and the door to the manager's apartment in the rear was shut. There was a bell sitting on the counter next to a sign that said to ring the bell after 1:00 AM for service. Caje could see the keys in narrow wooden mailboxes behind the desk, on little lanyards that were supposed to look like dream catchers, brass rings with a little feather on one side. Most of the boxes had two dream catchers, his room—number fourteen—only one, same with room four and a couple others. He assumed there was some little alarm that had gone off in the manager's apartment when he'd come in, a light or a buzzer or something, so he waited, but with the bell and the sign, maybe not. Let's see, he thought, about five seconds to get there around the end of the counter, and five seconds to get back with the second key, the way things been going, the manager'll come out from his apartment just when I'm back there grabbing it, but I can just say I locked myself out.

The manager did come out too, not the lady who had checked him in, but a flabby guy in a white shirt and pajamas and a comb-over that apparently wouldn't stay combed over. "You need a room?" But Caje was already opening the door to leave again.

"Oh no thanks. Just wondering if you have a Coke machine. But then I seen the sign and figured you didn't want to be woke up." He smiled. The flabby man looked him over but said nothing, and he left. Caje slipped into shadow at the empty parking spot and found Hal standing with the rifle sling over his arm. "Here ya go. I just slipped back and got it. Got it clean."

Hal's eyes were adjusted to the shadows and he tried to look Caje in the eye.

"What you gonna do?"

"Not sure yet, but I'm gonna try to get that guy off your back. Yours and Tara's. You get going now."

Hal didn't think the little bastard was in the room, or anyone else for that matter. Unless maybe he's in there all bandaged up and trying to recover from the slug that Tara gave him. But no, probably not; the big bastard didn't strike Hal as the nurse-along kind of guy. So no, the little bastard probably hadn't made the trip, lying around the camp or some clinic in Nogales. Still, Hal took his time entering, with his ear against the door for a count of sixty. And he didn't think the big bastard had taken any time to put a match or anything in the doorjamb, probably confident that Tara and Caje would never figure on him showing up there and probably in a little bit of a hurry to make sure he didn't lose sight of Caje and the Jeep, but he checked anyway, feeling all the way around the jamb and the header before he put in the key.

He turned on the light as soon as he closed the door. He didn't want the guy to see the light on if he came back just now, but he also wanted to know where everything was in the room. It was very like Tara's, same furniture and another cowboy painting, this time three guys around a campfire drinking coffee. Same double bed; Hal stepped over to it and tested it to see how easily it moved on the carpet—it didn't. There was plenty of room behind the door for a man to stand, he noticed, and no reason to look over there when you come back to your room after a night of chasing people around and shooting at them....well maybe make a half-turn back to empty your pockets on the night stand, so gotta be careful about that...nothing to stop the door though, so I better test that. Hal took the Henry from its sling and set it behind the door, butt on the floor, and he got as far as he could into the corner and opened the door again, wide. The damn thing did hit him before it hit the door stop. He closed it again. Gotta be careful about that too, damn it to hell. Need to make the first strike with a bastard that size, hard. Course, ninety-nine times out of a hundred, he wouldn't open the door that far…and his hands will be full, one anyway, with the bag or maybe a gun. And there's no better way I can see. He picked up the rifle and chambered a round and released the safety and set it in the corner again. The phone was on the night stand, but its line had been brought in from across the room, with the black cord stapled onto the wall, like phones weren't the first thing the owners were thinking about when they built the place and added room phones later. In the closet, another smelly, rolling, fold-up bed and some wire hangers, a wooden clothes rod, which looked too brittle to be used for skull-cracking. The small armchair was situated near the window, which made sense, 'cause of course the bastard had been watching them. He wondered momentarily why the big guy hadn't gone after Tara when he saw the kid leave, make her tell him about the meeting place, and finish her then. If there was anything to be glad about, it was that he hadn't.

He picked up the phone and used it as a handle to jerk the phone wire off the wall, the half-inch staples popping out of the plaster without complaint. He pulled the Wonder Bar from his belt and used its sharp hook end again, to chop the telephone wire off at the wall. He twisted the black wire around his hand and pulled it free of the phone, and then returned the phone to the night stand. Two steps away from the door, he tied one end of the cord to the air conditioner about ten inches off the floor, pulled it tight, and tied the other end to the steel bed frame. There was excess cord, about five feet, and he chopped that free with the Wonder Bar, put a slip-loop into it at one end and coiled it up and stuffed it into his back pocket. Then he locked the door, turned out the light and sat in the chair, waiting, now and then tapping the round side of the Wonder Bar into his left hand.

He thought about how he was going about it. Well, if he comes back tonight, he'll come to this room, even if he decides to go look in the other first. The broken door over there might get him edgier, but he'll still come over here. Besides, ripping them off like that probably already has him edgy. So the only chance to surprise

him is here, either putting the gun on him and tell him to get down
…or crack his skull enough to make him go down. That guy didn't
seem like the kind that would put up his hands like in some Western
movie. Nope, he seems like the guy that would turn and *do*
something, start shooting if he's got a gun handy or charge me if he
doesn't. He didn't seem too impressed with the Tommy gun, so my
Henry carbine won't even give him pause. So stand silent behind
the door… He listened and decided the air conditioner hummed
enough to cover him while he stood there…and take him out with
the Wonder Bar from behind…hope the bastard doesn't turn, doesn't
sense me there the way a guy can sometimes.

   He thought about praying for Tara. How would Mrs.
Thadbury's priest say it? For her safe return. Or more couched: for
those in distress, those who are suffering, or more like "if it be thy
will." Give God some wiggle room, in case. But really, the priest
would tell us to pray for spiritual gifts: courage, strength, stuff like
that. Mrs. Thadbury, the landlady, would pray for her soul. He
wondered if Doris prayed and guessed she had used to, when she
was still going to AA meetings, but it was a thing they never talked
about. He was pretty certain she wouldn't pray for Tara in any case.
He wondered if Judd ever prayed; he had used to attend church with
Midge, but Hal assumed she was the believer and Judd was just
tagging along. So maybe just pray for those good old spiritual gifts.
He could just hear what Tara would say about it too: "Hell, I got
enough of those without God. I may not be the bravest, strongest,
mentally toughest girl on earth, but I can come up with those things
when I need them, and all on my own. It's called will." And most of
the time, it seemed like she was right. If God doesn't answer prayers
for something that counts, something that has real value, why pray?
Does it do any good to pray for Tara's life? Wish I could believe it
did. I don't want more strength and courage so I can bear her
death—that's bullshit. I want Tara alive. He remembered praying
for his aunt's life, not her soul, not strength and courage to bear the
world's ills, for her life. For a cure, not for all people who suffer or
all people who have cancer, just for her, just her life, that's all. Just
one life in all the millions. She didn't need strength or courage or
wisdom; she had plenty of those. No, she needed to live out her
days, days she deserved. But no luck. God just didn't answer those

kinds of prayers. Or yes he did; he answered no, but if you want some spiritual gifts, I'm good at handing those out.

He thought about praying the Lord's Prayer, anyway, because he knew it by heart, and some part of it must cover this situation; "deliver us from evil"—that was it, but he didn't bother to say it. And then he thought about saying the 126th Psalm, When the Lord restored the fortunes of Zion…because he could say it without thinking, but it was too hopeful, and then he thought about the tenth Psalm again: Why do you stand so far off, O Lord, and hide yourself in time of trouble? Good Goddamn question, Why *do* you hide yourself? He rapped the Wonder Bar in his hand and wished he had a shot of Ezra.

He almost dozed off just after four and decided to stand, wondering if maybe the big bastard had decided not to come back. He hadn't left a damn thing here. He took one of the mugs from the bureau and carried it into the bathroom and ran the hot water until it was as hot as he thought he could stand and then filled the mug. He stepped back to the bureau and tore open a packet of Folgers and emptied it into his mouth and gulped some water and swished it around in his mouth to mix it and then swallowed. He tore open a second packet and drank it in the same way. He carried the empty packets into the bathroom to throw them away.

It was almost five o'clock when the Charger pulled in, stopping in front of the room instead of pulling into its covered parking spot. Hal was anxious, suddenly tingling with nervousness and wanting to get behind the door, but he made himself stand at the edge of the window-blind to watch, telling himself, This is just like crouching in a listening post and you still know how to stay cool, how to do this. Understand? He worried that the air conditioner wasn't going to be loud enough, wondered if he could be quiet enough, doubted that he'd chambered a round in the Henry. Sure you did.

The big bastard was alone for sure, a hulkish shape inside the car. He sat for a few minutes, in the deep shade behind the steering wheel but with the ambient light making his face glow, looking around the commons, mostly toward Caje's room it seemed like, making up his mind then, opening the car door and lighting himself up suddenly with the dome light. Moving to get out, but slow, lurching through stages, leaning to get one foot out, holding the steering wheel, turning, getting the other foot out, lifting himself. So maybe she hit him, or he's been out celebrating. Good if he's shot, weakens him. Bad if he's drunk, harder to bring down sometimes.

Hal knew that one tap of the Wonder Bar was not going to be enough to bring the big guy down, like you'd see on television. He'd seen guys take blows to the face and head, and it was almost never enough to end it, not even when the guy was hit hard and square, not even in a barroom, where a guy's life didn't usually depend on getting up again. But maybe it was enough to hurt him, slow him down so the second or third tap would stun him and make him pliable.

Then he glanced over and saw the Wonder Bar where he'd left it on the chair, and his breath caught. Forgot it 'cause I'm anxious, he thought. There was time to retrieve it, the slow way the big guy was moving, so he ducked low and snatched it off the chair and made himself small behind the door again, wondering if he'd forgotten anything else, wondering if there was a coffee smell. He heard the car door close and waited for the sound of the key in the lock, taking deep, controlled breaths, now wondering if the guy would be carrying anything, wondering if he'd turn and see.

Hicks was carrying something, the duffel bag, which he swung through the door with his left hand while he held the door open with his butt. He made a little gasping sound as the weight of it came after him. Then the light came on and the door was closing, and he was stepping into the room, not turning.

When the door swung closed, Hal stepped forward and swung the Wonder Bar as hard as he could, aiming for the soft spot at the top of the neck and just below the big bastard's skull, connecting, and pulling the bar back again for the next swing. And just as he thought, the blow didn't drop the guy; if anything, it sped him up. The bastard turned, looking for his enemy, still holding the duffel bag, swinging it up at Hal's head trying to club him, in pain and staggering but angry as hell. Hal ducked lower as the duffel bag went high and wide of his head, and he came up swinging the Wonder Bar again, this time aiming for the left side of the neck, trying to put the round part of it just behind the big bastard's ear, but it was too much of a roundhouse. The guy had let go the duffel bag and brought his left arm back and up in time to block the bar before it had even traveled far, almost stripping it from Hal. He couldn't swing it with any force now, so he pulled it back and then jabbed the blunt end forward and hammered him in the chest just below the nipple, wishing it was the sharp end and thinking how puny and desperate the blow was, that the big guy was going to beat hell out of him now, but instead the big guy gasped, really hurt. The big man was suddenly stunned but still not going down and still swinging at Hal, trying to connect with his fists, but in a wild, uncontrolled way. Hal easily ducked below one of the fists and drove the bar forward again, aiming for the same spot, hitting it and watching to see how the guy took it. Not well. He grunted and flinched, grabbed at the spot with his right hand. Hal drew back the bar again and paused, thinking the guy would go down now.

He didn't. His grimace turned into a rage, and he growled out, "You," recognizing Hal. "I'm gonna kill you." He lunged forward now, not trying to use his fists any longer, hugging Hal and lifting him, wrapping up like a tackler in a football game, driving his back square into the concrete wall and crushing the breath from him, loosing Hal's hold on the bar, the bar falling harmlessly to the floor. The big guy drew back then and punched with his right fist, catching Hal on the shoulder, drew back and punched in the chest. And drew back again.

Hal stayed low and went for the spot again, this time without the bar, driving his fist into it. The guy growled from pain and staggered back, trying to gather himself to come at Hal. And Hal punched again, hitting the spot, and the guy stepped back, trying to find his stance, and Hal came out of the crouch and shoved with both hands, making the guy stumble back till he hit the stretched telephone wire and went sprawling to the floor, landing full on his back and groaning, barely moving, reaching for the painful spot with his right hand. The big guy's olive vest had fallen open when he hit the floor, and Hal could see the white bandage there, some red on it now, but he didn't wait. Pulling the telephone cord out of his back pocket, he came down hard on the man's gut with his buttocks and jerked the big bastard's left arm up, holding it near the elbow, and dropped the loop of the cord over it and cinched it tight at the forearm.

The man's eyes were blinking and the rage was gone from his face, and he flailed weakly at Hal with his left hand, still trying to press his right down against the wound, knowing what Hal was doing, trying to stop him from doing it but not able to. He heaved to his right, Hal letting him, lifting the buttocks now and helping him roll sideways by pushing him in the back with a knee, pulling the cord and yanking the left hand behind him at the same time, and letting the big guy rise to his elbow and then getting the phone cord around his right arm and pulling it as he rolled farther, pulling his right arm to the rear and wrapping the cord around it. Then Hal dropped his buttocks onto the left arm and lifted the right arm with the rope until the hands were together behind the big guy. Then he wrapped twice and pulled the cord through, making a hooey, and the guy's wrists were bound like a rodeo steer's hooves.

Hal kept pushing, rolling the big man onto his right side and then all the way onto his stomach. Hal squatted again and used the leftover length of telephone cord to tie the wrists a second time, making sure. Then he stood and moved away, watching the big guy, letting him move if he could. He was aware of his own breathing now, heavy, painful on the inhalations. He picked up the Wonder Bar and tossed it onto the bed and retrieved the rifle and pulled the chair around so he could sit and watch the guy come around while he held the rifle at low ready.

It took a while. Hal could tell the big bastard was in pain, and he wondered if he should help him sit up. If things were reversed, he'd want the help...want to face the SOB who'd just taken him out. The big guy was making grunting sounds as he tried to change position. Daylight was coming through the gauzy curtains now, so Hal went to the window and drew the blinds shut and turned on the light.

When he finally came up to a sit, he was pale, the blood gone from his face. Hal wondered how much of it was the blood trying to go to the bandaged bleed spot and then just leaking inside him like water from a crack in a concealed water line. He was leaning forward. For the first time, Hal felt bad for the big bastard. ...just like some Chinese kid rolling into your LP and you're there waiting for him with your bayonet, he thought, personal with him so close, with time to focus on a man's face. He saw the name tag on the army shirt.

"Why you here, Hicks?" Hal said.

"Fuck you want to know for?" His top lip curled up, but he gasped.

"Just curious." Then he felt worse, being a smart ass again. He could see the red spot on the bandage. It looked like it was spreading. "Yesterday shoulda been enough for you."

"You're a son of a bitch, coming at me like that. Behind like that."

Hal thought he should agree or explain that it was the only advantage he'd had, but he didn't want to say anything that seemed like a response. Instead he said, "Really, what did you come here for? You need to tell me."

He didn't say anything right away. He crab-crawled backward, pulling his knees up, pushing down on the floor with his bound hands and lifting his buttocks off the floor and gaining a few inches, then doing it again. "The hell you doing tying me up like this?" He rested, gasping, and crab-crawled again, until he could lean against the far wall.

"Where's the other guy?"

"You saw. The little bitch shot him. What is this, for Chrissake, you gonna try taking me to jail? Cuz if you are, you're crazy. I ain't going."

Hal wanted to say he wasn't crazy, but he remained quiet, waiting. There was the faint sound of a siren somewhere and the big guy's loud breathing. He glanced down at the rifle, making sure the safety was not on. He looked at the guy, how robust he was, young and tall, maybe fifty pounds heavier and four inches taller, and decided he was lucky not to be the one on the floor, lucky he'd struck the weak spot on the guy's chest. He said, "He didn't look that bad hit. Musta been worse than it looked, yeah?"

"What, you a fucking doctor now? Fifty yards off and you can see?" He snorted for emphasis. "She shot him. He's dead and that's it. Figures though. The poor dumb bastard goes halfway around the world and dodges slimy little gooks for a year and then gets wasted by some skinny little blond bitch after he comes home. Fuck she get a gun like that anyway?"

"Yeah, it's too bad it happened that way. Looks like you caught one too. That happen yesterday?"

He snorted again. "So who the fuck are you? I made the little Mexican piss-ant for her boyfriend, so that makes you what? Her daddy or something?"

Hal felt old suddenly, wanted to correct the big bastard about the Yaqui piss-ant, to try to define the 'something', but didn't respond. "Too late for your partner, but you're still alive. You don't believe in taking a second chance when you get one?"

"That's why I'm here, asshole, making a second try." His ghost-pale face disappeared as his head slouched forward, as if it were suddenly too heavy to hold up.

"Doesn't seem like you're gonna get a third one. The little Indian kid from yesterday--he didn't shoot you, so who did?" Hal noticed how filthy the guy looked with his hair matted and streaked with oily grime, his coarse stubble full. He lifted his head again after a few minutes and took in a deep breath. His jaw muscles strained as he took the inhalation long and slow. He was off balance, straining to pull his left elbow forward, as if he was trying to protect the darkening red spot. "I need to get back to the doctor."

"Not yet. I need you to tell me what happened. You want some water? Coffee?"

Hicks's voice was slower now. "Sure. You gonna untie me?"

"Not yet." Hal stood with the rifle at low ready, but now he slipped his finger inside the trigger guard. He said, "Don't move your feet. I wouldn't like it." He kept the rifle pointed at him as he stepped over and past him toward the bathroom. He brought back a water glass filled with tap water, put the rifle barrel against the big guy's rib, and squatted and put the cup to his lips to let him drink. Hicks dropped his head a little, and Hal figured that meant he wanted to gulp instead of sip, so he poured the water into his mouth. He drank about half the water, the other half spilling down his cheeks. Hal brought him a second glass, and Hicks drank half of it again. Hal went back into the bathroom and now filled the glass with hot water and carried it back to the bureau and made instant coffee in the mug and sat down. "You found 'em here. What happened tonight?"

"So you ain't the dad. You must be banging her too. The little piss-ant know that?"

Hal thought about kicking him in the leg, remembering that day with Tara in his old bedroom, the blue room. He wondered if Caje was trying to call and wished he hadn't needed the phone line. He couldn't resist saying something. "No, I'm the guy watching you bleed."

"You don't wanna fuck with me, man." The words coming out in a low voice, a murmur, but angrier again. "I ain't gonna stay tied up down here forever."

Hal thought, See, Hal? Counterproductive being a smart ass. "Were you the guys supposed to get the … whatever you call it? The stuff?"

"Do I look like a connected guy to you?" He made a sound somewhere between a snort and a gasp.

"Looks to me like you ain't been back that long."

"I ain't gonna tell you jack till we get to the doc's. This gotta be sewed up again." He squeezed his eyes closed suddenly, clenching his teeth, and flexed his arms, fighting the telephone cord. After ten seconds, he relaxed again. When he opened his eyes, they seemed vacant. He opened his mouth as if he were about to speak, but he merely pulled in a breath and heaved the air out again, exhausted from the effort. "How 'bout it?"

"Not yet." Hal looked at the alarm clock. He waited, but Hicks didn't say anything more. Hal was glad that he had tied the guy's wrists a second time, remembering times when he'd seen a calf-roper's hooey fail, the calf hobbling away for a disqualification. And of course, the rubbery wire might stretch some. Well, the big guy wasn't going to hop up on his legs like a calf would, but Hal wasn't going to set the rifle down either. After he finished his coffee, he rose from the chair and backed over to where the duffel bag lay and hefted it up to his waist with his left hand and brought it back to the chair and set it in front of him and sat again. "Maybe there's some answers in here then, eh?" He kept the rifle vaguely pointed at Hicks, the stock nestled into the crook of his right elbow, and leaned over and unzipped the bag with his left hand. He pulled out the envelopes first, one at a time, the fatter one ripped open and the thinner one never sealed. He thumbed them, glancing back every few seconds to Hicks, whose eyes were drowsing. The fatter one was all hundreds, not stuck together but still crisp and flat, like they had been counted a couple times, the thinner one a mix of bills. He set them one on top of the other on the air conditioner. He took out a brick and examined it.

"That shit is uncut," Hicks said. "Worth a lotta money."

"Yeah? How much?" Rubbing the cellophane wrap on the outside of the brick, thinking the stuff looked gooey, trying to get one answer from the guy.

"Piss-ant said each one was twenty grand. Course that's after they cut it and get it out to the junkies." He was struggling to talk now. "May be high, but worth enough so they can pay the mule a few thousand every trip."

"By mule, you mean the piss-ant, I guess?"

"Him and the bitch," trying to needle Hal, his face set in a growl. He leaned left and looked down at the spot where blood was seeping into the bandage, his face tightening. The redness had reached the bottom of the bandage, and now there was a trail of blood across his grimy abdomen.

Hal dropped the brick back into the duffel bag. "So you interrupted the delivery, and there was some shooting. I guess you won that round, eh?"

Hicks lifted his head. His eyes were turning hollow now. He breathed through his mouth. "'at's right. Sheriff's gonna have a breakfast picnic with a dead Mexican pretty soon. Already, maybe." He chuckled and then his head went down to his chest again.

Hal reached into the duffel bag with his left hand again, feeling around and counting the slabs of heroin through his pigskin fingers. Twelve. He brought out the silvery slip of paper and read it. Has to be the same RJ, he thought, but what? He held it up. "Whaddya know about this?" When Hicks didn't look up, Hal kicked him on the bottom of his boot. General issue, he noticed.

Hicks raised his head, slower now than before and squinted at the slip of paper.

"Okay." He stared at the phone numbers. The hand is too neat to be Tara's, he thought. So who wrote the note and who put it in? He dropped the slip back into the bag. He watched Hicks for a time, watched him breathing irregularly, waiting for his head to come up again. When it did, he said, "So how'd you get hit? The Mexican or the girl?"

"I shot the hell out of that big greaser. Bitch shot. Lucky ass bitch shot. Some little pop gun, goddamnit." He was grimacing, either from pain or from what was left of his anger. "Hey. Get me to the car, man. I need the doc."

"Sorry. I don't think I can do it."

"Whatcha mean? You help me, I can get there."

"Trouble is, Hicks, I can't let you have another chance. I came in here thinking I's gonna have to shoot you. Apparently I don't have to--just gave her bullet a second life. 'cause you're right, sarge. She's important to me. Not the reason you think, but she is."

Hicks breathed hard. "Well, you're too late mother-fucker. She found out she can't fly very good 'thout her fairy wings."

Hal tried to act as if the words hadn't shaken him, but his heart fluttered with pain and his eyes flared wider. He struggled to find the same tone in his voice, and he failed when he said, "What the hell is that supposed to mean?" He stared into the big bastard's eyes, probing for a lie, praying he'd find a lie behind Hicks's eyes and not finding one.

Hicks chuckled and then tried to rouse his anger again. He flexed against the telephone cord, widened his hollowed-out eyes. He tried to yell, but the sound came out a cough.

"We'll see," Hal said. He put the envelopes of money back into the duffel bag. He stared into Hicks's eyes until the big man lowered his head.

At seven o'clock, Hicks's breathing was shallow and arrhythmic, and Hal didn't think he needed to keep the Henry on the big man anymore. He set the safety and put it back in the sling. He turned out the light and opened the shade. He read the sign on the back of the door, looking for the checkout time. Noon. He opened the door wide enough to hang out the do-not-disturb sign and closed it again. By eight o'clock, Hal couldn't hear any breathing at all, and he knelt next to the bulky frame. He removed a glove and set the backside of his fingertips next to the nipple and felt for the heartbeat. Weak but pumping. He retrieved the Wonder Bar from the bed and wrapped it in one of the hotel hand towels and laid it in the duffel bag on top of the heroin.

He sat down, his eyes crawling across the commons, frequently peering through the chain link fence at the door to room fourteen, figuring what might be the most anonymous way to exit. He wished that he'd thought to put the do-not-disturb sign on the doorknob over at fourteen but told himself he couldn't think of everything. Wouldn't do to have a patrolman come by to take a report just now, but so far the broken jamb hadn't caught anyone's eye. He watched a guy load bags and an ice chest into the New

Mexico car and leave just after nine, wearing slacks and a tie and shiny brown shoes, a brown-skinned woman rolling a service car up to his door right after he left. A couple came out of room six at ten o'clock and left in the car that had been backed into its stall, Arizona plates. The guy was about Hal's age, maybe a little older, wearing a light blue sport coat, and the gal a lot younger wearing a lightweight dress. Apparently, they hadn't bothered to unload their luggage the night before. She was dark-haired and not very tall, but her slender frame reminded him of Tara. He wondered if Caje had tried to call and remembered Hicks's last remark. "Goddamn it," he muttered, without conviction.

Hal checked Hicks's heartbeat again. When he knelt, he had to be careful of the blood that had run down the big man's side and pooled on the carpet. He kept his fingers on him for a minute and felt nothing. "Don't think I'm sorry, big man. Seemed like the only way."

The maid went to fourteen after she finished in the couple's room. When she knocked, the door gave a couple inches, and she started to nudge her way in, tentative about interrupting some guest's privacy, but scurried to the office as soon as she recognized the marred door frame. In less than a minute, a man came over, tending to fat, carrying a bat. He pushed the door open and then stepped away for a moment, gave himself an angle to peer in and then disappeared inside. Hal lowered the visor of his cap.

When the fat man headed back for the office, Hal was already holding the duffel bag in his right hand. When he disappeared, Hal moved. He opened the door, slung his rifle and left, closing the door behind him. He walked. Not too fast, he reminded himself.

It was a longer route, but Hal went left at the sidewalk so that he wouldn't have to cross in front of the office windows. He strolled. West to the next intersection, south for a block, east, and finally north to the titty bar. There were three cars in the parking lot besides his pickup. Not unusual then, he thought. He threw his cap into the duffel and put on his Stetson and drove away, the bag next to him on the seat of the pickup.

Eleven

At Tara's, Hal couldn't help scanning for the Jeep. The pain coursed through his heart again when he didn't see it. There weren't any sunbathers, but Caje was sitting on the concrete porch outside her front door. There was a hopeful look in his eyes, but Hal shook his head slowly and watched the look fade and saw Caje turn and retreat through the doorway. After a few minutes, he followed him, toting the duffel. When he came inside, Caje was standing at the counter in the tiny kitchen, staring at the phone.

He thought about saying he was sorry, like you would at a funeral, but he resisted. He figured there was no one going to say that to him.

"What happened with that tall guy?"

"It wouldn't help anything." Hal sat on the sofa with the duffel bag in front of him on the floor. "Besides, not much to tell. Tara put a bullet in him. Must have finished him."

He looked imploringly at Hal now. "She might still be coming."

"Yeah, she could." Hal nodded.

"But you don't think so, do you?"

Hal examined his round face, the owlish eyes puffier now. He wondered if the kid had been crying. "Caje, you know her good enough, how tough she is. She put a slug in both those guys, not the other way around. It wouldn't be the first time she surprised me."

His eyes dropped and he said, "I feel like I've been stupid, never knowing what the hell to do the last few days, having to be told. And me all the time just thinking of myself. Ready to take the money, to take whatever Tara gave me. Ready to run like a rabbit anytime something started to go wrong." He brought his eyes up again, making himself look right into Hal's eyes, holding the gaze.

Not easy for a Yaqui, Hal thought. "Least you grabbed the opportunity when it came along. There's plenty of time for soul searching later. You still have problems to solve."

"I just want her to drive up here in my Jeep. I gotta believe she will. Or the phone will ring. Somethin'."

"Could be, but suppose it don't happen that way. Suppose a sheriff car comes in here next, or city police. Then what? You know they're gonna get here at some point, no matter what happened to her."

"Maybe she seen that coming. I don't know how well you know her, but she's smart enough to know that the cops'd come. Maybe she's already fifty miles south of Nogales."

"Sure, or sipping margaritas in Guaymas. She's okay or she's not. But either way, we need to make some decisions."

He shook his head slowly, suddenly hopeless again. "If she's not okay, then I don't care what happens to me."

Hal stared for a long moment, then said, "Well, let me know when you're done with the self-pity, and we'll decide what to do next."

His eyes flared open, angry now.

"Look," Hal said. "We both know Tara had a lot going on inside her. She was smart and tough, but all the same angry and confused, 'specially about men. You weren't her first boyfriend and you damn sure weren't gonna be her last." They stared at each other momentarily; then Hal said, "Didn't mean to be ironic." And now Hal was the one who looked away.

Caje said, "I wanted to be. I mean, everybody talked about her...in school, you know, how she'd get with different guys. And she'd never stay with a guy, you know? I thought maybe it was different for me…this time."

"You were hoping, you mean."

His eyes opened in surprise now.

"It was your fantasy. You wanted to be the boy that got to her 'stead of the other way around." He paused. "Oh, I ain't saying it wasn't ever gonna happen. I may be outta line saying it, but I got a hunch you wanted it to happen for *you*. For your sake."

"You're right. You are outta line." He was glaring at Hal. "Mister, I was born out on the rez … government house, you know. And I can't remember a single thing from when I was young that wasn't broke or messed up some way; busted windows, my cousins huffing gas and trying to get me to try it, my little sister's raggedy clothes, even my family was all damaged. When I first seen Tara, she was like the opposite, even though everybody talked about her, the guys anyways. And me afraid she'd catch me looking at her, thinking she was this precious thing. I even went to girls' basketball games so I had an excuse to watch her. She seemed like the one thing I saw every day that wasn't damaged. We ran together, on the cross country teams, ever since we were freshmen, and then every fall. She always tried to stay up with me on training runs, even after I was state champion, she'd try to hang right there, never stop running. Sometimes I'd let her get even with me and even pass me, just so I could watch her, her arms and neck all white and lovely and streaked with sweat, her blond hair in a tail behind. But everybody said she was slipping around, one guy to the next. A slut, you know? Every guy wanted to be with her, of course, and when he was, he'd brag on it until she moved on, and then it was like she was just nothing to him after that, somethin' ready for the trash can. It was always the same. And maybe it was cuz I never thought she'd give *me* a chance, but I swore it would never be like that for me. If I got to have her, even for a night, I wasn't gonna talk about her afterward like she was trash, you know. And then she did pick me. We were juniors. We were together for a two weeks, and then it was over. Guys always asked me what I got off her, but I wouldn't say nothing, mister, not even after she went on to this college guy she met."

"Okay. But Tara could sense the me-first in a man, any man. Anyways, we may never get to find out now. One thing I'm sure of is it's time to get out of here though. I just need to know what you're gonna do so I can decide what I'm gonna do."   He looked expectantly at Caje.

"You can moan all you want about what a fool you are right up until some guy with a snub-nose kills you for that shit in there, but I am not interested in being there with you."

"It was gonna be okay, I think, till that guy showed up. Lacho was letting me go, getting in his pickup."

"You figure he's the one got shot up?"

Caje nodded. "There was this note from RJ..."

"RJ! Like RJ Jasper, the guy who hangs out at the Sahuaro Bowl." When Caje nodded, Hal fished the silvery paper from the bag. "This?" Caje nodded again. "Just numbers, what is it?"

"Tara said that RJ was promising to take care of it somehow."

"With some phone numbers. All that talk about RJ ain't just horse feathers then." Caje shook his head. "And he's still in it, somehow." Caje nodded.

"Then he's still your best chance. Complete the delivery, maybe it goes away."

"It won't help anymore. Not after what happened out there."

"You don't know if it will or it won't, but havin' that bag gives you a better chance than not havin' it." Caje's eyes had dropped again. "Look at me, damn it." When Caje looked up, he went on. "Somebody's gonna find you, Caje. It might be the cops, and it might be the thugs. Hell, it might even be Judd if something happened to Tara. And no matter which one it is, you're gonna get around to telling 'em about me. That means I'm in it now too. You might think different right now, like you can lie your way through, but I didn't do what I did just to wind up dead or in jail 'cause you're busy feeling sorry for yourself. You got that?"

Caje's eyes were flashing, but he nodded.

"Okay. Let me tell you how I see it. Your biggest problem is these guys," motioning at the duffel bag, "the assholes who were expecting this. They want their stuff and the cash, and they want you both dead, you and Tara. How well you know RJ?"

"Not much. Tara made that connection. I don't want nothin' to do with that shit no more."

"And you didn't know anybody above Lacho?" Caje shook his head. "Then you get your wish. If the cops ask you about it, you don't know what they're talkin' about."

"What if RJ ask?"

"If one of his pals come around, they probly ain't askin' anything. Means our long shot didn't play out right, and we're just grease spots in somebody's garbage can. What's your story for the law?"

"I don't know. Something like the truth, I guess. Only I want to keep her out of it."

"Yeah, all good lies start with the truth. But I don't see how."

"I don't know how yet, but I'm gonna try." He stared at the ceiling for a moment. "Maybe if I disappear for a while."

"The village?"

Caje nodded. "Where my grandfather lives. I'm gonna find *her* first though."

Wordlessly, Hal went to the phone and dialed. "Hey Johnny, this is Hal…yeah, it *is* my day off, just wanted to see if they posted a shift for me tomorrow. Judd said something … what happened? …oh, my God. …When did *this* happen?...Yeah, it'll kill him….uh-huh…instantly, you say…uh-huh…" When he hung up, he looked at Caje and said, "The coroner's got her." And then he couldn't hold it in any longer, couldn't pretend he was the older brother or the barroom supervisor or the father's employee or a roping cowboy or even a wartime soldier alone in a listening post. He went back to the couch, making a low sound in his throat, as if he were whispering a howl to himself, and lowered his head. If only it could be a mistake, he thought. Maybe Johnny didn't have it right. Maybe I should call Doris or someone in the lounge. Johnny is always exaggerating, dealing out drama when there isn't any. He rocked back and forth. If only she's still alive, he bargained, everything would be mended, every pain healed. If only… "Gone forever," he whispered.

"You were hoping too," Caje said.

He nodded but kept his head low. He started to speak but his breath turned to a gasp. He inhaled deeply and brought his head up and said, "I owed her and now there's no way to pay. That's all." There would be tears, he knew, but not now, not in front of this kid.

"You got the bastard that was chasing her."

"It was Tara did it. My part was just luck." He finally looked at Caje. "And don't say that again."

"Yeah."

"How did you feel about her? Were you in love with her? I mean, if you had got to her the way you said you wanted, would you have wanted it forever?"

He dropped his eyes to his shoes. "I don't know. To me she was still the precious blond girl in the sun trying to beat me on training runs through the desert. So I think that's why she came back to me when she seen me at the college. She was surprised I was there at all, of course, a Yaqui boy on scholarship, driving my uncle's Jeep to campus every day. But we been together a while now. Since before Christmas."

"That's not what I asked. I asked if you loved her."

"And I said I didn't know. What I knew is that she saw me for something more than just an Indian boy. I wasn't just part of her collection. She knew I wanted to be something more than a white girl's symbolic fling"

"The Twentieth Century Caje'eme, huh?"

His eyes narrowed, shocked now.

Hal said, "She told me some things, her dreams, a couple of yours too," and looked at the duffel bag again. "Anyway, time to go." He stood and lifted the bag. "Try not to let the bastards track you down. The cops either, for a while. If you're smart, you'll skip the funeral." He went out the door to his truck, and he drove away.
*****

Hal watched Linda make her way to the booth in the corner where RJ was sitting with two other men. One of them looked like a builder, a white guy, about five-ten, who'd come in with a roll of papers that was spread out on the table now, blueprints, Hal figured. He was pointing to the prints and talking a lot, mostly to RJ. The other guy looked Mexican, tall and thin, listening mostly. They were on their third round, RJ drinking Black Velvet shots with draft chasers, the other two sticking to beers. Hal was having trouble thinking about anything but Tara, but he noticed that the three guys didn't look like thugs. Linda smiled as she set the drinks down, trying to spike her tip. Hell, go over there and sit down and introduce the builder and the Mexican to the local drug guy, see how they all react. But he didn't. He waited, hoping the other two would leave RJ alone by the fourth round. He kicked at the duffel bag where he'd stashed it under the counter to reassure himself it was still there and poured drinks.

His sorrow was solitary. Before she died, Henrietta had given him the advice to divide his grief, and then, after, there were at least the other hands and the cousins who came to her funeral and listened to him talk about her, so he had done his best to let them carry away their own share and he told himself that it lightened his load. But this time there was no one. Not Caje, because Caje was gone now, and Caje was not really a friend, and anyway, he had enough of his own. Not Midge because he'd let Midge die too. Not Doris, though she had come back to his apartment the previous day, talking about Judd's pain and Judd's anger. He had thought about dividing it with Johnny. Johnny was, he supposed, his best friend, and it would have been safe enough sharing some of the story with him, since Johnny could keep both a secret and a promise. But no, not Johnny either, for some reason. There were fifty or sixty drinkers now, Friday late afternoon, three busty waitresses and another bartender, but Hal knew he was quite alone with his grief. He'd set out a vase with wattle and yellow bells.

After a while the late afternoon crowd, a lot of them blue collar guys in their sweaty trade clothes, made their way out the doors, and they were replaced by the early evening crowd, salesmen and tellers in their bowling league shirts and their wives and girlfriends, some of them wearing dresses and glittery costume jewelry, a lot of them ordering food too. RJ was in the booth with the same guys, the blueprints still rolled out flat in front of them, on the fourth round and no sign of anybody leaving.

Until RJ got up suddenly and went off to the rest room. Funny looking, Hal thought, or out of place, his white hair combed perfect like he'd just left the barber's chair, the tony shirt and sandals.

The first time Hal could remember seeing him, RJ had been meeting with Judd, papers spread out that time too, and in the same booth, five years ago now. The server had been delivering an order out in the bowling alley, and RJ called him over to speed up the next round, not wanting to wait for the server. RJ said, "Wanna freshen these up, my man?" Like I worked for *him*, not Judd, and like where the hell you been. After that, Judd usually stopped for a sit-and-chat if he noticed him in the bar. It had been rare but enjoyable watching

Tara serve him, her sauciness obvious even though you couldn't hear her voice, and rolling her eyes on the way back to the bar.

The builder was rolling up the prints. So maybe they were leaving together. He tapped Gary on the shoulder and told him he was going on a break, Gary looking irritated.

On his way back to the booth, RJ got Linda's attention, wanting the tab. Linda knew he didn't like to wait, so she came to the bar still carrying a full pitcher. Hal said, "I got this," and took the ticket with him, along with the duffel bag. He knew it looked a little odd, but he moved slowly, the bag almost dragging across the floor, and pretended to stare at a poster that said WOMEN'S LEAGUE FORMING: REGISTER AT THE MAIN DESK BY JULY 1ST.

RJ didn't seem to notice him. He heard a couple words of their conversation about breaking ground on something. To Hal, it seemed strange for them not to be talking about Tara, the builder mentioning something about September and then looking up at Hal because now he was standing there. RJ's eyes followed too.

"Evening Mr. Jasper." He remained standing but set the bag on the bench seat next to RJ so that all three of them had to look at it, RJ glassy-eyed with Canadian whiskey and fascination. "I'm wondering if you have a minute."

"Well, well. I never thought about *you*." His voice was lower than usual, but still quick and full of crust. The Black Velvet wasn't slowing him down any. "You carrying around other people's dirty laundry?" He smiled a little, but forcing it.

"Why would I wanna do that?"

"Get it cleaned, I guess. Better'n hanging your own underwear out in public." His eyes narrowed and he turned to the other two. Hey, you two, thanks for bringing these by." He patted the rolled up blueprints. "I'll look them over good this weekend and get 'em back to you Monday. Tuesday at the latest. 'kay?" They nodded and scooted out, silently, looking from Hal to RJ and back again. When they'd stood, they reached in front of Hal and shook RJ's hand. Hal smiled, but no one offered an introduction. When they were gone, RJ said, "People been trying to find that boy, the Indian, so they can figure out what to do with him."

"I don't know," Hal said. I was thinking more like that wouldn't be necessary. He let his eyes wander around the room, then over to the bar where Gary was filling a pitcher, Linda waiting for it.

He noticed tiny streams of cigarette smoke rising. RJ was saying something about things going too far to make the sale now.

"No, the sale was complete. The money's in there too." He turned a little and looked through the glass doors into the bowling alley. The pins crashed, louder every time the door opened. The place was just smoke and noise and booze smells, but Hal imagined it was the duffel bag that had ruined it. He didn't think he would be working here much longer, but he wanted RJ to be the one to leave. And take the problem away with him.

But RJ said, "What did you want to get mixed up in this for? Even if it's all there, the Indian kid's problems ain't goin away. And now you got the same problem."

Hal brought his eyes back to RJ in his extravagant shirt, slick hair, turned in the seat now with one leg up on the bench, like he was completely relaxed and suave, or at least wanting to look that way.

"What are you, like the laundromat's advisor? You never touch the laundry yourself but you tell other people how to do it? When to do it and where? I think this one time, you could get the laundry where it's supposed to go, and everybody gets to go home and start over. Even the kid." He wanted RJ to just say sure, what the hell.

"I don't do other people's laundry. It's all smelly. Sometimes there's stains too. Sticky stuff and blood. You wouldn't want to touch it either."

"I don't mind delivering the stinky laundry one time. You just tell me where."

"Not possible." He was smirking now, but Hal watched him shifting around in the seat, as though he couldn't find a comfortable way to situate his butt and still stare up into Hal's eyes.

"How long you been in the liquor business?"

"Bout fifteen years."

"Well, you're a big bug now. You always know the right guy for everything. And you make sure everybody knows that, don't you. Maybe that's why you got them into it in the first place. But you're still coming into the Sahuaro Bowl to get wasted just like everybody else. And fifteen years ago you were delivering laundry just like Tara and the Yaqui kid. And now you're gonna sit there and tell me I *can't* finish this job and you *won't*? That what you're saying?"

RJ kept staring up at him, nodding a little bit now, like he was getting ready to say something. Hal gazed out the glass doors now, waiting.

"I'm saying they'll want blood for Lacho's blood. There's no way you come away alive. They get the bag and all you get is dead. You're crazy if you think otherwise."

Hal thought about telling him there wasn't much difference between insanity and grief. But when he looked at RJ again, he said, "It's all I got. So I can do one of three things: take the laundry out to your car, deliver it myself, or get it to the sheriff. Your note's in there too."

RJ's face went white for a moment, but then he said, "It don't mean a fuckin' thing, my man," shaking his head and smiling.

"No, I reckon you're right, but they'll at least want to chat with you." He looked at the duffel bag for a moment, then took it up and gathered it against his chest, staring down at RJ, but remembering the way Tara felt when she had pressed herself into him.

In a moment, RJ nodded. He slipped along the bench and stood and said, "Wait a few minutes anyway, then take it to the loading dock." He put two twenties down, took the rolled-up plans and left through the glass doors.
*****

For the second time in two years, there was a Sahuaro Bowl funeral. The memorial mass was said at Saint Thomas, Father John Saxon presiding there and also at the interment, where Tara's walnut casket went into a hole a few feet from her mother. Standing there, Hal remembered she'd said she wanted to be cremated, with her ashes scattered among pine trees on Mount Lemmon or someplace like that, and he wondered if she'd ever mentioned that to Judd. At the mass, Father John had read from Philippians and urged everyone to obedience, especially to maintain their innocence in the midst of our crooked and perverse generation. Graveside, he read the twenty-third Psalm, along with something from Corinthians that said something about resurrection.

Hal had warned Caje'eme not to attend the funeral, and he was relieved when he did not see him at the mass, but the kid came to the interment, wearing a loose white tunic cinched with a belt at the waist and a turned-down gray hat with an eagle feather angled in at the band. The police were looking for him, and Judd had promised to kill the little Indian fuck. He at least had sense enough to wait until Judd left, until everyone left.

...except I only pretended to leave and circled back so I could do my crying in secret...and there he was...and then I wouldn't cry, after he noticed me, giving it up because he was there...

Judd held the reception at the bowling alley of course, with the lanes quiet and the front doors locked. Funeral guests used the café entrance on the south side. When he arrived, Hal looked over the reception scene as if it were a tableau. Used to giving crowd counts for Judd, he counted. There were about a hundred people in the café, two groups. Bowling alley people, Judd's group, were near the bar. A younger set, Tara's friends from school, milled around the catering tables. The glass doors connecting to the main part of the alley stood open, and a few people were out there in the darkened bowling alley, talking quietly. Judd sat at one of the round tables with Doris and another woman. Doris sat behind a bloody Mary with her hands covering Judd's forearm.

Hal moved slowly to the table and extended his hand. "I'm really sorry, Judd," saying it for the fourth or fifth time.

Judd looked up and absently shook his hand. Then he sipped his bourbon with water and stared.

Hal glanced at the two women and sat down.

Doris said, "This is my friend Colleen." She smiled.

"Nice to meet you, Colleen." He smiled with his lips. "It's nice you're here."

Hal noticed tapping at the outer door and peered through the semi-darkness. A few people stood at the glass looking in. "I should go change the marquis."

Doris said, "Yeah, why doncha, Hal. That's about the third group."

Hal nodded. As he rose, he wished he were somewhere else. He spoke briefly to Johnny, then went to the storage room to retrieve the letter case and out the café door toward the marquis. Johnny brought the ladder, climbed it, and they began changing the message: CLOSED FOR PRIVATE MEMORIAL.

He thought, I should just leave now while I have the chance, as soon as we get the sign changed. But he didn't. Instead, he went back inside, Johnny too, and watched, catching snatches of conversation. One at a time, or in twos and threes, people came to Judd at the table and gave their condolences, trying to lift him somehow—some of Tara's school girlfriends, who cried loudly, Hal thinking he recognized one of them as one of the sunbathers, the Mexican custodians who worked ten-hour shifts for Judd, along with their wives, saying Es triste and Lo siento, a priest who had presided with Father John at the funeral mass, and who told Hal that Judd should eat something, Johnny's wife and daughter, and the rest—all of them saying their words to him as they were leaving.

Finally, as evening approached, there were only the three of them. Judd had stopped adding water to his bourbon an hour before. When he said, "She made her own bed," Hal thought that perhaps he hated him and had to suppress an urge to slap him. …doesn't know what he's saying…drunk on whiskey and bitter sorrow…at least he said it after everyone left…

Doris swayed on her chair, sitting behind a virgin vodka now. Hal wondered if she regretted the times she had called Tara "that slut with the cute little ass." And he thought maybe he hated her too. Instead, he cursed himself silently for not knowing what to say to either one of them and for drinking a beer along with his chicken salad sandwich. Then he went home too, wondering if Doris would come there.

Twelve

Hal met Caje's uncle before anyone from the sheriff's office even came to talk to him. He was still tending Judd's bar, still setting out flowers for Saturday shifts, desert marigolds or poppies that appeared after the rain or aloe from Mrs. Thadbury's garden or, if tips had been good, crimson roses.

It was the end of August then, the monsoon over half-spent. There was an afternoon thunderstorm, which seemed like any other summer storm, but the weather man said it was a tropical depression that had come up from the Gulf of California, had a girl's name like some Caribbean hurricane. A lot of lightning and rain either way, Hal thought. Uncle came in through the bowling alley doors, wearing a broad, flat-brimmed hat and a shirt and pants that were wet from the armpits down. He was looking for Judd, wanting to get his Jeep back.

"I don't think he can help you with that. It's probably in county impound."

"His daughter, she was driving it."

"So I heard. But Judd ain't got the Jeep. Never had it." Hal started to wonder about Uncle, whether he really thought Judd could help get the Jeep back to him, whether he was really the uncle, but only for a moment; he had Caje's round, owlish face. "Besides, he's out of town right now."

He was thin, like Caje, but taller, and about Hal's own age, he judged. He had yellowish teeth and there was a soft raspiness in his voice, as if maybe he was a heavy smoker. Hal pictured him out on the reservation, thinking of him as a rez Yaqui, wondering if Caje counted him as one of the broken things there. He stared at him across the bar, waiting for Uncle's eyes to come up, but they didn't. Uncle stood watching the television screen high on the wall, its sound barely audible but broadcasting images of storm damage somewhere.

"You want, I can tell him you were in."   Uncle kept his eyes on the television screen, paying no attention to him.   "Have you checked with the sheriff's office? Maybe you oughta start with them."

He kept looking at the television screen, but he said, "It was very bad in Mexico--did you hear?" He pronounced the x like an h, like a Mexican would. "Sank a lot of pangas."

"Boats? Yeah, across the sea from Rocky Point mostly. Washed out some houses too. There was a story in the paper."

It got Uncle to look at him.

"I saw a little article this morning while I was drinking coffee. San Felipe." Hal said San Fuh-*leep."* Too bad about all that damage. Know anybody down there?"

Uncle nodded, agreeing, but he said, "No, I don't know no one in San Felipe." He said Sahn Fay-*leep*-ay. There was damage in Sonora too, on the east gulf. I have some friends and relatives there."

"Yeah, I think I know one or two people might be down in Sonora."

"Might even be the same people."

"Could be, I guess. You walk over here today?" Hal watched him put his hands on the mahogany bar rail then, the fingers so brown they almost looked black, the fingers a little crooked and angled away from his thumbs.   Hal noticed his wet clothes again. "Course, that Jeep wouldn'ta kept you dry anyhow."

"If I had my Jeep, I wouldn't be out looking for it."

It reminded him of Tara, the smart ass remark, but he tried to smile. "No, I reckon not.   Well, you're welcome to sit here and dry out some. Can I get you something to drink? Coffee maybe?"

"That'd be good." He slid onto a stool and set his woven hat on the bar with the brim up. Pinned to the underside was a service ribbon, blue with a white bar in the middle. Hal had one like it in a drawer.

When Hal brought him the coffee, he said, "Guess I'm wondering what you're looking for…besides the Jeep, I mean."

Uncle looked at him hard, in the eyes, like he was deciding something. He put cream in the coffee and stirred and sipped it. "I'm looking for my nephew to come home. You know him? Caje'eme is twenty years younger than me. But he's older in his soul, I think. I always felt like he was gonna do something, you know? Something important and good too. He used to take his books from school and go out to this old Chevy parked in the yard and sit there and do his school lessons. He was good at writing, you know. He'd read some of it to me, reports and things."

"So you thought a lot of him."

"Mister, Caje'eme was the best boy I ever knew. That's why I lent him the Jeep, so he don't have to worry about wheels, so he could go to college and be a teacher or a lawyer or something, not have to lay no block. I never would have done that for another kid, well, maybe my own boys. He wasn't even baptized in the church, you know, cuz his mother thought he was gonna die right then when he was born. He was real small, like under five pounds. They called the priest in to do the baptism right there, didn't even wait for the father, my brother."

"So, your kids going to college?"

"Not as I know of."

"But you'd like 'em to."

"I don't wanna talk about them. How 'bout if I asked about your kids?"

Different than talking to Caje, Hal thought. He could tell Uncle was only going to talk what he felt like talking about, Caje, getting the Jeep back, maybe the weather. He wondered what the guy's name was, whether it was Yaqui-sounding like Caje'eme, but didn't ask. He pictured Caje sitting in a parked car and writing in a theme book, the cousins trying to get him to go someplace to sniff gasoline. Uncle's hair was straight and black and long, pulled back over the ears and held in a tail by a red band. He wondered if the guy would give a direct answer if he asked his name. Uncle--Uncle Remus, Uncle Sam, *Uncle Tom's Cabin*…say uncle. None of them seemed to fit. "Never had kids--always seemed like kind of a risky thing to do." He scanned the room, but nobody seemed to need a fresh drink. He looked at Uncle, waiting for him to say something.

"There's not many things riskier, I guess, but most guys don't know that when they get it all started."

Hal glanced at the hat and then looked at Uncle again. "Korean service ribbon. That was risky too, I reckon."

"Eighth Cavalry. There was a couple of us Yaquis signed up cuz we heard stories about them Navajo in the big war. We was too young for that one. Thinking we'd go to school to learn about codes. But instead, we wind up in Unsan with just a rifle."

"I heard something about Unsan."

"Yeah, you probably heard it wrong. That bullshit about losing our colors. We ran them Koreans all the way up north, was easy. Then come a goddamn jillion Chinese with their truck rockets. Cut us off on three sides, and we had to start falling back to the east. Then the ROK gave way, the bastards, and we was encircled. Dug in around the Nammyon. Couldn't even get resupply. We slaughtered Chinamen for three days and nights with their own ammo before command gives the word we should try to break out on our own. Sneaked out in squads, and half of 'em got captured."

"Nobody who knows anything ever believed that bullshit about losing your colors. Crazy talk, like you were some kinda horse brigade in the Civil War."

Uncle nodded. "Preciate that."

"Want a little something in that coffee? On the house?" Hal lifted his little glass of Wild Turkey from under the bar.

"No. Every drink I have tastes like more."

"Here's to the 8th anyway." He took the shot. A middle aged couple came in and sat down at the bar, and Hal moved away. When he turned, Uncle was gone.
*****

It was a Saturday in November when two deputies from the sheriff's office finally came to interview the bowling alley staff, in light brown shirts and black ties. The first news stories had already linked the accidental death of Tara Judd to the shooting death of one Horacio Antonio Barrera, who had been discovered by early morning hikers. The local papers theorized that the young woman had chanced upon the picnic table scene during the commission of a crime and had lost control of her vehicle in her terrified dash to escape. They referred to her repeatedly as the 'daughter of local businessman Wayne Judd.' After a few days some other details came out that didn't fit the original theory: the recently-fired Marlin revolver found downslope from Tara, the Jeep registration to one Francisco Martinez, Uncle Frank, a stolen Dodge Charger and its driver that had appeared at the crash scene, then disappeared, then reappeared at a Miracle Mile motel at a second murder scene...

The deputies came into the bar through the double glass doors, accompanied by Judd. One of them, the older one, stood with Judd just inside the doorway, the two of them talking a little but not looking at each other. The younger one walked around the bar, inspecting closely, as if he expected some evidence to jump out from one of the vinyl cushions. Hal thought he might have seen some too, if he would have just come in on the right Friday afternoon. He had neat black hair, looking like he'd just left the barber shop. He nodded at Hal and Gary behind the bar. Then the deputies went to Judd's office and started calling the staff in one at a time.

They called Gary first, and Hal wondered about the order. Alphabetical? Maybe--Gary was a Bingham. But after twenty minutes, they called Linda in--she was a Vargas. Then he wondered about the time--couldn't get much information in twenty minutes, and Linda's interview lasted forty-five, so maybe they'd asked who Tara had been chattiest with, flirtiest with, her favorite and least favorite co-workers and customers...

When Hal entered the office, the older deputy stood to greet him. "Hello, Mr. Mull, I'm Pete Caldwell." Hal shook his hand and looked at the name tag. "Go ahead and sit down, okay?"

The younger deputy didn't say anything. Hal said, "Sure," and sat in one of the leather-upholstered chairs facing Judd's desk. He told himself it was all right, that he knew when to stand a little apart from the exact truth, but pictures of Tara kept tugging at his memory, and he suddenly wanted to mourn out loud. He fixed his eyes on the brass star on Caldwell's shirt, higher than his heart, above his left pocket, and it made him think of Hicks's wound again. He counted the points on the badge--seven, which he thought was an odd number for a star. Five or six sure, but seven?

The older guy was taller than he'd originally thought, and older, probably in his early fifties, gray hair creeping into his mustache and hair. He handed Hal a business card then, and he thought it was strange that a sheriff's deputy would have a business card. It had the same seven-pointed star, and it said he was an *Investigator* with the *Pima County Sheriff's Department.* Near the bottom there was a motto, *Keeping the Peace Since 1865.*

"We're trying to piece together what happened the night that Miss Judd was killed."

Hal nodded. "Yeah, it's a shame."

"Let's start with your own knowledge of this girl. How well did you know her, exactly?"

"Oh, you know, she worked in the café most of the time when she was here, so I've known her since she started work here. So it's been a couple years." He noticed the younger deputy starting to take notes.

"Well, I'm sure it's a minor point, but I didn't mean how *long* you'd known her; I was trying to get at the nature of your relationship."

"I guess you'd say I was her boss. Me and Gary were supposed to keep her busy waiting tables and so forth, ever since Judd had her start coming in. But she didn't really take to getting bossed."

"Did you know her outside of work as well?"

"Well, when she moved into her apartment, I helped her move a couple of the bigger things--desk, bed and such."

Caldwell stared and nodded. Hal stared back but didn't nod.

"Any reason you did that?"

"She asked me to." He paused. "Well, actually, she asked if she could borrow my pickup, and I don't really let anybody else drive my pickup."

"Any other times?"

"Mmmm," he said, trying to look as if he was searching his memory, "Well, Judd used to bring her in once in a while before she worked here. You know, when she was younger." He wondered if saying 'well' so much was raising a flag for Deputy Caldwell.

"Any other times?"

So now it was time to trust Tara, which he did, and time to trust Caje too, which he was not sure of. And there were Tara's sunbathing neighbors and the wait staff at Mija's, that south-side restaurant, and perhaps a dozen others who had seen them together, people he didn't even remember, and he would just have to hope he hadn't made an impression on any of them. "No, that's it."

"Do you remember Miss Judd ever talking about things besides work? School... boyfriends...anything like that?"

"Sure. She liked to pass the time."

"With just you, or with other people too?"

"Me and Johnny, I guess. Maybe one or two of the waitresses." The young guy looked at a list of names then. For someone named John, Hal guessed. "John's his middle name. He doesn't like his first name. Heywood."

"I can see why," Caldwell said, smiling for the first time.

"Heywood Gale?" the younger guy asked. Hal nodded.

"What's this Heywood do here?"

He listened to the name, Heywood. "Funny how you guys always use the names nobody else ever uses. Johnny's the lead mechanic. He keeps all the pinsetters working. Does some other maintenance too. The air conditioners and what-not."

The young deputy staying with it then, the older one letting him, "How'd she come to be spending time with *him*?"

"We'd hit a slow patch in the bar, and I'd send her back there to see if Johnny needed a gopher or anything. Better'n letting Judd see her sitting at the bar."

"Her dad wouldn't like that?"

"He could get a little crossways with her, right after she first started anyway."

"Cuz she was underage and sitting there?"

"That too maybe, but he was a little upset with her anyways, to begin with, 'cause she got in a jam at school."

"What kinda jam?"

Hal shrugged his shoulders and said, "Beats me. You'd have to ask her dad. She got suspended for a while is all Judd told me."

"So you went outta your way to make sure she didn't get in trouble with her dad."

"If that's how you want to look at it."

The young deputy pressed, "Would you go outta your way to protect her from somebody else?"

Here we go, he thought, but he kept his voice low and spoke slowly. "You know, I've had a few speeding tickets 'cause I got kind of a lead foot, but once I got a ticket I didn't deserve. Fuckin' sheriff deputy pulls me over, Pinal County that time, just west of Superior, and says I passed across a double yellow line. I say to him, respectful and all, I thought it was okay long as I started the pass maneuver across a dashed line. He says, No, you came out across a double yellow, which was bullshit."

Both deputies stared at him.

"Reason I mention it is sometimes a deputy will get an opinion in his head, and once that opinion's out of his mouth, it's already a fact, leastways in that deputy's head, you know what I mean? Like that Pinal County son of a bitch writing me a ticket for something I woulda never done. So listen to my answer, okay? Yeah, I'd protect her. She was a teenage girl. Course I'd protect her."

Then the older deputy said, "Don't get worked up, okay? My partner didn't mean anything. She mention any names you remember? First names even."

"Not really. Names came up. People I wouldn't know though, Professor X and student Y. Don't remember."

"You must have met this Caje, yeah?" He was unbuttoning his shirt pocket and then reaching into it.

"Yeah. He came here to pick her up a couple times. The papers said you was looking for him, right? "

"The deputy showed him a photograph. "This the boyfriend?"

"Yup. Looks older than that tho. What's 'at, a school picture?"

"Mm-hmm."

"He's got a mustache now too, you know? And wears his hair long like the kids do these days."

"You know anything about this kid that would be helpful to us?"

"So you *are* looking for him, huh?" Hal watched the deputies, who were deadpanning it. He waited for a moment, but they still didn't bite. "Well, he's got an uncle came in looking for him…I guess 'cause the kid was using his Jeep. Did he ever come in trying to get it back? … Reason I ask is I told him it was probably in your impound, told him he should go see you guys. Did he get the Jeep back?" They didn't answer, but this time Hal waited longer.

"Yeah, we met the uncle."

"He get the Jeep back? Said it was his."

The older deputy nodded. "What you know about this Caje besides he has an uncle? Where he comes from, what he does, anything like that?"

"Just stuff she told me. Not much. Met him in high school. On the cross country team at the same time. Wanted to be a teacher, I think. Lived out on the rez."

"You ever meet any her other associates?"

"Associates?"

"Might be friends … might be people she was doing business with." The deadpan look from both of them.

"I'm not with you. Business?" Hal imitating the deadpan now.

Caldwell set out another photo. "Ever see this guy?"

This one was easy. Heavy-set Mexican guy, Lacho. "No, never saw that guy around. That's that dead guy, right? The one who got shot?" They waited without saying anything. "Same picture they ran in the papers. The picnic table guy, right?"

"Guy's name is Barrera. Name used to come up sometimes in drug investigations. Been arrested a couple times. Not a nice man. We're wondering if she might have had any contact with him."

Hal twisted his face into an are-you-nuts look and said, "Tara with that guy? Can't picture it." Probably overdoing it, he thought, but he shook his head anyway.

"Well, Mr. Mull, that's why we want to talk to this Caje'eme. We're wondering if he can picture it. He disappeared for *some* reason, partner."

Hal thought about telling them, Yeah, Goddamnit, the kid's got a hell of a head for imagining things, but didn't think it would be in anybody's interest. "Maybe you should ask one of Barrera's friends. You guys are right, they're looking for Caje too, don't you think?"

"Believe me, Mr. Mull we've been doing that when we could." He set out a photograph of Hicks. "You ever meet this man?"

He shook his head again. "Don't know him either." He wondered if any more pictures would come out of Caldwell's pocket, maybe a photo of the smaller man he'd seen from a distance near Ruby. He had a hunch he wouldn't see a picture of RJ.

"You're sure then. Never saw him with Miss Judd? Maybe picked her up after work once or twice? Came in for a cold one one time and chatted with her at the bar?"

"Not on my shift. I'd remember that. You ask Gary?"

"Mr. Mull, I'd appreciate you answering my questions without asking so many of your own." The look on his face was of a guy trying to restrain himself and not succeeding very well.

"I'm sorry. Have I been doing that?"

The young deputy said, "Like you're trying to change the subject." Caldwell gave him a look to silence him.

"Well, it's not the most pleasant subject. We all miss Tara."

"You mean everyone who worked with her?"

Hal nodded. "It's been real hard on Judd especially, her dad that is, even though he tries not to let it show." He thought a psychiatrist might say he was projecting, but he guessed the deputies weren't really here to shrink his head. "Judd has anything to say about it, somebody's gonna pay for his girl's life."

"Could be somebody already has." The three of them staring at each other again.

"Gotta be up front with you Mr. Mull, we're exploring a lot of possibilities here." He paused. "One possibility is that Miss Judd was involved in something illegal. And if that's true, then she had to be getting help from one or more of her friends, maybe this Caje fella, and maybe someone else besides. Was Miss Judd the kind of girl who might have had more than one boyfriend?"

"Never struck me that way."

"How about phone numbers and such? We been through her apartment, but we're wondering if she mighta had an address book around here we don't know about."

"I doubt it. I never saw one."

"Any chance this Caje fella ever left any hints about where he mighta gone off to? Something he mighta said or something she said?"

Hal shook his head.

"Somethin' you mighta forgot. How 'bout the uncle? He mention other places? Other relatives?"

"The kid's cousins, the uncle's own kids, out on the rez. But he never mentioned their names. Like I said, he was after the Jeep. That it was a CJ-2A."

There was another short silence. Then Caldwell said, "Okay, Mr. Mull. We appreciate your time. Hang onto the card I gave you, case you think of anything else."

"Will do," he said, standing. When he had opened the door to go out, he heard Caldwell call after him, "Oh, by the way, you got any travel coming up? Vacation or anything?" He turned and said, "I should be so lucky." Holding the doorknob and making eye contact.

"Reason I ask is we may need to talk to you again."

"People generally know where to find me, but I get out hunting now and again. Douglas or thereabouts. Like the bass bite at Parker too sometimes."

"You ever get to Patagonia? I like the largemouth fishing over there better."

"Hmm. Well, I did hear that they had opened that up to the public."

"Hell yes. It's been open for a few years now."

"Okay, well I'll give it a shot."

Hal was careful to time all the remaining interviews, though he didn't know what good it would do. Couldn't ask anybody else about their interview without getting Caldwell and the other guy wondering. His own visit with the deputies was about thirty minutes. Johnny's had gone for an hour, but then Johnny liked to talk. Chances are, he thought, that Johnny would yap away about his interview without any encouragement. All he had to do was wait.

Thirteen

Hal woke up, not groggy this time, but with his eyes alert and wide, knowing he would not sleep again. He remembered Tara, then Doris. He glanced at his silent alarm clock, wondering what had interrupted his sleep. Six o'clock, still dark. But then the telephone rang again and he reached for the receiver. Thinking it might be Judd, he made his voice crisp. "This is Hal," he said.

"Hey, buddy. You still in bed?" Johnny. The always-teasing tone, like What the hell you still in bed for?

He relaxed and talked low. "The goddamn middle of the night."

Johnny laughed. "Listen, Hal, I need you to come down and give me a hand this morning. The temp called in sick, and I still have some shit to do with a couple pinsetters."

"What's the big deal? Thought the tournament didn't start till tomorrow." He lay back on his forearm.

"Pro-Am starts today. C'mon, lazy-ass. Judd finally got the tour to come and put us on the map, and it's on us."

"You'll need to pick me up. Tore into my carburetor yesterday."

"Twenty minutes."

"Fuck you. Half an hour."

Johnny laughed again. "Jeez, Hal. You can go to hell for swearin' same as for lyin'. Say, is Doris awake?"

"No." He said, "She ain't here," thinking she wouldn't have heard the phone anyway.

"Hey, she was s'posed to have a list for me—confirmation for the amateurs—Batman said to get it from her. Did she go into work already?"

Johnny *had* to know the way things were now, Doris over at Judd's most of the time, but he guessed Johnny felt like he needed permission to know it. He said, "She was still thirsty when she left here, so she either raided the bowling alley bar, or she went over to Judd's house." Tried to make it sound casual.

There was silence in the earpiece for a moment. Then Johnny said, "Well," not quite stuttering. "Maybe down at the bowl then. Batman's still in Vegas."

He appreciated Johnny playing along, pretending. He wished she was there in the bed next to him. "Yeah, but I'd call Judd's first to make sure. And let the phone ring for a while. She couldn't be sober yet."

"Okay. I'll see you in a few minutes."

"Thirty minutes," Hal said and hung up. He sat up in his bed, scratching his chest and staring at the empty place in his bed, hoping that Johnny was right—that Judd was still out of town. That way at least she didn't sleep with him this time, he thought. But then, who am I to be jealous? Not exactly Romeo to her Juliet. "Poor screwed-up woman," he said quietly.

He sighed, slowly shaking his head and swiveling to plant his feet on the floor. He hung his robe over his shoulders and moved toward the tiny kitchen, thinking of how Doris would tease him about wearing it. Hell, it's cold.

He opened a cupboard to reach for the frying pan before remembering he had not washed it since using it the night before. He went to the stove, scraped opaque grease and hamburger bits from the pan with a spatula, spooned in some bacon grease and started frying two eggs. He broke the yolks with the spatula and tried to brush the yellow into a 'Z' the way Tara said she always did, because she wanted Zorros, not crybabies.

He cinched the robe around his waist. ... what little things make Judd think about her? And about Midge. Christ--losses like that, first your wife, him knowing I could've protected her and somehow not hating me for not doing it... and then your only daughter and not knowing about me having the chance to protect her too, and still not hating me, but hating pretty much everything else. Losing Midge had isolated Judd, but losing Tara had hardened him-- made him a hater.

He remembered when she'd given him the frying pans, saying they were an extra set from her "hopeless chest," to thank him for helping her move out, but no, more like to thank him for helping her defy her father. He wondered momentarily about the phrase she'd used, "hopeless chest"--was she being ironic about her prospects for marriage or her small bosom? He thought, if Judd had known about any of it, he would have just fired me.

He noticed the eggs were hard on the bottom, like leather, and turned them. "Terrific." ...Doris always got them just right, even when she was hung over ...was good to have her here, but impossible. "I'll leave you to your ghosts," she told him after she'd gotten her own apartment.

He finished frying the eggs, made toast and ate it like a sandwich, with milk because he'd forgotten to make coffee. He went to his bedroom and turned on the radio, listening to Loretta Lynn for a moment, nodding along with the steel guitar. He toggled a switch on a panel near the bed to turn on the speaker he'd put in the bathroom, and went there with clean underwear. He stepped into the shower and turned on the water, standing under the cold spray waiting for it to turn hot, letting it stream straight down through his short black hair.

He wondered if he had unlocked the door for Johnny. ...wouldn't want him to hear me talking to myself—he's got enough to tease me about...wonder why I do that...Probly do it more now Doris isn't around... He shrugged. ...really do miss her sometimes, like here in the shower. "I'll leave you to your ghosts," she had said, but I keep trying to understand it some other way. Things would be different about her too, if Tara were still alive, maybe living here, maybe drinking less. Maybe she blames herself for what happened to Tara, even though it made no sense, she was always ugly-mean to her, jealous of her…

He shook his head. …don't flatter yourself… she didn't like Tara because she knew Tara was just teasing me. But then he remembered the secret times with her, eating breakfast with her at Mija's, cutting flowers for her, keeping the cold grigio for her behind the bar, doing whatever she asked, her offering herself to him and his damnable self-control. So no; Doris *said* she resented Tara's teasing me like some poor bastard she was playing for tips, but what she really resented was she probably knew Tara *wasn't* teasing me. He remembered one time when Johnny had caught him staring at Tara as she walked away and said, "Would ya fuck her?" He'd said, "A little young for guys like us, eh?" Johnny had grinned and said, "I would. In a heartbeat."

Well then, maybe it's Doris's way of punishing Batman, she was calling him that too now, even though she was sleeping with him, blames him 'cause he was drunk and sent Midge to make the drop, wants to make him miserable…and me too, 'cause she thinks I must have been indecisive. Maybe Tara would have even agreed. What did she say? That I do what I do because of inertia…that my life could use a little disruption? Plenty of that now.

He assumed he would be getting another visit from Deputy Caldwell, but he didn't really have a feeling about whether they would be coming for him or not. He had been right about Johnny; once he got started talking about the interview, there was no stopping him: "Didja see the pictures of those mother fuckers got shot? Jesus, those two were a piece of work, specially the one. Asked me, for Christ's sake, if I ever ran into those guys. I said no, and I hope I don't either. That one guy looked like his daddy shorted him on chromosomes or something, like the human part got left out. You know the one I mean, he made the Mexican guy seem like Friar Tuck sending out vibrations of goodness and mercy. They musta asked you the same shit. Wanted to know if I ever seen either one of 'em with Tara. Fuck is the matter with those guys, they just got through asking me if I ever seen them before and I tell 'em no and then they asked me if I ever seen 'em with Tara. How the fuck, I said, could I see 'em with Tara when I never seen 'em at all." Hal laughed at the way he told it.

I think too much …that's what Doris says……makes me too careful. Johnny thinks I read too much—sure isn't his problem—he gets a notion, he just does it…says whatever pops into his head…be easier sometimes, for sure. Water under the bridge, water under the bridge. I keep telling myself it's water under the bridge, but if I'd gone sooner, followed them to the drop…or maybe the day before done something smarter…

*****

When he was dry, he went back to his bedroom and snapped himself into a yoked shirt and pulled on his jeans and boots. Stuffing a bow tie into his pocket, he heard Johnny come in. He moved toward the front room with his hat in his hand. "How ya doin', Boss? You get your list?"

"Yeah, I got it. Took Doris like ten minutes to answer the door, but her car was out front, so I kept ringing the bell."

The answer was obvious, but Hal let it out of his mouth anyway. "Over at Judd's?"

Johnny nodded. He said, "She says that Indian kid is around too."

"Caje'eme?" His face creased. "Well, shouldn't be a big deal. Cops are still looking for him--Probly run him in before long." But there was an edge to his voice. "Shit, I thought we'd never see that guy again."

"Yeah, Well, Doris is pretty worked up about it. He wants to have a sit-down with Batman. 'at's why he's back."

"A sit-down!"

"Yeah. Thinks he can clear things up with a talk." He chuckled. "I always thought that kid was on peyote."

Hal wrinkled up one side of his face and scratched his head. "He just doesn't understand Judd."

Johnny shrugged. "I'm just tellin'ya what Doris told me. He told her he needs purification." He lips turned up when he said 'purification,' mocking. "Been through some kind of a ceremony while he was in Mexico."

He asked, "What kind of shape was she in?"

"Goddamn, she looked sorry. I thought she'd quit last night when you took her home. When did she leave?"

He felt his face redden. "Yeah, I shoulda never let her drive." He put on his hat and said, "I gotta call Mrs. Thadbury and tell her I can't take her to church this morning." He sat and picked up the receiver.

"Church? Has she still got you doing that? It ain't even Sunday." He leaned against the wall, watching Hal dial. "Hey, when is she gonna get you a Twentieth Century phone?" He chuckled again.

"...can't make it today... yeah, sorry. They need me down at the bowling alley...we'll go together on Sunday...Yeah, light a candle for me. Thanks..."

"Okay, let's go." He moved to the door.

"Hey, Hal, is she Cath'lic or somethin?"

"Yeah." Outside, the desert sun angled onto them, gathering heat.

"Remember when my cousin talked me into goin' to one of his revival meetings with him, and you went along?" He didn't wait for an answer. "I figured that gave you about all the religion you could stand." They went down the stairs toward Johnny's truck.

"Yeah, I reckon that's about right," Hal said. "Reminded me of the stuff I used to go to with my aunt up at the ranch. People shouting amen half the time and standing there with their arms spread out. Like they were inviting the Spirit. Henrietta sure wanted me to get the Spirit. Never felt it though. But I started going with Mrs. Thadbury when her son left for college and, I don't know, I kind of like it. Brings her peace anyways."

"Say, do them Cath'lic preachers really go in a little booth and listen to all the stuff you been doin' wrong? That must be hard to do 'thout telling your friends and whatnot--about people's drinking and slippin' around, I mean."

"Don't know."

"Say, what kinda things you s'pose your landlady's got to go tellin' a preacher?"

"I don't know. Her priest never told me. How ya like the new truck?" He glanced at his own Dodge, thinking that he still had to put it back together. "Next truck I get, I gotta get air conditioning."

"Yeah. Whyn't ya get one that runs first?" He laughed.

Hal wanted to hear more about Doris, so he said, "So she was hung over?"

"Huh? Who?" Johnny's face tightened. "Oh—Doris! Yeah, no shit! She looked about half-dead."

Hal frowned. "Well, that's good in a way," trying to sound casual again, "At least she didn't drink all night."

Johnny drove south along the curbless street, passing open stretches of desert and a hodgepodge of low concrete block buildings set like outposts amid the creosote and desert broom—the new Canyon Bank branch, Diego's Overtime Tavern, Buddy's Barber Shop, Dunham's nursery, the Wongs' little market...

Johnny pulled in at Burke's Honk 'n' Go and eased up to the Esso pumps. "Twenty-cent gas today. I'll take some of that." He smiled sidelong at Hal, hopped from the truck and trotted inside to pay. Hal got out and started to pump the gasoline.

"Stop at three," Johnny said when he trotted back.

Hal watched the dials spin on the pump and slowed as it reached the three dollar mark. "So what else did she say about Caje?"

"Not much. Came there in his Jeep lookin' for Judd. Didn't you say that it b'longed to his uncle? She heard it comin' way off and knew it was him from the sound. Still ain't fixed that muffler, I guess."

Hal did not answer, wondering how he'd got the Jeep back. They climbed back into the truck and continued south. There were new homes on their right and untouched desert on their left, the city spreading east toward the Rincons. After a couple of lights they turned west.

"I guess he hung around and had coffee. She told him it was a bad idea. Looking for Judd, that is."

"Coffee? She needed a bloody Mary, more like."

"Yeah, I think she was puttin' something in it. Hair of the dog."

Hal wondered if Johnny knew how often she went to Judd's now. "Sometimes she gets to wanting a drink about two or three in the morning and heads out."

"Jesus, that could drive a guy to the poorhouse. Don't buy any."

"I never buy vodka, but she brings along a pint or two in her purse...leaves when she runs out. Doesn't even sleep sometimes.

"Ya gotta keep her busy all night." Johnny smiled.

Hal shook his head and forced a smile. "So why the change in Caje you s'pose? I mean why you s'pose he's even back?"

"Mentioned a sweat lodge. I thought them Yaquis was all Cath'lics, carryin' they statues on Easter, but there you go. Well, maybe he'll get tired of hangin' around and head back out to the rez."

"Yeah, like hell," Hal said. "You ever read about them Yaquis? Used to sit behind a bush all day, waitin' for one clear shot at a soldier.   And Judd's only s'posed to be gone one more day. He ain't gonna miss this tournament after all he went through to get them pros here. So what was Doris tellin' you all this for?"

"Worried, I guess. Or just running her mouth about problems the way women do. I dunno."

They were silent for a moment. The new truck smoothed out most of the bumps in the asphalt. My Dodge would be shaking apart, Hal thought. "Didn't you tell me he jumped Caje once?"

"Yep, for jackin' stuff outta cars, like always. But ya gotta believe the kid, I think, said he was just cuttin' through the parking lot. That was before Caje and Tara hooked up. Few years back," Johnny said.

"Judd sure screwed the pooch trying to break them up. Hell, if he'da stayed out of it, she probably woulda got tired of him on her own." It was a theory he'd considered lately. "I figured she just took up with him 'cause he was another guy the old man wouldn't like." He was thinking, I was too old for her but maybe she felt different about me.

"Everybody coulda seen it 'cept Judd."

"Just wanted to get the old man's attention."

"Well, she always had that. I reckon she liked the idea of it too—being with an Indian. She had that one black boyfriend, 'member? Hell, if most of them Indian gals weren't so damned fat, I'd be chasing 'em too. I wonder what Indian pussy is like." Johnny sighed, like he was trying to imagine it. "Tara was always so damn nice, you know. She used to bring me beers when I was fighting the pinsetters in back."

"It was always fun her sitting and talking with me at the bar when things were slow. Seemed like she mostly told me the sad shit though."

Johnny mimicked his voice, "...she mostly told me the sad shit." He chuckled and steered through the bowling alley parking lot and rolled to a stop in a space near the employee entrance. As they climbed out of the truck, he asked, "Didja have breakfast?"

"Yeah. Watcha still need to do?"

"Polishing and pinsetter work."

Johnny unlocked the thick wooden door, and they went straight to his little foreman's office where Johnny punched in the two time cards. They walked to the end of the row of lanes and turned left and moved single file down the narrow corridor that led to the service hall door. Johnny called it 'thunder hall.'

"Why don't you check out the decks down on twenty-nine and thirty? I think they got too much tilt. I got some bearing work here on number two."

"Sure," Hal said, "by the way, what would you do if I didn't know anything about these things?" He grabbed a tool tray from the shelf and walked down the hall. Setting the tray on the floor next to the machine numbered thirty, he took off his shirt and hung it on a broom end nearby. He checked the switches on the machine, pulled out the fuse retainer to make sure it would not come on and raised the guard panel. At least we don't need ear plugs, he thought.

He squatted and duck-walked partway in, staring at the hard maple deck, remembering the last time he had helped Johnny in the hall. ...she was alive then...wished I was young enough for her sometimes...maybe that would have changed things...

He backed out and retrieved a screwdriver and socket wrench from the tool tray. Squatting back under the lifted guard, he could almost hear her voice when they had joked about being lovers: "We'd never make it, Hal. You're too much of a shitkicker for me." And then there was her laugh—the soft cotton of it. ...yeah, a shitkicker surrounded by bowlers, drunks and city cowboys... her funeral had come a few months later.

He sighed, backing out of his crouch within the machinery, he lowered the guard panel.

After an hour, Johnny said it was time for coffee. "How you doin' down there?" Johnny asked as he walked behind Hal on the corridor next to the lanes.

"I got one of 'em so far. Is the coffee shop open already?"

"Every morning at six-thirty. At least this week for the tournament. And afterward, Batman thinks he can get a few guys on their way to work out south."

They were the first two customers in the coffee shop. The waitress poured coffees and asked, "Cream?" She was a dark-skinned Latina with a thick middle.

"Sweetie, you know I like my coffee the way I like my lovers—dark brown and full bodied." He watched her.

She looked at him but moved off without a comment.

"Hey Linda, how 'bout a doughnut?"

"You going to pay for it?" She did not turn.

"Put it on Judd's bill, sweetie." He sipped. "Christ, that tastes good."

"Yeah, no kidding."

The waitress was returning with two doughnuts, half-wrapped in paper napkins. She glared at Johnny, dropped them in the middle of the table and moved away again.

"What, no jelly-filled?" He watched her again. "You know how I like it with jelly in the hole." When she did not react, he said to Hal, "I am gonna get some of her some time."

Hal looked out the window as cars streamed past. "Ya know, one thing I like about bein' a bartender is that I usually don't have to get up so damn early to go to work.

Johnny chuckled. "At's why I always call you when I need a hand. You need reminding that you're just like the rest of us poor slobs."

"Hey you freeloaders," the waitress called, "since you're getting' everything for free, why doncha spring for a couple quarters in the juke box."

Hal pulled change from his pocket and fed the coin slot of the selector at the table. He pressed D9 for "The Hungries" by Buck Owens and A13 for Johnny Cash's "I Walk the Line."
"Whatcha wanta hear?" he called to her.

She strode back and slid in next to Hal in the booth to leaf through the selector, making it obvious she wouldn't sit next to Johnny. The pages clicked.

"Plenty o' room over here," Johnny said.

She smiled and kicked him under the table. "You forgettin' that ring boy?" She punched buttons. The Buckaroos crooned about their old two-button suit.

"It comes off pretty easy," Johnny said.

She finished with the buttons and slid away again. "Hmmph!"

"Playing hard to get," Johnny chucked. "Hey, I meant to ask you. I'm goin' down to Sasabe to look at a piece of land after the tournament. I thought maybe you could get off a couple days and go with. Maybe raise a little hell."

Hal shook his head, half smiling. "Sasabe—there's nothin' there but a bar. Besides, last time we went border hopping, I almost got to leakin' blood."

"Those bastards. I still think they all needed their faces rearranged a little. Teach 'em some manners. 'sides, it makes for a good laugh now."

The smile was still on his face, but Hal had never been able to laugh about their last trip south of the border—the five hard-faced Mexicans surrounding them, smelling of sweat and mescal, the silence that hung in the air with the dismal smoke, waiting for Johnny to strike with his coiled fist, thinking he would never back down, vaguely sensing it wouldn't be just fists, speaking softly, "John, time to leave." Silence and smoke hung in the tension. "John, let's go." Swallowing hard, Johnny finally uncoiled and said, "Yeah, I hear ya," staring at the brown face in front of him. And seeing him lower his head finally, turning away. Feeling the tension ebb back a notch, hoping that was enough for the Mexicans, waiting for Johnny to lead the way out of the cantina, praying there would be no taunt to reignite Johnny. Then they were outside, feeling the night air, and his own heart was slowing, but sensing Johnny's anger at him now.

"Well, maybe I got a real customer now," the waitress said. She was looking out the window into the parking lot.

Johnny and Hal turned and looked through the glass and saw Caje'eme climbing out of his Jeep and moving toward the café door. The Jeep's front fender and bumper were still twisted, and they could see the bullet hole in the windshield.

Caje'eme couldn't see inside through the café windows, but he smiled and waved at the two men when he came inside and saw them in their booth. He sat with them, and the waitress brought him a cup of coffee, glancing at Caje'eme and then staring at Hal.

"Is Judd…is Mr. Judd going to be here?"

"No," Johnny said, "He won't be back—not today at least. What you need to see him for?"

"I need to talk to him. About Tara. About what happened."

"Let it go, Caje. It won't do no good," Johnny said. Hal listened, wondering what he would tell the police about the Dreamland.

"Can't." He looked into the mug of coffee as if he were reading it. "I just...need to talk it out with him. I knew it in the Temescal."

"Temescal--What the hell is that?" Johnny said.

Hal shook his head.

"Listen, Caje—let us talk to him first, at least," Johnny said.

Hal's narrowed his eyes at Johnny. Us?

"You are not part of it, Mr. Gale."

Meaning I am part of it, Hal thought, wondering if Johnny would take it the same.

"C'mon, Caje. You know how he is. People don't call him Batman for nothing. He still sets up on the roof looking for thieves."

"I have to own it--what happened to her. I wasn't driving, but without me, it wouldn't have happened." He looked at Hal, who was still shaking his head, and scratching at his scalp now. Then he said again, "You are not part of it."

Hal said, "We're *all* part of it. It's part of *us*." It was silent for a moment. Then he said, "You might be ready to say you're sorry, but he isn't ready to hear it. You go see him when he's had a couple drinks, and there's no telling what'll happen. You need to forget about this apology stuff or whatever it is and get back to the rez. Better yet Mexico."

"I need him to understand. It's the only way."

Hal knew he had not made a dent. He looked for grief in the Indian boy's face, thinking there was none, and wondering if the spirit he'd met in the Temescal had made him forget what Tara was supposed to have meant to him, remembering that Caje used to have her, and knowing now he'd always wanted to.

"Well, that's all very nice," Johnny said. "But you know just as damn well that Batman ain't gonna listen to anything you say. You'll just stir up something that's over and done with."

No, Hal thought, it was never really done with. Blankly watching Johnny and Caje as they moved their lips, he quit listening. After a few minutes, Caje'eme left.

"Hell," Johnny said, "what a time for that kid to show up." He gulped his coffee.

Hal sipped from his mug. "That sure tasted better when it was hot."

"Yeah, before that crazy Indian came in." He watched through the window as Caje's Jeep left the parking lot. "We should think of a way to get rid o' him before Batman comes back."

They had not heard the waitress approaching the table, and they turned when they heard her voice. "He might be back already." She was holding out the cash register receipt for Johnny's signature, smiling, expecting a tease from him.

Johnny ignored the receipt and the smile. "How do you know?"

"He called first thing this morning. I thought he was checking to see if we'd opened up, but he wanted to know if you had gotten some list or other. Sorry. Shoulda told you."

"You sure it wasn't long distance?" Johnny said.

"Oh yeah," she said, waving the receipt at him, "it was long distance. But he was just getting his plane fueled up to come home. 'bout seven o'clock."

"Well now, this should be interesting." Johnny signed the receipt and they stood. Silently, they walked back to the hall. Hal walked toward his tool tray while Johnny pulled out the wax and buffing machine. He hung up his shirt again and set to work on the next pinsetter. He raised the guard and slipped under with a wrench in his hand, thinking about Tara and Caje, Doris, Johnny and the way he always says what's on his mind, even to Judd…gets away with it 'cause Judd needs him back here.

The wrench slipped, and he felt pain in his hand. He set it down and watched the blood ooze out on his knuckles and licked it away.   …bartenders are easy to replace, but not bowling alley mechanics…or maybe I just don't have the cojones…

Fourteen

When noon came, Hal was in the lounge, taking glasses out of a dish strainer and drying them and setting them in neat rows on the shelf above the counter. The bar was long and straight, with stools for thirty drinkers. There was a lunch crowd now, sitting at the booths and tables, eating griddle-fried burgers or pastrami sandwiches and fries from plastic baskets—airmen, carpenters and drywall hangers wearing sweat and dust, three deputies sitting together in a booth, a few ranchers. Linda and a chubby woman hustled between them and the kitchen. Hal wondered if Judd would make Doris put on an apron and help them. He wondered if she would be sober enough. There were bowlers too, and bowling fans, seated sparsely at the bar, or out in the alley, bowling on the end lanes or claiming seats in the temporary bleachers. Contestants were checking lockers and inspecting lanes and bowling practice games.

Hal put up the last few glasses and leaned against the bar, looking into the bowling alley itself, listening to the intermittent clank and crash of the contained collisions of balls with pins, thinking that it was going to be a long, tiring shift. He looked over at the little stage where the Mavericks' amplifiers and drums stood in a jumble around the microphone. He wondered if there was a way to hook their equipment into his sound board behind the bar so that he could control the volume....turn it down a little at a time, and they might not notice...damn amps.

Natural light poured in suddenly from the door to the parking lot, penetrating the dark moodiness of the barroom for a moment. Hal turned and squinted into the frame of light and saw a woman's silhouette. When the door eased closed, he could see that it was Doris. She took a stool near Hal.

"Well, it looks like you could use another customer." She was wearing tear-shaped pilot's sunglasses.

He waited for a moment to pass, measuring his silence. He could not remember the last time she had come alone to the lounge while he was working. "How are you?" His voice was soft and even.

"You really want to know?" She sat straight and careful on the stool. Her face seemed blue in the thin lounge light except for dull dark rings below the glasses, partially hidden with makeup.

"Need a drink?" he asked.

"You're still crooning the same song, aint't ya, Hal." Her sunglasses stared at him. "But yeah, I can use a drink.Vodka."

"Tonic?"

"Just a twist. Very little ice."

He mixed it and brought her the glass. She had set her sunglasses down on the bar. He could see redness in her eyes and the dark rings. They swelled puffily, like a frog, he thought. "You feeling all right?"

She smirked. "I'm feeling just fine."

So don't tell me, he thought. "Some night you're gonna get in a damned wreck driving home like you did last night."

She chuckled lightly. "Home? I guess I don't know what that is any more."

An aching swelled up within him. He felt his face flushing, and he was glad for the dim bar light. He scratched at his scalp. "Just want you to be safe is all."

The little smirk left her face, and her eyes narrowed. She drew a gasp as if she were about to say something, but then just held it for a moment and let it out. Her eyes widened again. "It don't matter. Did Johnny tell you Caje's back?"

"Yeah. Me and Johnny talked to the kid this morning too. I s'pose Judd knows he's here." It was a question.

She nodded. "What's he gonna do?" She reached out suddenly and touched Hal's shirt sleeve.

He wanted to touch her hand, but he did not. "Who? Johnny?"

"Caje."

"I don't know. Johnny tried to talk him out of coming around, but you know how it is." He felt her fingers let go of his shirt and draw back across his hand to her drink. He watched her sip.

"It was before we knew Judd was back, so we just sorta let him leave."

"Maybe if you were there with them…" She frowned at him. "Or Johnny."

His face flushed again, and he picked up a towel and wiped it through his hair. "Probably wouldn't do no good. They're bound to meet up eventually, 'specially if Caje is looking for it." He wondered why she had come. …Caje or her and me?…you thought you could handle Judd, his anger… "Where's Judd now?" …why the worry over Caje?...you used to call him Tonto and ask where the Lone Ranger was…because he liked Tara…everybody liked Tara…

"I left him at home." She stared at him. "At *his* house."

"*Home*. You don't have to dance around it." He looked hard at her, wondering if she was trying to apologize or if she wanted him to come to the rescue.

"Don't flatter yourself. I ain't dancin'." Her eyes flashed at him. "What are you gonna do? Is Johnny looking for him?"

"Like I said, no point in it."

"So you don't do nothing?" She drew her eyes away from him and raised the glass to her lips. She swigged this time. "Judd'll be looking. And if he can't find him, he'll come here and wait."

"Well, maybe you can keep Judd away then. Stall him so Johnny and me can head the kid off and make him see how it is."

She raised her voice. "You son of a bitch. You was always ready to go run and help *her*. You gotta do something now. What are you waiting for?"

"I'm sorry," he said softly. "There's nothing to be done." He reached to touch her face.

She lurched back, her eyes flashing again. "I don't even know why the hell I'm here," she sobbed. "I might as well be talking to my vodka glass." She was off the stool now, backing away. "What does it take to make you mad, anyway?"

A group of three businessmen at the bar stopped talking and stared.

She turned and went out the door to the parking lot. Hal moved down the length of the bar, lifted the gate and followed her. When he swung the door open, he saw her Cadillac pulling onto the street. He stood for a moment holding the door open, his eyes hurting in the brightness and squinting after her. Then he sighed and stepped back inside, letting the door close out the Arizona light. Aware of the eyes on him, he looked at the two waitresses, who continued to hustle for the lunchtime crowd. He moved back behind the bar, wondering if Doris would come back and this time talk to Johnny. To the three businessmen, he said, "Need another beer?"

Unlike most days it picked up after the lunch hour passed. The crowd grew and the noise surrounded Hal, growing in a disharmony of voices and laughs—drink calls louder than the rest, with juke box music twanging, the low consistent rumbling of heavy balls on lacquered hardwood lanes and the intermittent explosion of pins. He poured drinks automatically, smiling mechanically when customers spoke to him, just nodding to the waitresses. Hal was glad for the noisy chaotic camouflage.

…the way she touched my hand… the way it used to be when she was staying with me…could it be that way again?…the tears… gotta remember Doris chose Judd…had me and went with him… so that's what she wants, and what if I leave?…new job, new life…run cows for Johnny in Sasabe…would she really quit him?…go with me?…or maybe Caje spills it all to the cops and I don't get to make those choices…

"Hey, Hal, where's that pitcher!" Linda glared at him. "You tryin' to kill my tips?"

He stepped to the tap and twirled a pitcher into place. "Coors?"

"A-One."

He tipped the pitcher and filled it.

The camouflage seemed to disappear when Caje arrived. About an hour had passed since Doris left. As soon as Caje came in, Hal realized he was only pretending he had some cover with all the noise. Caje came in through the parking lot door and sat down right away in a stool at the bar. He was wearing a white tunic that lapped over his white trousers, with a belt at the waist. He stared at Hal from the far end of the bar, obviously there to meet Judd or wait for him. As Hal moved toward him, he thought about carding him and sending him away. Wouldn't do any good, he thought, the kid would just hang out in the café or maybe outside, waiting for Judd.

"Whatcha need?" he said.

"Draft beer would be fine," Caje said. He looked thinner, especially in the face, so even with the mustache he didn't look owlish. He sure as hell is the only guy in here dressed all in white though.

Hal nodded and moved off and brought him a Coors in a Pilsner glass and set it on a coaster. "He's still not here, you know."

"I figured. I can wait." Hal wondered if it was the Temescal sweating that had made him look so thin.

When Gary arrived, it was late afternoon and the Mavericks' manager had finished setting up their equipment. The pace slowed for him, and he thought about slipping back to the hall or using the phone to see what Johnny would think about involving the police. But he figured he already knew, and he kept pouring drinks.

The house phone rang and Hal answered.

"Hal? It's Johnny. Can you bust away for a second?"

"Sure. Gary's here. Whatcha need?"

"Hey pour me a beer, will ya?"

"Okay. Want me to bring it back there?"

"Nah, I'll come get it. This junk is all working fine right now. Did Doris talk to you before? She just called me back here raving about Batman—even called him Batman."

"Yeah, she came in a while back. Was she drunk?"

"I don't think so. All worked up though. Talking about calling the sheriff. Wanted to know if I'd found the kid yet. I'll be up there in a minute."

The phone came down abruptly in Hal's ear. He hung up and started filling two of the chilled mugs with A-1. He looked down at Gary at the end of the bar, wondering what Johnny was thinking.

"Quite a crowd you got."

Hal turned his head and looked at the man who had spoken. He set the beers down beside the tap. The man was in a dark suit, slim with dark features, alone at the bar, sipping at his whiskey. "Yeah. It's the tournament."

"Bowlers any good?"

"PBA. Supposed to be some of the best, yeah." Hal forced himself to chat. "Gonna stick around and watch?"

"I don't know," he shrugged. "Never been much for bowling, but looks like the crowd might be fun. Is the band any good?" He tilted his head toward the stage.

"They're okay. It gets kinda loud in here with the amps." He glanced at the door just as Johnny entered. He nodded toward an open booth when Johnny looked at him. "Scuse me, fella."

Hal took off his apron and called to Gary, pointing to himself. "Going on break," he mouthed. Gary didn't like it, never liked it. He picked up the two beers and carried them to the booth where Johnny was sitting. "What's up?"

Johnny took a gulp of beer. "Damn, I'm thirsty. Your girlfriend is crazy, you know that?"

"Yeah, but she ain't my girlfriend anymore."

"Well she's crazy, but she's right. She said Judd's headed down here with his rifle. We gotta have a plan for tonight in case Caje shows up."

"Didn't you notice? Look down the end of the bar."

"Fuckin' fabulous," he said when he saw Caje. He took another gulp of the beer. "How long's he been here?"

"An hour I guess." Johnny looked at him. He felt like he had to explain. "Figgered if they're going to meet up, it's better right here than out in the parking lot or something. Doris was in earlier, before she called you I guess. You know, worried about what would happen. I guess she wanted to see what we were going to do. Cussed me." He sipped.

"Well, I got an idea if he does." He looked straight into Hal's eyes.

…same look he had in that greasy Mexican bar…

"We gotta be ready." His eyes never moved or flickered. "I need you on this."

"Waddya need me to do?"

"Not much of a plan but it's all we got, I guess. We're gonna get the guns from him. Maybe it gets him to give it a second think.

So first, let me know when he gets here. He'll go to his office, right?"

"Yeah, 'less he sees Caje first."

"Yeah, but he won't do nothing in front of the crowd. So we go in together and talk to him. You need to get over on his right side though."

"We're gonna talk?"

"Yeah, but you know how that'll go. No, we gotta take those guns from him—his colt and his ought-six. Might take some persuading…"

Hal didn't say anything.

"Don't worry. I'll do it. You just back my move when he gets tough." His eyes didn't waver. "We're doing him a favor." Like he figured Hal wouldn't have the nerve on his own, and Hal knew that's what he meant. For a few seconds, he wanted to tell Johnny about the Dreamland, wondered if he'd even believe it, but he let the urge pass. Johnny said, "Besides, he's gotta know he won't get this tournament again if something happens to screw it up. Maybe he'll understand that and we won't have to do anything but talk."

"Yeah." Hal sipped. "Maybe if we make him see that…"
*****

Judd cursed mildly when he saw that his reserved parking spot was taken, then idled his way through the rows of parked cars until he found a spot for his wide-bed dually. It's already a big crowd, he thought, glancing at his wrist watch—seven o'clock. He got out of the truck and looked at the sky. The sun had disappeared behind the low western hills over an hour before, and the crescent moon had already risen well above Mica Mountain in the east. The neon Saguaro Bowl sign beamed into the darkness. The message read, 'FIRST ANNUAL PBA PRO-AM--7:30.' First annual, he thought, let's hope so.

He lifted his Springfield 30-0-6 off the rack behind the seat and held it in his left hand as he locked the driver's side door with his key. The rifle felt good in his hand, and he rotated it up and aimed momentarily at the moon, then lowered it and cradled it in his elbow and walked back toward the bar entrance.

There was the noise, the crowd, the drinks, but Hal thought mainly about what Johnny had said last, Call me on the house phone when Batman comes in. Maybe another hour had passed from the time Johnny had gulped down the last of his draft and headed for the mechanical rooms. A couple of the Mavericks had come in, but they weren't even tuning their guitars yet. Now Judd was walking across the open floor and along the bar, carrying the long-barreled ought-six in his left hand and crooked into his elbow, the tip of the gun barrel about a foot above Judd's head the way he carried it, and anyone in the bar who was looking that way could see it. Judd looked ahead though, catching Hal's eyes at first, then ignoring him and heading for his office. He didn't see the bar customer dressed all in white, and with his back to the door, Caje didn't see Judd until he'd half-crossed the room. Hal watched them both. Judd kept walking, pretending it was an everyday thing, carrying the rifle in that way with most of the bar patrons staring and wondering about it. Caje had been sipping a second beer, but he stiffened when he finally recognized Judd from behind.

Judd walked all the way across the lounge to the door that led down the hallway to his office. Turning, he leaned against the door and turned the knob with his right hand, still pretending he was invisible to the staring crowd, and keeping the ought-six in front of him as he did, too fixed on pretending he was invisible to recognize Caje. Or at least that's what Hal figured. He stepped through the door and disappeared into the hallway, and Hal lifted the receiver on the house phone and set it down on the counter and pressed the square button for the mechanical room. When the button started flashing, Hal set the receiver down and turned around again.

One of the waitresses was leaning against the bar at the service area trying to get Hal's attention, but he didn't even look at her. He was aware of Caje off to his right, still sitting at the bar perhaps but probably about to get up and follow. And off to his left was the doorway to Judd's office. Time to make him see the sense of it, he thought.

Hal put a towel over his shoulder and stepped back to the house phone, the extension button not flashing anymore, and hung it up. He went to the register and reached under it and pulled out the Beretta and pushed it into his pocket as far as he could, wondering who would notice. First, you got a crazy bastard parade through, holding a rifle up like it's a flag, and now you got a second crazy bastard going around with a pistol grip sticking out of his pocket. One more gun in here and we can scare off *all* the customers. He

walked the length of the bar and lifted the gate and followed Judd
through the same door. In the hallway, he turned and looked back
toward the bar, his foot holding the door. Waiting on Johnny now,
he saw Caje rising from the bar stool to follow. Well, Johnny gets
here in time or not, but either way.

He'd already pulled his foot away when he saw Johnny
coming straight for him, biting on a toothpick, and he pushed the
door open again. When Johnny came inside and the door closed
completely, Hal set the deadbolt. He waited for Johnny to pass him
and lead the way down the hallway before he pulled the Beretta out,
flicked the safety off and stuffed it into his rear pocket, where it
could be extracted easier.

*****

Judd said, "What's up with you two?" He was standing
behind his desk, where the ought-six was lying. There were three
five-round stripper clips next to it. Now he looked hard, at Johnny
and then at Hal and then back at Johnny, who stopped just inside the
door.

Hal didn't say anything, but he didn't stop, edging over to the
right of Judd's desk.

Judd said, "Hey, what's wrong with you. You never seen a
rifle before?"

Hal said, "Yeah, we seen rifles before. But not since we
went turkey hunting. You kinda made a commotion coming in here
through the bar like that."

Judd shrugged a little and made a what-the-hell gesture with
his hands. "They'll get over it. They're here for the tournament."

Johnny, leaning on one of the chairs that faced Judd's desk,
looked at him with hard eyes, expectant. He said, "Like you said,
you need them to come back *after* the tournament, Judd. What are
you up to with that Springfield?"

Hal didn't say anything. It didn't seem there was anything to
say that would help. Judd's face was setting harder with every
second that passed, and Johnny was acting as if Hal wasn't even
there. Johnny would make his move and Hal could just stand there
and watch for all he cared. And now, Judd was straightening up, no
longer thinking about the Springfield, and he was resting his hand on
his belt an inch or two from the Trooper, daring Johnny to say some
more or to make his move. He wouldn't shoot him; that part of it

was bluff. What he would do is jerk the Trooper out and club Johnny's head with it. Judd said, "Maybe you ought to think about getting back to work and minding your own business." What Hal had to do, and right away, was to figure a way to get around the desk and neutralize Judd's right hand before the Trooper cleared its holster. He slipped his hands into his rear pockets, thumbs hooked outside, wondering if it looked natural. The pocket gun was there under his right hand now.

The phone rang, and Johnny said, "That'll be Gary calling to tell you Caje wants to see you. How 'bout we put away all the cannons now and give him a listen." He stood straight up and began to inch his way around the chair toward the desk. "You musta walked right past him when you came in through the bar. If it's anybody else, you can just tell them you're tied up right now." He rolled the toothpick across his upper teeth with his tongue.

Judd let the phone ring. He said, "It'd be stupid for you to get mixed up in this, Gale. And you come any closer, you're gonna get a Colt sandwich." His hand went to the Trooper, and Johnny stopped. The phone stopped ringing, but then it started again, and Judd pressed a button on the phone. "Yeah?"

The bar noises surrounded Gary's voice, but it was still easy to make out what he was saying. "Hal back there with you?" Wondering first where the other bartender was. Judd said, "Yeah, but he's finished. He'll be right out." Then Gary's voice again, "Hey Judd, there's a guy here asking to see you. Young guy. Already told him you were busy but he asked me to check with you anyways." And then Judd, "Yeah, Hal's gonna unlock the door when he goes back to work." He rotated his head then, like a hawk, without twisting his body and still squared up on Johnny. And then, like Judd's answer wasn't enough, Gary said, "Well, can you ask him to hurry it up? We're getting behind." Never one to overdo it. Judd told him he was sorry, that Hal had just made a mistake, still looking at him, and Johnny edged forward. Judd said, "He thought I called him back when I didn't, I guess. Must've been he got mixed up from all the noise out there. Or he listens to the wrong people." Hal thought maybe Judd was right. He'd listened to Judd and Doris and Johnny, plus the army recruiter and the cousins way back when. But then maybe not. There was Tara… Johnny was close to the desk now, looking like he was about to reach down for the rifle.

Hal said, "Maybe I've listened to you too long." He watched Judd's eyes narrow, watched him punch the button on the phone to hang up.

Judd said, "You need to get your ass out there behind the bar."

Johnny stood in front of the desk now, upright, looking like he was where he wanted to be now, taking his time. Hal had dropped his eyes to the desk, pretending to look at the Springfield lying there. Judd still had his eyes on Hal, expecting him to start moving toward the door. "You ever use an ought-six like this, Hal?" Johnny said.

It caught him by surprise. He'd been thinking that Johnny would take control of the rifle just then, while Judd was still trying to run Hal out of the room with his eyes. Now both of them looked at Johnny for a moment. Hal said, "No, never bothered with anything but the Henry."

"Well, you need to get something else purty soon. Can't get them rimfire cartridges any more."

Judd said, "You need to get back to work too, Gale." His jaw was set square.

"Jesus, you see that, Hal? Sometimes he even looks like Batman. Look at him. The square jaw, the pointy nose?"

Jesus, what the hell was he doing? He watched Judd's face going red, Johnny leaning in and taunting him and still not taking the gun.

"You must notice the resemblance yourself, eh Judd? That why you comb your hair up high on the sides, wear the gray shirts, huh?" This was making him see the sense of it? He was grinning at Judd for Christ sake.

Hal surprised them both when he spoke, and they looked at him. "Except your daughter. She never called you that. Thought it was mean." Judd's face softened a little and Hal could tell he liked hearing that. "She wouldn't let anybody say it, ever."

Judd pinched down on his face again. "She was a slut."

"She got around some. Most girls do nowadays. But I think she only loved two men in her life, Judd, and you're one of them." Hal watched to see if he liked that. He'd never thought about it before, but when he said it, he was sure it was true. Girl loves her father--most natural thing there is. It was hard to tell if the lines on

Judd's face were going softer or not, but there was a question playing
out from his eyes, like maybe he was asking who the other man was.

"Had no respect. No respect for me, or her mother either."

"Just she couldn't trust people. Cuz no one ever protected
her. Specially not the men."

That's when Johnny decided to grab the Springfield. Maybe
it was the right thing, Hal didn't know, but he wished he hadn't done
it. Johnny put both his hands down on the rifle as if to lift it, and
Judd pulled the Trooper and lashed Johnny's head with the barrel,
hard, at the temple. Johnny crashed against the wall to his right, and
the Springfield came free and clattered back down on the desk.

"How'sat for a Batman move?" Like that was the end of the
conversation. Hal's right hand came out of his back pocket holding
the Beretta. Judd was watching what he'd done, laying Johnny out on
the floor dazed for the moment, not even seeing the Beretta. Hal felt
to make sure the safety was still off. He said, "You gotta listen this
time," aimed the Beretta at Judd's big right buttock and shot him
there. The sound of it was shocking, not loud. Judd gasped, but he
seemed surprised more than wounded, and his head came around at
Hal first. He was still holding the Trooper. Then the hips rotated
too, and the revolver came around, and Hal shot him again, this time
in the front of the thigh, and the Trooper came out of Judd's hand
and landed on the floor, and Judd flopped down into his chair.

"You gotta stop," Hal said, "I can put another one right in
you."

Johnny was rolling onto his side, wanting to shake off the
daze but afraid that his head would hurt more. He could hear Hal's
voice, but it didn't sound like Hal, and Hal was letting his breath out,
like he'd been holding it underwater. He was trying to roll up on his
elbow and hold a hand to his stinging forehead at the same time. He
saw Judd sitting down now, behind the desk, and he heard Hal say,
"Thank you." Johnny mumbled, "Welcome."

Hal set the safety on the Beretta and returned it to his back
pocket, and stepped over to the Trooper and lifted it. Staring at Judd,
he thumbed the latch to release the cylinder and then ejected the
shells. He opened a drawer on Judd's desk and tossed the big
revolver in, then the shells, and then the five-shot stripper clips. He
closed the drawer again.

"You fuckin' shot him," Johnny said. He was standing now.

"Yeah, only thing I could think of."

"You fuckin' shot him in the ass." When he told about it later, he would always tell about Hal putting the shells and clips in the drawer along with the big Colt. He would sometimes say that Hal shot him because he'd called his own daughter a slut; sometimes he wouldn't say that, but he never said Hal shot him because it was the only thing he could think of.

"You guys are both fired, God damn it," Judd said. He was grimacing and holding the thigh wound with both hands.

"We didn't figure you were going to give us a raise," Hal said.

"You're dead, Mull." He was sitting rigid in his chair.

"Johnny, maybe you better sit down here. You don't look so good." Hal moved to the door. When he'd opened it, he looked back and said. "Just don't let him load anything."

When he returned, he had a bottle of Wild Turkey under his arm. Caje, carrying four small tumblers in one hand, followed him in. "Put them down and set in that chair, Caje."

He looked at Judd and set the glasses down. "I didn't want it to happen like this, Mr. Judd."

Hal said, "Well, tonight, Caje'eme, I don't know if anybody gets what he wants. But what I want is for us all to walk out of here okay."

Judd shot a look at him. "Yeah, you go to the hospital and I go to jail, but tomorrow, it needs to be okay. You're wearing a couple bandages, but you're watching the PBA tournament; Johnny gets me out on bail and goes back to running your bowling alley; and Caje goes back to…" Hal looked at Caje then, "whatever he goes back to." Hal poured the little tumblers half full of whiskey. He said, "Sorry I shot you, Judd."

"It's not okay. If you think you can fix everything like this, Mull, you're fucking crazy." He lifted one of the glasses and took half a mouthful and swallowed it. Johnny lifted a glass and said, "Salud," and drank off the contents of the glass. Hal and Caje lifted and sipped. Caje set his glass down.

"I'm here to say I'm sorry, Mr. Judd." Caje waited until Judd's eyes had narrowed on him. "I'm sorry for your loss."

"You have a lot of damn gall, coming in here like this, you know that?" Judd said. Hal thought about telling him to shut up and listen but decided it wouldn't do any good. He sipped again.

Caje went on as if Judd hadn't interrupted him, like he had thought it all out while he was sweating in the Temescal, every word, and then had practiced it a thousand times since. "I'm sorry for your loss...and I'm sorry for my part in what happened. It wasn't *all* my fault, what happened to Tara, but I know I carry a lot of it. I know you hate me, and that's your right, but I want you to know that the sorrow I feel, the shame I feel, is worse than anything you feel toward me, anything you can do to me. Tara made me feel like I could do almost anything...because she could do almost anything herself...because she was never afraid. Maybe you don't know what a gift that is." He stopped talking then, and moved his eyes down into his lap, where his hands were.

Hal took a bigger swallow from his glass. He thought of the fresh flowers he'd cut every Saturday, and the pinot grigio bottle he'd kept at the bar, and the lovely way she'd felt when she'd pressed into him, and her voice, soft and gentle and low, when they'd sat together. And he was jealous of Caje, for the feeling of power she'd been able to give him and for the way he'd talked about her. He wished Johnny would say something then. Johnny, who never seemed able to tolerate silence, said nothing. He finished the bourbon and set the glass down on the desk and squeezed the words between his teeth, "Now's the time to say anything you got to say, Judd."

"You, an Indian for Christ sake, you were banging her, like every guy she ever knew."

Caje didn't lift his eyes. In a low voice he said, "I am sorry for my part in what happened, and I am sorry for your pain, but I am not sorry for what I had with her."

"You're not, huh?" Judd looked up at Hal then, that same question in his eyes again. He looked at Johnny then. "You believe this?"

Johnny still said nothing.

"Or were you guys screwing her too? Jesus, ain't there anybody you can trust? This sweet girl Hal says loved me so much." He knocked off the bourbon and refilled the empty glasses, with his left hand, letting the blood ooze out the front of his thigh. Johnny drank his down.

Hal was thinking, That what a father's love looks like? Better to die childless. For a second, he wanted to bring out the Beretta again, put one in Batman's heart. "Anything else to say, Caje?"

Caje looked up at Hal and shook his head. "Thank you, Mr. Mull."

"Time to go then, Caje." He waited for Caje, who looked Judd straight in the eye again, then rose and turned to go. He followed.

Caje stopped at the door to look back, and something new came into his face, like a cat that's just seen the shadow of a hawk descending. Hal pivoted and saw Judd there, the ought-six leveled. Johnny hadn't moved.

"One in the chamber, Mull, like every other gun I got." He pulled the rifle to his shoulder and put the site on Caje.

Hal didn't know why, but he stepped in front of the kid, not letting the fear show. Caje had said she was never afraid…

Johnny pushed the barrel away, but for Hal it was a quarter second too late.

What Johnny heard was the explosion of the round magnified by the confines of the office and barely a foot away from him, crashing into his ears, and what seemed like echoes set off a ringing inside his head. What he saw was Hal getting hit. He thought it strange that Hal never flinched, never even brought his hands out in front like a shield, like he thought anyone would have done. And he saw Hal jerk backward, as if he was taking a fist to the chest. And weirdly, there didn't seem to be any shock in his face, eyes fierce and flashing and jaw set hard, like he was fighting pain more than he was fighting Judd. Then he staggered half a step, forward this time, and fell, first to his knees and then sideways to the floor. And he heard some kind of sound from Hal, like breath leaving him for the last time, like he was saying, "Huh!"

The big bullet had taken him in the lung and the heart as well. There was a lot of blood.

Johnny was still gripping the barrel. He looked down at Hal and he knew he was dead. He faced Judd and said, "Put it down on the desk," but Judd, looking where Hal lay, held it for another moment. Caje crouched motionless, waiting for a second shot, but then he remembered Judd saying "One in the chamber," and stood erect. Johnny said, "Put it down," and now he did.

Judd said, "He shouldn'ta shot me." Like saying, Look what the son of a bitch did to me.

Johnny said, "Yeah, maybe not," and took the rifle and carried it to the far side of the office and leaned it against the wall. He looked at Hal again and said, "But the angels are takin' *him*."

Judd was saying something about his wife then, slumping down into the chair, holding his bloody pant leg, but Johnny wasn't paying any attention. Caje said, What? and Johnny said, "Maybe you should go. I gotta call the cops."

*****

It fell to Mrs. Thadbury to make arrangements for Hal's funeral. When Doris came to get the last of her things, Mrs. Thadbury asked her what she wanted in the services, "...you living with him for upwards of five years and all." but Doris said, "Things changed for us," their eyes meeting, and she added, "It's not my place anymore. Maybe it never was."

"Didn't he ever say anything to you about how he would want it?"

"It wasn't the kind of thing he talked about."

"You can't erase a man like him, you know. He was one of the good ones," Mrs. Thadbury said. She waited for Doris to turn her eyes away. When she didn't, Mrs. Thadbury said, "And shame come upon them that try."

Doris said, "It's not right you judging me. Hal's heart left me way before I walked out the door." She didn't attend the services.

Caje did come. Afterwards, he went to the sheriff's office. He was not a good story teller. He tried to keep Hal out of it, said he hardly knew the guy, never saw him anywhere outside the bowling alley, didn't know why he'd shot Mr. Judd, couldn't remember much of what had come before and maybe there was a grudge.

He tried to keep Tara out too, but of course that was impossible. The kids at her apartment knew Caje, said he lived with her. The manager at the Dreamland thought maybe he had taken a room that night, but he couldn't be sure. The sheriffs couldn't place him at the picnic table nor at the camp near Ruby nor in Hicks's room. They made Lacho for the Ruby assault and Lacho's associates for finishing Hicks, though they still wondered about the hooey knot. Caje was charged for smuggling marijuana, since they'd found some at the apartment, and illegal border crossing and was assigned a public defender and finally bound over for trial. His public defender was an older man who used a cane to get around; he told Caje he had nothing to worry about.

The sheriff's office questioned Judd after he was released from the hospital and recommended that no charges be filed against him. Clearly self-defense. The County Attorney's office agreed.

The services were not Catholic. Father Scotia, the rector at the Church of the Innocents, said he could not say a Catholic mass for Mr. Mull because Mr. Mull was not of the Roman Catholic faith. Mrs. Thadbury said, "Could not or would not? I'm sure he was baptized a Christian, and he's been coming to mass with me for two years now, not every week, mind you, but regular enough." Father Scotia said it was too bad he had not received the first sacrament in a Catholic church. Mrs. Thadbury appealed to the Bishop, who listened to her patiently and said that in terms of church doctrine, her rector was quite right. She carried her broken heart to Saint Jude's Parish, where Father Birdsong promised to help. No one knew Hal's favorite Psalm, so Mrs. Thadbury asked for her own favorite, the 126th, and Hal went into the ground after an Episcopal mass, not quite as blessed as Mrs. Thadbury thought he should be, but still quite dead.

Johnny attended the mass, which he described later as gobbledygook, and the burial too, with his wife, who was a bit more generous. In the eulogy, Johnny rambled a good deal, as he sometimes did, avoided references to whores and mescal, and told funny stories about him and Hal staring at stars and chasing javelina near Sasabe, laughing at the stories as he told them, and called Hal a prince: loyal above anything, obstinate in friendship, agreeable to a fault and, finally, a man who did what needed doing. No one disagreed. But then, there was not a crowd, though Father Birdsong had exhorted attendees at the Sunday masses to come. Mrs. Thadbury was there of course, attended by acacia and brittlebush arrangements she'd made, but her son was away at vet school in Colorado. None of the cousins came, though one, Edwina, sent a floral arrangement that said "Peaceful Memories" made of yellow carnations.

Uncle came, in plain slacks and a khaki beret with his Korea service pin attached. When he'd seen the obit, he called the funeral director and requested a burial flag from the VA to drape the casket. After the commendation, he got Johnny to help and folded the flag in a triangle and handed it to Mrs. Thadbury and told her since it was cotton, she should only display it on holidays. And he'd recruited a guy he knew at the VFW to come and play "Taps" after the committal, and he saluted when it was played. "Mr. Gale was right," he said, "this guy never lost his colors."

www.ingramcontent.com/pod-product-compliance
Lightning Source LLC
Chambersburg PA
CBHW050927120626
46552CB00001B/85